LAKSHMI'S SECRET DIARY

LAKSHMI'S SECRET DIARY

ARI GAUTIER

Translated by Sheela Mahadevan

Columbia University Press
New York

Columbia University Press
Publishers Since 1893
New York Chichester, West Sussex
cup.columbia.edu

Library of Congress Cataloging-in-Publication Data

Names: Gautier, Ari, author. | Mahadevan, Sheela, translator.
Title: Lakshmi's secret diary / Ari Gautier ; translated by Sheela Mahadevan.
Other titles: Carnet secret de Lakshmi. English
Description: New York : Columbia University Press, 2024.
Identifiers: LCCN 2024000899 (print) | LCCN 2024000900 (ebook) | ISBN 9780231212045 (hardback) | ISBN 9780231212052 (trade paperback) | ISBN 9780231559188 (ebook)
Subjects: LCGFT: Novels.
Classification: LCC PQ3989.3.G378 C3713 2024 (print) | LCC PQ3989.3.G378 (ebook) | DDC 843/.92—d23/eng/20240325
LC record available at https://lccn.loc.gov/2024000899
LC ebook record available at https://lccn.loc.gov/2024000900

Cover design: Julia Kushnirsky

Cover image: Shutterstock

Columbia University Press gratefully acknowledges
the generous contribution to this book provided by
the Florence Gould Foundation Endowment
Fund for French Translation.

CONTENTS

TRANSLATOR'S NOTE

TWO KEY FEATURES of Gautier's writing are its hybridity and multilingual character, and I have sought to reflect this in the translation, retaining vocabulary from French, Sanskrit, and other Indic languages. On occasion, Tamil words have been included in the English translation in order to convey that a dialogue is taking place in Tamil, even if the dialogue may be presented in the French language in Gautier's writing.

Certain French words and spellings—in particular, names of locations and buildings in Pondicherry—have been retained, echoing Gautier's act of French heritage preservation. The inclusion of French vocabulary in the English translation also resists the hegemony of English, the former rival colonial tongue of India, gesturing to the constant tensions between the British and French empires that were apparent during the colonial history of Pondicherry.

Above all, I hope to have conveyed and captured the powerful and vibrant images of Pondicherry and the vitality and psychological depth of the characters, along with the tragic and comic tones that shape Gautier's imaginative, moving, and evocative writing.

LAKSHMI'S SECRET DIARY

Chapter One

WHY? People often say that without this question, life would have no meaning, the world wouldn't be as we know it today, and humanity wouldn't have reached this stage of evolution. The whole world seems to revolve around this question. But why this question *why* in particular? Why not *who*, *what*, *when*, *where*, and all other kinds of questions? Why does the question *why* control our existence? And what would life have been like without this question *why*? And why am I asking myself this question? And since I don't know the answer, why should I ask Tripod Dog Baba? Interrupted mid-siesta, he considers it beneath him to answer me; he merely rolls his eyes as if my question was the most stupid thing he'd ever been asked, or as if the answer had been so obvious that the question wasn't even worth asking. I wait a few seconds, and then, since there's no response, I wake him up by prodding him with my trunk.

"Hey, Dog Baba, you could at least make an effort to answer me! You're always sleeping; you've got nothing else to do all day long. Can't you give it a bit of thought?"

Tripod Dog Baba is lying on his side; he opens his eyes, stretches, gives an enormous yawn, and starts licking himself, ignoring my question. There are days like this when I just want to scoop him up with my trunk, fling him into the air, and volley him so he goes flying into the shop opposite us. That would remind me of my time with the Gajarastas, who taught me how to play football. What's more, it's disgusting to see him like this with his three and a half legs, hind leg raised and the stump of his foreleg dangling down. He looks ridiculous.

■ ■ ■

That's why he's called Tripod: because he only has three legs—well, actually, three and a half. And Tripod became Tripod Dog Baba after his pilgrimage to Rameswaram.

Once he's licked himself clean, he sits on his hind legs.

"Firstly, you'd better call me by my real name: Tripod Dog Baba! Not Tripod, not Dog Baba, and not Tripod Baba either! I suffered my whole life long because I didn't have a name. Now that I've got one, I don't want it to be mangled. Understand?" He growls.

He's in a foul mood.

"But, Lakshmi," he continues, "I don't need to think about it; I know the answer."

"You do? So, what is it then?"

Licking his stump, he acts all high and mighty, which I'm well accustomed to.

"I've spent my whole life pondering over this question—it's been a dog's life, I'll tell you that—and I think I've finally found an answer. I'm still not sure if it's the right one! But at least I've got a theory about it. And you think I'm going to give it to you just like that, so easily? All you need to do is rack your brains, you great big beast! You're enormous, but your brain is the size of a shrimp."

Now he really deserves to be hurled into that shop! But I can see that he's in a bad mood, because I roused him from his siesta. For if there's one thing that Tripod Dog Baba considers to be sacred, it's most certainly his siesta. I've never seen such a lazy dog. This dog really is the epitome of idleness and passivity; he's capable of whiling away entire days on end doing nothing. He only ever adopts two positions: sitting or lying down. Whereas the other dogs roam about all over the place, either fighting among themselves or doing other things, Tripod Dog Baba does nothing. He's either lying down or sitting beside me.

It's true that Tripod Dog Baba is old and half-blind, which somewhat restricts his travels. But when it comes to eating, or rather, when it comes to looking for food, he can roam the entire town, from boulevard Sud right up to boulevard Nord, avoiding all dangers that this may entail in a most remarkable manner: Pondichéry has, after all, become a bustling town where moving about is almost suicidal for a three-legged dog who is half-blind.

However philosophical and spiritual he may be (or at least that's what he claims to be), Tripod Dog Baba loves eating. He's a true connoisseur of good food; he likes nothing but the finest of cuisines. Well, when I say philosophical and spiritual, that's all a pretense; I'm sure he knows very little about that sort of thing. But ever since he came back from Rameswaram, Monsieur has been acting like a guru and even organizes spiritual satsangs from time to time with the other dogs of the town, who admire and worship him infinitely.

■ ■ ■

So, most of the time, the responsibility for finding him food is taken on by his disciples. Unsurprisingly, his favorite restaurant is Satsanga, not because of its spiritual-sounding name, but because of the steak with green pepper sauce that Ramesh, the chef, excels at cooking; Tripod Dog Baba even boasts of knowing the cook. He knows exactly where the best restaurants are, and there's a different one lined up for each day of the week. For example, on Monday, it'll be Annapurna for its Andhra-style mutton curry; on Tuesday, it will be Aristo for its Mughal-style chicken; on Wednesday, it will be Le Café for its Creole beef; on Thursday, it will be Rendez-Vous for its Mangalore-style fish curry, or its Goan-style pork vindaloo, which originates from Portugal; on Friday, it will be Salem Biriyani for its famous mutton biriyani; on Saturday, it will be Satsanga for its steaks, and on Sunday, it will be La Promenade, because of its excellent buffet, and because he enjoys devouring an assortment of different dishes.

How do I know all of this? Tripod Dog Baba very much likes to boast; he takes a mischievous delight in filling me in on the details of everything he eats. It's as if he needs an external accomplice to know about his secret vice. For Tripod Dog Baba claims to be vegetarian and pretends to eat the meals served in the Sri Aurobindo Ashram or in one of the vegetarian restaurants run by Brahmin cooks on the other side of the canal. However, he already has two disciples who are devoted to him and know his secret. Why should he take me into his confidence? Sheer vanity. He just wants to show me how much he is respected and worshipped.

Every day as the clock strikes eleven, he sends off his trusty disciple, who reveres the guru; this subservient dog takes on the responsibility of finding his guru something to eat. And when the disciple returns with his meal, Tripod Dog Baba thanks him, bestowing his blessing on this dog with his half leg. He barely touches his meal and leaves the rest for his disciple. This disciple takes it and sets off to share it with the other dogs of the district, as if it were a religious prasad, convinced that it's an honor to share the master's leftovers.

Everyone, including those who live in the temple neighborhood, praise the ascetic qualities of the guru dog who eats very little and devotes his time to meditation and contemplation. But at around one in the afternoon, when the temple closes, the road becomes deserted, the shops shut, the beggars seek shelter to escape the searing heat, and Pondichéry prepares for its hour of siesta, two accomplices appear with the master's actual meal. The three of them then hide behind the temple's power generator and tuck into these delicacies. Once their meal is over, they take care to hide or remove the leftovers from the temple, for if anyone should discover that Tripod Dog Baba ate meat, he'd risk being chased away from the temple. And then this mask of sanctity that he has created for himself would be destroyed. It's easy for him to deceive his own kind with this pretense of sanctity, putting on an act as a pseudo philosopher, but deceiving man is another matter altogether. So the two accomplices take great care to ensure that Tripod Dog Baba's true identity is not revealed. Especially the female dog, who I believe is more or less in love with him.

Incidentally, one day, I saw people kicking her and throwing stones at her, because of him.

All this happened because Tripod Dog Baba had devoured an entire biriyani with a juicy joint of mutton, and had then dozed off with the bone still in his mouth. And at around four in the afternoon, when the temple reopened, the first stallholders began to set up their stalls, and the priest opened the temple doors, Tripod Dog Baba was still asleep with his bone. The female dog noticed this and leaped onto her guru, removing the bone from his mouth, hoping to hide it. But it was too late. The people nearby had caught her red-handed; they shouted, kicked her, threw stones at her, and beat her with a stick, and then she fled, tail between her legs, whining continuously. Of course, amid all this chaos, Tripod Dog Baba woke up. He barked a little and pretended to chase the female dog away. No one even questioned the sincerity or sanctity of the guru dog.

One day, I asked him why he didn't eat the ashram food, and why he put on this whole act. Tripod Dog Baba looked at me with a mischievous smile, lowered his voice as if he was going to reveal a secret, and said:

"You know, Lakshmi, it's obvious that you've never tasted man's food. You don't eat like them; all day long, you eat sugarcane, bananas, and goodness knows what else. I've noticed that you're always hungry. If you ate a few kilos of vindaloo, you'd see the difference. Anyway, of all the domestic animals, we are the closest to man; we're their best friends. We eat exactly like them. The areas where I grew up shaped my culinary habits. Meat, rice, fish, and leftovers were thrown over to me. Not the kind of food served at the ashram. The food in the ashram is bland and tasteless; it's the simplest kind of food: a piece of bread, a bit of dhal and rice, a banana, some yoghurt, and that's all. They call that satvik food."

"Why's that?" I asked.

Tripod Dog Baba scratched the back of his ear and began to act like a scholar. He always put on airs and graces when people asked him questions.

"They say that back then, upon arrival in Pondi, Sri Aurobindo decided to devote himself to prayer and sadhana, and he decided that his spiritual companion, the Mother, would take care of practical matters. Everything went smoothly until the day when a revolution almost broke out at the heart of the ashram because of culinary issues. The disciples who had followed their master to establish the ashram came from different states of India, each with their cultural, linguistic, and, of course, culinary differences. Each community demanded that the food be prepared to their taste; everyone wanted to add their pinch of masala. Needless to say, an anarchic atmosphere began to prevail in the dining hall . . . The Mother tried to find a solution somehow. She tried all kinds of recipes, but the disciples just wouldn't have it. They each stood their ground firmly, and even wanted a dining hall to be set up for each community, but that was simply impossible in practice. Can you imagine? One for the Gujaratis, one for the Bengalis, another for the Oriyas . . . there were also Europeans among the disciples . . . It was sheer madness. The Mother was completely helpless dealing with these disciples who were acting like spoiled children, and so she went to see the master and asked him for advice.

"It was well-known that Sri Aurobindo, as revered as he was as a great yogi and a spiritual leader who completely devoted himself to his sadhana, was also incredibly pragmatic. And so he said to the Mother:

"'It's very simple. If all my disciples are here to pursue a spiritual life and practice my form of yoga, well then, all you have to do is give them a spiritual diet. A bland diet without salt or spices: a simple diet that we will call satvik food. From tomorrow, instruct the volunteers who do the cooking to throw away all the spices, and you'll see that the problem will be resolved.'

"And so that's what happened. From that day onward, there were no longer any problems in the dining hall; everyone was satisfied, and even happy to eat the spiritual food."

Tripod Dog Baba lay down again as he concluded his tale, and then proceeded to explain his situation:

"But you see, Lakshmi, I'm just a dog. Even if I'm a guru, I can't eat like that: I like meat too much, and I'm too fond of spices. You don't know the taste of a decent mutton curry or the taste of a good pork vindaloo . . . if ashram food is spiritual, the meat I've just described is simply divine. But I have to be credible in my role, otherwise I wouldn't be respected. To them, I'm the one and only dog who doesn't eat meat. I'm the only one who doesn't fight for a bone. I'm the only dog who not only eats satvik food but also shares it with others."

■ ■ ■

That he had chosen this temple among so many others in Pondichéry was not accidental. For the Ganesh temple is located in the ashram complex, just a couple of meters away from the tomb of Sri Aurobindo and the Mother, where an atmosphere of sanctity and spirituality blends with scents of incense, camphor, and fresh flowers. The Ganesh temple is the only temple in the quartier blanc. Tripod Dog Baba can reign alone as the supreme leader in this district where there are very few dogs. No need to compete, fight, or tire himself out asserting his authority and guarding his territory. Moreover, the proximity of the temple and the ashram only further emphasizes his spiritual and religious traits.

I had often wondered why this dog was here, for the ashram complex consists only of houses and buildings that are linked to the different activities of the ashram. It isn't really a residential district where a stray dog can easily find something to eat.

■ ■ ■

In the center of the ashram complex is Aurobindo's former residence, which currently houses both his tomb and that of the

Mother. It is situated on the corner of rue de la Marine and rue Manakulla Vinayagar. The ashram complex occupies a large square, which extends from rue de la Marine, where the main entrance is located, to rue François Martin on the right, culminating on rue Saint-Gilles behind it.

Legend has it that in a bygone era, the sage Agastya had set up his ashram at this very location during his mission to bring Hinduism to South India. It was here that Aurobindo spent his final days; before this, upon arrival in Pondichéry from his native land of Bengal, he had resided in a road that is presently called rue Aurobindo.

The main ashram complex stretches from the north to the south of rue Saint-Gilles, extending up to rue Rangapillai, and from the east to the west of quai de Gingy, up to avenue de Goubert. It consists of various buildings, including the school, an engineering unit, a parfumerie, the post office, the famous dining hall, two sports halls, a library, and a pâtisserie, which no longer exists today . . . Essentially, it's a collection of buildings that contribute to the smooth running of the ashram. They are easily recognizable because of their gray and white colors, and they are all more or less identical, owing to their colonial architecture.

Nevertheless, some buildings stand out in this gray square because of their yellow-ochre color. These are the official French buildings, such as the consulate, the Institut Culturel Français, and the Foyer du Soldat, where the veterans meet up.

And just there alongside the Foyer du Soldat is the Ganesh temple, where I work. It's located on the corner between the Law de Lauriston and rue Manakulla Vinayagar; this latter road was formerly known as rue des Tisserands, subsequently renamed rue d'Orléans, before becoming rue Manakulla Vinayagar. That's where the main entrance is located. In any case, there is only one entrance, because this temple is architecturally unusual.

■ ■ ■

Before the arrival of the French and the missionaries, the temple must have been near a pond surrounded by sand, and this is where it gets its Tamil name Manal Kulam, meaning "sand pond." More than three hundred years ago, a Hindu saint named Thollakadu Siddhar attained a deep state of meditation beyond consciousness known as Jeeva Samadhi in the location where the temple was erected. The French, who arrived in 1673, were granted permission to construct a fort and dwellings in the vicinity of the temple. On several occasions, the temple was almost closed and destroyed. As early as 1699, the presence of the temples in the region aggravated the Jesuits, and they asked the Pondichéry council to destroy them. For commercial reasons, the council refused the request. August 15, 1702, marked a religious festival for both Catholics and Hindus. The Jesuits persisted with their request, and so the governor, François Martin, forbade all ceremonies and public events, and he then got hold of the keys to the temples. The following day, the local residents and some workers, especially the weavers, bricklayers, and road workers who were directly involved in the export trade and in the construction of the fort, headed toward the Porte de Madras to express their unhappiness. They wanted to flee the

French enclave of Pondichéry. François Martin rushed before the residents and promised them that he would no longer prohibit their religious ceremonies. The residents turned back and resumed their activities. The Jesuits and the missionaries initially gave in to the demands of the residents and the governor, but they came back later to ransack the temple and beat up the priest in charge. But that didn't mean the devotees were going to abandon their worship of their favorite god . . .

▪ ▪ ▪

Originally, the deity was called Bhuvaneshar Ganesh, because the idol faces eastward, looking out over the coastline of the Bay of Bengal; the name also alludes to one of the sixteen forms of the Lord Ganesh. However, his peaceful existence was to be interrupted by the Montbrun family, an illustrious family originating from the Principality of Monaco, who had come to settle in Pondichéry in the nineteenth century. Armand and Lucien Gallois Montbrun were the town mayors, and to the servants and people of Pondichéry, they were both known as Bambaram Durai meaning "Lord Spinning Top," because the local population struggled to pronounce "Montbrun." Armand was mayor from 1884 to 1893, while Lucien held the same post from 1931 to 1934.

Bambaram Durai—it's not clear which of the two mayors, but probably the first, according to old wives' tales—could not tolerate the fact that a pagan god was located close to his beautiful colonial house. The little shrine was actually next to his magnificent villa, and the right wall of this house was adjacent to that of the temple. Overwhelmed by the racket made by the pilgrims and the smells of incense and camphor, he repeatedly instructed his servants to go and throw the stone idol into the sea. But each time he was thrown into the ocean, Ganesh would reappear unscathed, back on his small plinth, waiting to be tossed into the sea yet again.

Despite their religious zeal as newly converted Catholics, the servants did not want to incur the wrath of Ganesh. Some of them even worshipped him secretly, such as one particular servant from Coimbatore, the gardener, who was responsible for throwing the idol into the sea. This servant had experienced the same fate as Montbrun; people called him Tanniglass, meaning "water tumbler" in Tamil, but Stanislas was his real name. He would leave each time with the idol under his arm, throw it away, and return empty-handed. Then, at night, he would go and find the idol and set it back on its plinth. And the following day, when Bambaram Durai would become enraged upon noticing that Ganesh was still there, Tanniglass would roll around on the ground in tears, begging his master to punish him if he had lied; he would swear by all the gods (in any case, he had only one ever since he had converted to Catholicism) that this could be nothing but a miracle. The exasperated Bambaram Durai didn't know what to do in this situation. He no longer knew whether he should trust Tanniglass, who was so convincing, or if he should send him packing, delivering a few well-aimed kicks, not only for having disobeyed him, but also for having taken him to be a fool.

Who knows what state of mind Bambaram Durai had been in when he decided to abandon the idea of getting rid of the idol of Ganesh. Was it the heat of the tropics that had got to him, preventing him from thinking rationally, or was it all this Hindu mysticism, which he couldn't get his head around? Or maybe he just used his common sense to avoid another revolt from the local population. For the supposed miracle was already well-known among the Tamilians who lived on the other side of the canal that divides Pondichéry into the Indian district and the ville blanche.

■ ■ ■

Now, a new wave of local residents fleeing Pondichéry was simply unthinkable: it would have dealt a fatal blow to all the activities of the town, and especially to the Compagnie des Indes, the French East India Company.

And so Bambaram Durai decided to leave Ganesh in peace. And then, much later, when the ashram purchased the Montbrun villa, the Mother donated part of it to the temple. A true mockery of history, for it has become the most popular temple in the town.

Owing to the proximity of the temple to the ashram, the two sacred places attract a large number of visitors on weekends. Very recently, this spot has even become the most popular religious site, visited by the local population and tourists alike. So, predictably, shopkeepers have set up their stores there. I still remember that when I first started out at the temple, there was just one store opposite the entrance that sold the items necessary for puja: coconuts, bananas, camphor, and incense sticks. A little farther on, toward the ashram, a woman would sell lotus flowers to adorn the tomb of Sri Aurobindo. The devotees of the ashram particularly like this flower, for it is as satvik as their meals: only slightly fragrant, but nevertheless beautiful. Hindu temples, in contrast, favor jasmine and other heavily perfumed flowers.

But when the temple suddenly became popular, other stallholders with miscellaneous items came to sell their wares. Of course, for the most part, they stock religious items, but they also sell souvenirs intended for tourists. And so it wouldn't be surprising to see photos of Ganesh, Sri Aurobindo, and the Mother rubbing shoulders with one another, and a whole load of bric-a-brac sold in a shop selling shells, rosary beads made of sandalwood and rudraksha seeds—"rudraksha" means "the eye of Lord Shiva" in Sanskrit—lingams, and other religious figures. Sometimes, if you look carefully, you can even find items that have absolutely nothing to do with religion. What are the portraits of Gandhi and the famous film star Rajnikanth doing there, right in the middle of the Shiva family? I, Lakshmi the elephant, couldn't tell you that, but it all seems quite normal.

This world made up of vendors—some with stalls, others wandering about selling their wares—autorickshaw drivers, beggars, the elephant who blesses people, the spiritual dog with three legs . . . all this contributes to exactly what the foreign tourist is looking for: folklore. Religion mixing with the absurd, the absurd with the surreal, the surreal with reality, and reality with truth, for all of this is reality: it is visible and tangible. Local residents who flee the French enclave to defend their god; a statue of Ganesh who is thrown on several occasions into the sea, only to return to its plinth each time; the rational mind of a mayor named Bambaram Durai trusting a servant named Tanniglass, who was fearful of his former gods despite wearing a cross around his neck; a Hindu temple making an appearance in the most European part of the town; a bored temple elephant who begs, and an idle, fake-spiritual dog. All this undoubtedly belongs to the realm of the absurd.

▪ ▪ ▪

Thinking of Tripod Dog Baba's story and that of the temple, I realize I've completely forgotten my original question. And since this pseudoguru dog still hasn't come up with an answer, I begin to think about my own life.

Why am I here? Once again this *why* . . . Why me, and why not anyone else? What stroke of fate and what circumstances have led me here? If my life hadn't been as eventful, I could have been elsewhere. And why this temple? Why should I spend my time standing here, posing for tourists, blessing pilgrims and terrified children who burst into tears as soon as I place my trunk on their head? And why do these people seek blessings from an elephant in a Ganesh temple? I'd very much like to see them receiving blessings from a tiger in an Ayappan temple, from a lion in a Kali temple, or from a monkey in a Hanuman temple. They'd come out covered in scratches and bite marks.

Whoever came up with the idea of this ridiculous and pointless ritual? It's a bit like these superstitious people who come and buy hairs from my tail to make bracelets or rings out of them; apparently, this brings you good luck. You'd have to be truly featherbrained to think that, firstly, you can buy good luck, and, secondly, that it can be found in my body hair. Do you ever catch me pulling hair off your head to make myself a bracelet? Do you ever see me tethering you to a tree to bless all the animals of the forest? What is it that drives man to this height of stupidity? What is it that drives man to de-animalize us, to make us resemble him?

And to make an even greater fool of me, this idiot Tokuram, my keeper, has made me wear a kolusu to adorn my left foreleg; this anklet has become an object of interest for the residents. When I walk past, I hear them say: "Oh, look how elegant Lakshmi is wearing her kolusu! Look how beautiful her makeup is today!"

I'm the one earning the money, and this fool Tokuram spends it to make me look even more ridiculous.

Yes, that's exactly what I'm paid to be: an object of ridicule. In fact, I'm actually a beggar. During each blessing, people slip their grubby coins into my trunk, which I must then pass to Tokuram. I pose for photos, which tourists take home as souvenirs. So, I find myself featuring among the stereotypical tourist photos: slumbering autorickshaw drivers, feet dangling out of their vehicles with overgrown toenails that have never seen nail clippers. Then there's a photo of a cow who is supposedly sacred. I say supposedly, since a sacred cow does not eat from trash cans. It wanders about in the middle of the road looking important, chewing some plastic bag. And here's another snap: fifty children crammed into an autorickshaw who are trying to get to school. I say trying, because you can't be certain they'll get there. And of course, there's the must-see statue of

Gandhi, who looks like he's just finished a gym session, abdominal muscles sufficiently toned to make any Tantex model go green with envy.

Just thinking of all these things, I can feel anger and frustration surging within me. Tripod Dog Baba has fallen asleep again. I watch him sleep, his chest rising and falling to the rhythm of his breathing. That's all he has to do: wait for his disciple to come and serve him food, and take away the leftovers before he nods off again. Whereas I'm still standing here, blessing my millionth pilgrim; my legs ache, I'm tired and hungry, and I just want to lie down and do nothing.

Which makes me think that my life is worse than a dog's life.

Chapter Two

"IF YOU CARRY ON LIKE THAT, Lakshmi, you'll end up as a circus elephant! Is that what you want? Do you want to live among the clowns like a nomad without ties, stay in a circus tent and fool around, balancing on a stool on one leg?"

Each time I did anything silly, my mother would repeat this well-worn mantra; in her view, the life of a temple elephant and its training required a particular degree of discipline, restraint, and a good education. She was determined to pass on this familial tradition to me, or at least, this tradition of our caste. Yes, alas, we too have our caste system. No one can escape it. A curse for some, a cosmic order for others, it's woven into the very fabric of our society, but I'm not here to challenge this system.

Our social structure is exactly like that of man. Right at the top of the hierarchy are the Gajahramans, which is the caste I belong to; we are allocated roles in temples, processions, and religious ceremonies. We represent knowledge and wisdom.

When Vyasa set out to compose the *Mahābhārata*, he called upon us. Next in line are the Gajatryas, who are the warrior elephants. They continue to take pride in the fact that they defeated Alexander the Great. Ever since wars have ceased in India, these elephants have been used for military parades, and many have changed career to become polo players. Then come the Gajasyas, who represent economy and labor. They are divided into several subcastes; some work in tourism, transporting people on their back for palace tours, and others work in national parks. Below them are the Gajasudras, who work in forests on deforestation projects. Some work in sawmills, transporting enormous logs; this is the work of slaves. Some elephants suffer the unfortunate karma of being exhibited in zoos, and others work in circuses; this is the fate that awaits me if I continue like this. On the bottom rung of the caste system are the Gajavasis, the wild elephants who live in the forest and spend their time fighting one another and sabotaging the work of farmers. But we aren't as cruel as human beings, who go as far as establishing a caste of pariahs.

There are very few animals in India who can boast of living like humans and having a social structure similar to that of man, who considers himself to be the most evolved being in the universe, a theory that is yet to be proven. And if we have this privileged status, it's because people believe that we are endowed with a distinct intellectual capacity. For that matter, the elephant god Ganesh was modeled on us, and not the other way around.

But I digress: I'm here to tell my story. So, my mother, Meenakshi, was working in the very ancient temple of Janardana

Swami of Varkala, which is two thousand years old. It's an important place for the worship of Lord Vishnu, known as Vaishnavism. For those who know Varkala, this peaceful village besides the sea was, until recently, an idyllic spot, known for its ayurvedic schools and sacred waters that can cleanse you from sin.

If you wander along the cliffs in the north of the village, you can reach lake Kapili with its backwaters—a network of canals linking the saltwater lakes and lagoons of Kerala—which merge with the sea; this confluence is known as Sangamam. We would share this spot with the Gajavasis, who also came there to bathe. This is where I encountered these boisterous, undisciplined, and quarrelsome creatures for the first time. What struck me above all was the sense of freedom they exuded. Even if I wasn't yet aware of the concept of imprisonment or freedom, something about these elephants appealed to me. Perhaps it was their casual, carefree nature, or maybe even their wild side. In contrast, we temple elephants were much more reserved and restrained in our gestures.

This was always the most enjoyable part of the day, for we could bathe at leisure, spray ourselves with as much water as we pleased, roll around in the sand, and rub ourselves against the trees; at last, we could wash ourselves like elephants in the wild. This moment of leisure belonged to us. However, we were formally prohibited from mixing with the Gajavasis. In any case, a good distance separated us from them, but we could see them, hear them, and also smell them. I loved their trumpeting, but when I began to imitate them, my mother would scold me, saying: "Shhhh, be quiet, stop trumpeting like a wild elephant!"

■ ■ ■

The temple of Janardana attracted many visitors. Its festival was known all over Kerala, which gave my mother a special status—for our status can be measured by the fame of the temple to which we belong. So, understandably, my mother wanted me to be her successor, and she did everything to ensure that I could have the education of a temple elephant. But I had other ideas; I didn't mind what I would do, but I didn't want to follow in my mother's footsteps.

It isn't easy to become a temple elephant. It involves years of apprenticeship and training, standing on your feet for several hours. Bestowing ashirvads left, right, and center. You have to get used to festivals, along with their sounds, smells, and the hustle and bustle of thousands of people, jostling and shoving one another. You have to get used to fireworks and musicians with drums and trumpets blasting music right into your ears, creating a deafening racket. Unsurprisingly, from time to time, we become violent and lose our self-control. This whole phase of training is intended to help us acquire good self-control, learn how to keep calm, and, of course, how to conduct ourselves well. You can't just have fun, spending your time eating or doing your business in front of everyone. A temple elephant should exude a certain degree of sanctity and inspire respect. And should an elephant be assigned to a Ganesh temple, the work is even more demanding, because it involves representing the very god himself.

I began my training at a very young age. Chacko Chattan, my mother's keeper, was very thorough and strict in his training, but between him and my mother, there existed a beautiful bond, almost a love story. I never saw him lose his temper with my mother; I never saw him beating her or prodding her with his cheru kol. I should also say that my mother was docility personified. Like me, she was born in captivity. She was of a gentle temperament; moreover, she was very beautiful: average in size, a beautiful light shade of gray, and not this reddish color of the Gajavasis, a color they acquire because of their frequent mud baths. If by some coincidence my mother was also reddish in color, she would have been treated as a wild elephant, and not a single male Gajahraman would have wanted to woo her. My mother had beautiful eyes: they were fish-shaped and laughing, with a mischievous twinkle about them. That's why she was called Meenakshi, meaning "fish-eyed" in Sanskrit. Meenakshi was also the name of the goddess of Madurai.

When Chacko Chattan applied makeup on my mother, it was evident that he was taking care of her. He would take her first of all to Sangamam and give her the freedom to wash herself. She would take her time. My mother was certainly vain! During this time, he would wait for her patiently, smoking his beedi. Once she had finished bathing, my mother would splash herself with water and let herself be rubbed by Chacko Chattan, quietly trumpeting with pleasure. None of the raucous trumpeting of the Gajavasis. Back at the temple, Chacko Chattan would apply kohl to her eyes so as to highlight their beauty; he would use kohl of good quality, not the kind that leaves streaks trickling down your trunk.

Chacko Chattan was a talented makeup artist and chose the most beautiful designs. In fact, he had a pocket manual, which he would consult for hours on end. Since the beauty and elegance of the elephant are also a reflection of their keeper, he did everything to ensure that his elephant was beautiful, and he dutifully took great care of her.

My mother and Chacko Chattan were of a similar age; they had grown up together. Chattan's father had been my grandmother's keeper, and when my mother was born, as a matter of course, he entrusted her to his son so he could take care of her. My mother had been educated at the gurukulam, a boarding school in Kanjirappaly in the district of Kottayam. She would speak nostalgically of this carefree period when she had wandered through the plantations of rubber trees, where she had trained to become a temple elephant. She also told me that even if the training had been hard—spending entire days on her feet, confined to a tiny space, controlling the need to relieve herself, and eating a restricted diet—she had adored these long walks with the other Gajahramans, who were there for the same purpose. She had also enjoyed getting to know those who would share her fate. A fate that was difficult to escape. She told me that this had been the most joyful period of her life.

■ ■ ■

Unsurprisingly, Chacko Chattan decided to send me to the gurukulam. But ever since my mother had become an elephant of the Janardana temple and thus had an elevated status, I was advised not to attend the same gurukulam as her. It was therefore decided that I should be sent to the gurukulam in

Masinagudi in the Bandipur Forest. It's the crème de la crème, the most prestigious of gurukulams, educating the elite elephants among the Gajahramans. It is attended only by the offspring of elephants belonging to renowned temples, and is reputed to be one of the best in South India because of the quality of its education and its surroundings, which it shares with other animals of the forest. From time to time, this gurukulam also accepts Gajatryas and some Gajasyas, but really only the very privileged ones. They either belong to maharajas or are children of film-star Gajasya elephants. Sometimes, they are eager to climb up a rung on the ladder of the caste system.

The film stars of the Gajasya caste are among the most respected and admired elephants. We're in awe of these lucky elephants. Whether we're Gajahramans or Gajatryas, we all aspire to star in a film one day, even if this is prohibited by our caste.

And so, understandably, in my rêveries, I would picture myself being chosen to act in films alongside the greatest Indian film stars.

I impatiently awaited my departure for the gurukulam; I found this prospect very exciting. I must say that I was beginning to get seriously bored in Varkala, where there was nothing much to do. Apart from bathing in the backwaters, there was nothing of interest. I would spend my days sheltering between my mother's legs right until the moment she departed for work. Once she had left, I would remain alone in the temple courtyard gazing at the sculptures, playing with the squirrels, chasing the crows, and dreaming. For I was a great dreamer!

Sometimes I would escape through the back of the temple to daydream undisturbed on the cliffs, those majestic cliffs overlooking the breathtaking ocean. Here, my thoughts would take flight, soaring like a bird. As soon as I settled at the cliff's edge and scanned the horizon, I'd start to dream of becoming a film star or a polo player. I could imagine myself climbing down these high cliffs and crossing the sea. I would tell myself that life on the other side must be more exciting, that something else awaited me, that I would become something other than a temple elephant. I had this uncanny feeling—a small voice within was telling me that I wouldn't have the same life as my mother. That I had to change the course of the destiny that a villainous hand had sketched out for me.

But how? Where to start? Maybe I could escape from the gurukulam? Fine, but where could I go? I knew very little, and I didn't know anyone either. As kind as my mother and Chacko Chattan were, and as secure as my life as a temple elephant was, I felt sad and imprisoned in this village, though it was charming. I wanted to see the world, discover it for myself, and not through the eyes of my mother. In any case, what did she know? Apart from her Kanjirappaly plantation and her temple of Varkala, she knew very little, the poor thing. Her fate had ground to a halt there, as if it had reached an impasse, blocked by an invisible wall in front of these cliffs. As if the same villainous hand that was to write my destiny had halted there, paralyzed, refusing to progress for lack of inspiration, or maybe just out of idleness, or even malice.

■ ■ ■

I sensed that my mother was both anxious and uneasy each time I brought up the topic of freedom and asked her if she was happy. On occasion, I caught her shedding tears as she watched me play without a care in the world, undaunted by what tomorrow or my future might hold. I could read her mind. I knew she didn't want me to suffer a similar fate. She would have very much liked me to become something else, but what could be done? When one is born into this system, how can one escape from it?

When she was in this state of sadness, I would nestle against her; I too would feel like crying. Then she would wrap her trunk around me, and rock me to sleep. And I could feel the embrace of her maternal gaze, this gentle, warm gaze that only mothers can provide.

As much as I loved my mother, I was also aware that all of this was going to come to an end, and that our separation was imminent. I was aware that life wasn't always rosy, and that sooner or later, I'd have to confront its harsh reality. All our attachments to people and places must be severed one day. We must set off, sail away, confront the calm or storm, and find our own harbor. And the sooner, the better, before I succumbed to this comfortable way of life, sinking into torpor, and wallowing in emotion.

At the same time, I wasn't going to settle for any old destiny. That would just be ridiculous; it couldn't be that life boiled down to such a situation. I just could not and would not accept the predicament of ending up in a temple, confined within its four walls, blessing people and listening to mantras all day long. Oh no, I absolutely had to escape my destiny. I wasn't afraid of ostracism, and the prospect of no longer belonging to this caste didn't frighten me either. In any case, I've never believed in such a social system: a structure that confines you to one particular way of life, where there is no means of escape, a social system that is both restrictive and authoritarian.

This system, ancient though it was, did not correspond to my concept of life. For me, life was synonymous with freedom. But equally, I was not naïve; I had of course noticed that life entailed compromise, sacrifice, and even suffering. But it was up to me to decide if I wanted all this. No one had the right to impose it on me. The very thought that one could be forced into a certain way of life, forced to take up a path that had already been mapped out, disgusted me.

Although I was happy about my imminent departure from Varkala, the thought of the future also filled me with fear. But it was a delicious sensation: fear mixed with exhilaration, almost like intoxication. The anxiety of beginning a new life all alone without my mother's help, making my own decisions, confronting this merciless world all by myself. I began to wonder if it was fear, or merely apprehension.

■ ■ ■

I wanted to spend the final days before my departure with my mother. I wanted to smell and touch her, feel her caress, and listen carefully to her final words of advice. Until now, I had never paid attention to them, letting them enter through one large ear and go out through the other. These last few days flew by at an incredible speed, fueling the thought that I would never see her again, even if I was destined to come back to take her place in the temple after finishing my training at the gurukulam. But I'd made up my mind: I would not come back to Varkala. Come what may, I would defy destiny, and maybe I would succeed in my battle against my fate, which dictated that I should become a temple elephant.

Would I ever see my mother again? I had no idea. Was I bothered about this? I couldn't say. I was more preoccupied with getting ready to quench my thirst for freedom. As if by magic, my feelings had evaporated; I had anticipated a heart-wrenching and emotional farewell.

On the day of my departure, nothing dramatic happened. My mother, too, must have prepared herself for this separation. It was thus with a degree of indifference that she embraced me in her trunk for a few seconds. One ashirvad, and that was it. Twenty-two months in her womb, five years of life together, and then, just like that, we went our separate ways.

She had taught me everything, she had given me all her affection and love. She had protected me from the rages of Chacko Chattan when I did stupid things. She had lulled me to sleep with her wonderful stories, she had wanted me to have a happy childhood and life, and now she was distraught. At the moment of my departure, I saw a final tear fall from her expressive eyes. A tear shaped like a raindrop falling from a spectacular cloud trickled down her trunk, leaving behind streaks of black kohl. It was not the quality of the kohl that was at fault; no, it was the force of her tears!

Chapter Three

"**RIGHT, THEN,** as of today, you're no longer calves, you're grown-up and mature. You need to learn to live independently, and also in a community. You will make your decisions all by yourselves. You'll no longer have your mother, aunts, or extended family to help you. In your group, there are not only Gajahramans, but there are also some Gajatryas and Gajasyas, so I ask that you live in harmony with your classmates. I don't want any fights or arguments, and most importantly, don't ask me for favors, just because you are so-and-so. Everyone will be treated equally, fairly, and in an impartial manner. I don't need to remind you that our gurukulam is the best in this part of India, and that we have a certain reputation and standard to maintain. To this end, I demand an exemplary conduct of you; no violation of the rules will be tolerated. The first elephant to break the rules will be severely punished, and may even be expelled from the institution. I'm reminding you once again, and I hope I'm making myself clear: there will be no exceptions to the rule, whatever your status and that of your parents may be. From now on, you'll be divided into two groups: those with an elephant keeper, and those without. The lessons will begin in two days; until then, use the time to get to know each other, and get acclimatized to your new surroundings."

From this moment onward, a new phase of my life began. The gurukulam was located on the fringe of the village of Masinagudi in the Bandipur Forest, in the state of Karnataka. This forest was enormous; well, enormous for me, because I'd previously only ever known the temple and the Varkala backwaters. I was initially impressed by how extensive the gurukulam was. It was large, as it was not surrounded by a wall or enclosed by a stretch of barbed wire. Its only border was the river Moyar. It was, in fact, located on the left bank of the river; on the other side, the jungle sprawled out over vast hills.

I was awestruck as I discovered my new universe. The gurukulam was surrounded by majestic trees: teak and sandalwood, whose intoxicating scents I'd been able to recognize, but there were other trees that I couldn't identify. Everything was new to me: trees, plants, flowers, fruits, birds . . . other creatures whose existence I wasn't even aware of. I had a whole new universe to discover. Just knowing that I was going to spend several years in this heavenly location filled me with delight. It was as if the gurukulam and the forest exuded a sense of freedom.

The prospect of savoring the nectar of this freedom made me rapidly forget the moment of separation from my mother. But this newfound happiness was accompanied by a feeling of guilt. I could picture her thinking of me. Worrying about me. She had never known anything beyond the temple of Varkala. She would have certainly liked to be here with me, enjoying the splendor of this forest, listening to the birdsong, looking at the magnificent butterflies that fluttered above us in a rainbow of colors. She would have liked to bathe in the river Moyar and rub herself against the sandalwood trees to capture their heavenly scent . . . thinking of this, my eyes welled up with tears that instantly ran down my trunk. I then heard someone approach me from behind, saying:

"What's the matter with you? Are you sad?"

This was the first time that anyone had spoken to me since my arrival. I then realized that I had remained alone at the river's edge, lost in thought, whereas the others had already left to find their enclosure. I answered without turning around, for I didn't want him or her to notice my tears.

"No, I'm fine, I was just thinking of my mother."

My voice was stifled within my trunk.

"I understand," he said.

Meanwhile, I'd detected that he was a male elephant.

"That's understandable," he added. "All of this is new to you, just as it is for all of us. But don't worry, everything will be fine. You just need a bit of time to get used to it and you'll see that living in this gurukulam isn't as hard as all that."

His tone was almost maternal, and his voice gentle, friendly, and comforting.

"Thanks!" I replied, turning around to see who this kind elephant was that had come to comfort me.

He was a bit bigger than me and must have been about my age. Maybe a little older. He seemed to be somewhat mature, or rather, he seemed to exude a particular sense of self-confidence, which inspired respect and trust. He was of a grayish color, with beautiful eyes and small tusks, which were not yet fully formed. He didn't look like the elephants I'd previously seen or encountered; he was different. He didn't look like the Keralan elephants, and I was pretty certain that he wasn't a Gajahraman.

"And what about you, aren't you sad?" I asked, staring at him.

"Me? Never!" He replied proudly.

"Really? Don't you miss your mother? Doesn't this new environment make you scared?"

"No, not at all. I'm used to this kind of forest. And even bigger ones than this. As for my mother, it's been ages since I left her. I have only very distant memories of her."

As he spoke, he came up to me and looked out over the river.

"You see, even this river doesn't scare me. I've actually crossed rivers in the past. Big rivers like the Brahmaputra."

He was certainly about a head taller than me.

"You aren't a Gajahraman, are you?" I asked him, shyly.

"No, I'm one of these rare Gajatryas who attend this gurukulam and I'm originally from Assam."

"Assam? I don't know the place."

"Understandable. It's far, far away," he said, looking straight ahead into the distance.

I saw that his gaze traveled beyond the riverbank. It was as if he sought to be transported to his homeland simply by uttering this word "Assam." As if he had suddenly been overcome by a wave of nostalgia.

"So, you miss Assam, then."

"No, not at all. I was born in Assam, but I come from Odisha."

Now I was confused. Assam, Odisha, Gajatrya . . . this elephant certainly was unique. And interesting. I also knew that he was kind. He had a certain gentleness about him, and I now realized that this maturity and self-confidence were particular characteristics of the Gajatryas. It was the first time I'd met such an elephant, but I knew of them from the stories my mother used to tell. During my childhood, these bedtime stories of gallant warriors, their bravery, and countless battles had lulled me to sleep.

While we both stood there gazing at the river, the day gradually drew to a close. The sun disappeared behind the hill, and he said to me:

"I think it's time to go back. By the way, my name is Manmath. How about you?"

"I'm Lakshmi. But I don't know where to go," I told him, hesitating.

"That's why I came to fetch you. We're in the group without a keeper and we have been assigned a specific location. All you have to do is follow me."

■ ■ ■

And that's how a long-standing friendship between Manmath and me began. We lived in the same enclosure, which comprised a long corridor divided into several rooms, and each could accommodate one elephant. The master's house was located in the center of the complex. Each corridor consisted of about ten rooms in the space of about twenty square meters. The central position of the master's house enabled him to keep an eye on all the elephants. And the river Moyar flowed behind the house.

Manmath and I were lucky enough to live in the building that was closest to the river, and the farthest away from the master's house. We lived in the last two enclosures in the corridor. Manmath occupied the last enclosure, and he left me the penultimate one, so as to protect me from potential attacks or intrusions, should any animal manage to cross the river. This thoughtful act strengthened our growing friendship. At the same time, I found this comforting; as I'd just come from the city, our proximity to the jungle and its wild animals and unfamiliar sounds frightened me. I was more accustomed to falling asleep to the urban soundscape of cars and motorbikes honking and cycle bells tinkling. Film songs blaring out from a radio set near the temple. Ocean waves breaking against the cliffs. And in the foreground, the murmur of my mother narrating, for the umpteenth time, the story of Iravat the white elephant, the vehicle of Lord Indra. I would fall asleep to the sound of her voice melting inside me, her words forming a cloud of dreams that would keep me company at night.

My first few nights at the gurukulam were terrifying. I found it hard to get used to the silence and darkness. The moon and stars shone more brightly here than in the town, but above all, it was the silence that made me anxious. No matter how much I tried to prick up my ears so as to capture the slightest sound, all I could hear was the murmur of the river, pursuing its relentless journey toward an unknown destination. Every so often, I could clearly make out the sound of animals drinking fresh water. I could also hear dead branches snap, which prevented me from closing my eyes, but the presence of Manmath at my side quickly comforted me. This was especially so because, after the first sleepless nights, it turned out that Manmath was a very good storyteller. Having understood my problem, he began to tell me stories every evening. Of course, they weren't exactly the kind of stories my mother used to tell . . .

During those sleepless nights, I learned that Manmath had descended from an illustrious family of Gajatryas who had fought alongside Ashoka, an emperor of the Maurya dynasty (304–232 BCE). After Ashoka successfully conquered the Kalinga Empire, Manmath's family had continued to serve numerous kings in what is now known as Odisha.

Manmath belonged to Prince Shivendra, who ruled over Bhitarkanika; his kingdom was hidden away in the region surrounding the Similipal Forest, which was known for its tigers. His family had served this kingdom for several generations, performing various tasks. He told me that he had taken part in tiger hunts, not long before coming to the gurukulam. He painstakingly described the details of the magnificence of his palace, his luxurious home, and the splendor of his kingdom. He told me that he had been the prince's favorite elephant. I asked him why he was here among the Gajahramans, given that he was a respected descendant of these fierce warriors of Ashoka. He then explained the complexity of our caste system to me.

"The system appears to be rigid, unchangeable, and archaic, but this is just a facade. Since its conception, this system has been constantly evolving, changing with the times. By that I mean that those belonging to a particular caste can change their status. For example, a very long time ago, we used to belong to the Gajatrya caste, and this lasted for several thousand years. When the wars ceased, we were used for parades, hunting, and even for playing polo. But after the dissolution of our kingdom, which then became integrated into a new country called India, our kings and princes no longer had any power, and they lost all their former wealth. Now, the upkeep of hundreds of elephants requires both wealth and resources. No longer having the means to maintain us, our masters began to sell us, or they simply got rid of us in various other ways. And that's how the Gajatryas, who were once feared and respected warrior elephants, ended up in other castes, depending on where they lived. Gajatryas of the Travancore kingdom became Gajasudras and worked in the sawmills of Kerala. Others in the Rajput kingdoms ended up carrying tourists on their backs, taking them on a tour of the palaces and forts in which they themselves were guests. And the elephants in our kingdom were sold off to various temples. So our Gajatrya community made a radical transition into the Gajahraman community. But this can only ever happen to a community or a group; it isn't possible for an individual to make such a transition. That's why I'm here," he concluded, catching his breath after this long explanation.

"But," I said, "doesn't the same thing apply to so-called lower castes?"

"Of course, but it's a bit more difficult. You know very well that climbing up is always more difficult than going down. But there are instances where a caste that was previously considered to be inferior is no longer considered as such."

"It's now clearer in my mind, but I still can't help but feel appalled by the very thought that we can be divided into castes like this."

His explanation was exceptionally precise and crystal clear. But I continued to comment in a reproachful tone:

"It doesn't leave us much space for maneuver as individuals. The chances of leading our lives as we please are very limited. We have to follow the rules and customs of our community. Which means that your life as an individual only has value if you live in harmony with your community."

Of course, my intention wasn't to take him to task! But I wanted to know if he shared my indignation. I wanted to know his opinion on the matter.

He gazed at me for a long time, looking amused.

"You're the only one who shouldn't be indignant, if anyone is," he said, mockingly.

His words stung me, and I retorted vehemently.

"And why shouldn't I be indignant?"

He immediately burst into laughter, overtly mocking me.

"One is indignant when one is unhappy, and things are going badly. One is indignant when subjected to injustice. But, Lakshmi, honestly, what are *you* complaining about? Where's the injustice in your life? Are you complaining that you're being fed, that you've got a comfortable life in a temple, and that you're being worshipped? Come on, you make me laugh!"

He concluded by prodding my stomach with his trunk as if the whole thing were a good joke. This really made me furious. I pushed him away and faced him as if I were challenging him to a duel, and retorted, on the verge of tears:

"You're among those who believe that luxury, comfort, and an easy life are indicators of happiness. You don't understand the frustration of not being able to choose your way of life, you don't know what it means to be free. You have absolutely no understanding as to what personal ambition is. In your opinion, everything has to be done as a community. And I completely understand your point of view; you have lived in the splendor of palaces and forts, among kings and princes. You have absolutely no idea what it means to suffer; you're unaware as to what others may experience in terms of injustice or unhappiness because of their way of life."

Manmath was surprised by my reaction. His smile vanished, and I saw that my words had made an impression on him. He seemed to be a little ashamed of having hurt and agitated me, and as he came toward me, he said to me in a friendly tone:

"It's not worth getting worked up like this, my dear Lakshmi. I didn't mean to hurt you and I understand that this system makes you indignant, but what can be done about it? We each have our own karma!"

These last words only served to fuel my anger further. I looked at him and shook my head, unsettled. I no longer had the energy or desire to speak to him.

"You clearly don't understand. You've no sensitivity, you're just a fool! You'll never understand that your concept of karma is the very symbol of this injustice, and of the degradation of our entire society. You just stay locked up in your world of superstitions and false beliefs; I wish you a good karma!"

As I uttered these words, I turned my back on him and headed toward the river to avoid conversing with him. He let me go and remained rooted to the spot for a few seconds before setting off in the opposite direction, toward his enclosure. I was bristling with indignation, infuriated with Manmath; I had previously considered him to be a friend who shared the same values as me. A friend who would understand me, and my feelings, dreams, and aspirations. Someone who would console me in my moments of sadness. But instead, he had made fun of me. And when I had moved away, he hadn't tried to console me or apologize. I felt he had let me down.

■ ■ ■

The murmur of the river comforted me somewhat. The riverbank was my refuge for contemplation; each time my mind was in turmoil, this was where I came to seek solace. The rays of sun danced on the water's surface, glinting off the bodies of the fish, resembling sparks of fire darting in and out of the water, eternally ablaze. I felt the caress of the breeze, bringing with it an explosion of rosewood and sandalwood scents. I could smell the beautiful blossom of the flame of the forest tree, which, according to this irritating Manmath, was an incarnation of the Vedic god Agnidev; he had been punished by Parvati, having interrupted her moment of intimacy with Shiva.

This atmosphere calmed me down a little, and it made me think of Manmath. Maybe I'd been a little tough on him? Why had I lost my temper like this? All he'd tried to do was help me understand things I didn't know and teach me all the nuances of a particular belief and social structure. Of course, I had every right to dismiss it, but I didn't have the right to get angry with

Manmath. He had always been kind and gentle with me. He had taught me many things, and without him, I would have felt lost in this environment. He had been the first to show me the meaning of true friendship. I'd never had a friend before; he was my first companion. I couldn't destroy a growing friendship just because of a difference in opinion; that would be most silly.

While I was mentally trying to make peace with Manmath, the wind changed direction, and the scent of nature was replaced by that of my friend; I could sense he was behind me. I turned around and saw him standing there exactly like the first time, at the very same spot, looking at me. He looked apologetic and seemed to be lost for words. He managed a smile when he noticed that I was no longer angry, and he offered his trunk as an act of forgiveness. I took his trunk in mine, and we went back to the enclosure in silence.

This silence between us could express a thousand words. It was a pleasant, peaceful silence. A profound silence that was accompanied by the lullaby of the river Moyar lapping against the shores. And the birds and trees also fell silent, as if the forest too wished to partake in this moment. I gazed at the sky and saw that the moon, shrouded by clouds, was hushing the whispering of the stars.

Chapter Four

A GOOD DEAL OF TIME had already elapsed since my arrival at the gurukulam. I had grown accustomed to this new life and had made new friends. Varkala, Chacko Chattan, and my mother were now but a distant memory. The anxiety of the first few weeks had evaporated, now replaced by a degree of self-confidence, and a newfound mature side to my personality. Had I learned to accept the situation? No, it was more that I had developed a better understanding of life around me. My training as a temple elephant was progressing well, and I went along with it, even though my heart wasn't truly in it. It did, however, demand a lot of concentration, patience, and perseverance. I buckled down, and put a lot of effort into the training, all the while knowing that I did not wish to return to Varkala.

I must admit that this gurukulam was unique. It didn't match my mother's description at all. Her own gurukulam—the one in Kanjirappaly—was, according to her, restrictive, strict, and, of course, boring. There was nothing to do there except go on the occasional walk in the rubber plantations. How could one marvel at that monotonous landscape of identical trees, each with diagonal cuts on their trunks, with coconut shells fastened to them to collect the sap? My gurukulam was the opposite: it was bustling with activity, with this magnificent forest and misty blue hills in the distance. But most importantly, we were granted our freedom, which was especially valuable. Gradually, I came to understand that my education here was more about life in general than about becoming a temple elephant.

However, a significant portion of our time was devoted to training: learning how to stay still, how to interact with man, and how to control our emotions . . . we were taught how to stay calm when confronted with noise, how to endure a wave of pilgrims flooding the temples. We got used to being petted by them, and we learned to tolerate the sound of fireworks, our greatest enemy. But apart from this, we were completely free to do as we pleased, which seemed most odd to me. We could even take a walk outside our gurukulam; the worst thing that could happen would be bumping into the Gajavasis! My mother would certainly have had a heart attack if she had found out . . . All this seemed strange to me, and one day, I spoke to Manmath about it; we'd stopped arguing ever since the incident that I just recounted.

"Tell me, Manmath, doesn't it seem odd to you that we're enjoying such freedom in this gurukulam? My mother used to say that life during the training period wasn't pleasant, and that it involved many restrictions. But it's completely the opposite here! Is that to be expected?"

"Well, yes, to some extent. I have a cousin who was here not so long ago, and he told me that this gurukulam adopted a particular approach to education. So I was prepared for it, but I must admit that all this freedom has surpassed my expectations of this place. Its strategy is distinct and ingenious, because it not only makes us face our own responsibilities, but, at the same time, it also makes us believe we are privileged."

"I don't really understand what you mean, Manmath," I said, dreading yet another stormy discussion that could end in an argument. But this time, I was ready to hear him out.

"By giving us the freedom to discover the world in which we live, this gurukulam reinforces the idea that life is not so simple. By giving us the freedom to mix with the Gajavasis and the other animals of the forest, it makes us confront our destiny. It helps us understand how lucky we are to have a secure life. You'll see; gradually, you'll realize that the other animals of the forest have a price to pay in order to enjoy this freedom. And that price is none other than the fear of hunters, hunger, predators . . . all kinds of dangers that living in the wild entails. Now, you might say that this is to be expected, since this is their way of life, dictated by nature. But we elephants who live among human beings should be aware that we are privileged to live in this way. We have a standing in society. We are respected, and we have a longer life expectancy than those in the wild. But I know you, Lakshmi, and I know exactly what you're going to say: Isn't it better to live dangerously in freedom, rather than in safety, imprisoned in a gilded cage? Well, each to their own."

"But by doing this, aren't they afraid that we might choose to escape, opting for a life in freedom?" I asked. "I'm just wondering: What if they granted us this freedom? There must be some trap; there must be some kind of protective mechanism. Surely they can't risk exposing us to this kind of life without imposing certain restrictions."

I impatiently waited for Manmath's response. He gazed at me for a long time, as if to search my soul, seeking to discern what was going through my mind.

"Come on, let's go for a walk. I'll take you to the other side of the river, and maybe we'll have the opportunity to meet the Gajavasis."

This idea greatly appealed to me. At last, I was going to be able to roam the forest and meet other animals. I was excited to discover a whole new world with Manmath. I don't believe I would have had the courage to do it on my own. With him, I felt safe. This newfound freedom was unknown to me, and I didn't know what to do with it. Shaking my head from side to side to express my joy, I began to follow Manmath.

It was a glorious day, with a clear, blue sky, and it wasn't too hot. In any case, the gurukulam was surrounded by all kinds of trees, so the forest air was always crisp and cool. We walked past the last few enclosures, and turned left, heading toward the river. While we walked, Manmath continued:

"Do you realize how lucky we are?"

"We are? Why's that?"

"Because we are in the group without an elephant keeper, and that means we have more freedom. Those who already have a keeper have to more or less follow their master's instructions.

We'll be allocated a keeper at the end of our training based on our behavior and characteristics. We'll stay in this gurukulam for a bit longer than the others; once our basic education is complete, we'll have a further season of training with our appointed keepers."

I was beginning to better understand the workings of this gurukulam. Not that I hadn't already wondered about it, but, in a way, I had just got on with life without giving it much thought. I would get up in the morning, be fed and washed, and then we would all set off in a group toward the small temple, where we were taught to stand still. This was the most difficult exercise. Because after a while, your legs feel numb; the pins and needles make you sway from left to right. We were taught not to move too much, or to make sudden movements that might frighten people. We were taught to wait patiently for mealtimes, and we had to get used to the scents of incense and camphor, and other temple features; all potential aspects of life in the temple were accurately re-created.

But the hardest part was the chains. The first time I felt the icy clasp of metal around my leg, I was overcome by a feeling of disgust. A chain: symbol of submission, captivity, slavery, and the loss of freedom. A disgraceful object invented by man to destroy his fellow beings. A repulsive object that serves no other purpose than to restrain you. When I felt this chain around my leg, my eyes welled up with tears. My first tears of indignation, pain, and anguish. And the very thought that I was going to spend the rest of my life attached to this demeaning object filled me with rage and sadness. But what could I do? Accept my fate? Rebel against it? Flee? But how? All these questions crossed my mind, but I could not really find any satisfactory solution. And when dusk fell, we headed back to our enclosures, where we were fed; the day was over.

I found the training tiring and monotonous, even though we were surrounded by this beautiful landscape. I struggled to concentrate. Rather than listening to the temple bells, I was distracted by the cry of the peacocks, the song of the Malabar hornbills—with their yellow beaks and black caps to attract males—and the tapping of the green woodpecker against the tree trunks.

This walk with Manmath was therefore a breath of fresh air. We came close to the river, and the very thought of crossing over to the other side made me tremble with excitement. The sensation of water on my skin did me good. Feeling the current, listening to the soothing gurgle of the river, constantly flowing . . . I wanted to be swept away by this river, without contemplating where it might take me; I just wanted to go with the flow, see other landscapes, other people, and lead a different life. The contact with water transported me back to my time in Varkala, where I had dreamed of climbing down the cliffs, crossing the sea, and discovering other worlds. Lost in thought, I had forgotten about Manmath, who had already crossed over to the other side. Watching me from the riverbank with a smile, he inquired:

"So, are you coming? You really are a big dreamer. We must hurry because I'm famished, and I know a place where we can eat fresh bamboo."

As I emerged from the water, I found myself on the other side of the river Moyar. Just looking at the gurukulam from this side of the river gave me a curious sensation, one of freedom and relief. Only a few meters separated us from the gurukulam, but these few meters seemed to me like an abyss, as if we were in a different world. I turned to Manmath, who had already set off, and followed him.

On this side of the river, the forest was denser, with magnificent trees and scents that I had never known. This part of the forest, untouched by sunlight, was beautiful, and a single ray of sunlight falling upon a leaf or a flower was enough to set the forest alight with a profusion of colors, rekindling its hues of yellow and green . . . There was something mysterious about the forest. I had the impression that it was talking to me, that it wanted to reveal a secret to me. I felt welcome here. It was as if the forest had unfurled a carpet of dry leaves so as to receive me with open arms, like the return of the prodigal son. It was this, exactly this odd sensation that I had experienced at the start of our walk: a homecoming. A return to the native land. Back to my roots. Here, I felt at ease. This is what the forest was trying to convey: "Welcome home." Here, I could hear it clearly. The hospitable forest wanted to embrace me with its branches and offer me its riches.

This first encounter with the forest filled me with courage and gave me a sense of what freedom could be like. We continued to walk for some time, until we reached the edge of the forest, when Manmath said to me:

"This is where we're going to stop for food. Look at all these bamboo trees! I bet it's the first time that you've seen so many, isn't it?"

"Yes, you're right, Manmath," I admitted.

"But we have to be quick, because this is also the Gajavasis' favorite location, and I really don't want to meet any of them."

"Oh really? And why not?"

"They don't like us much, and also, it's their territory. As to why they don't like us, that's another matter altogether . . . but they find us arrogant, snobbish, and privileged, and they consider us to be slaves of man."

"I think I understand what they're like, but I would like to meet some of them."

"Don't worry, you'll have the opportunity to see some of them. But, you see, the Gajavasis have their own social structure. They move about in small, intimate groups, which consist solely of female elephants and calves. It's a matriarchal system. The female elephants keep to themselves, and the male calves live with the group only until adolescence, after which they leave the group, and spend their life all alone. The males form small groups and keep to themselves too. So, you see, it would be very difficult for you to mingle with the Gajavasis; all you can do is observe them."

I was impressed by Manmath's explanation. This elephant knew everything, and I enjoyed his company. We began to devour fresh bamboo with great relish. Manmath was ravenous, and said nothing during our meal. Once it was over, he took me to a watering hole. I could see that he was hurrying so as to avoid any unpleasant encounters, and when we arrived, other animals had also gathered there to drink. Here, I saw Sambar deer for the first time. These magnificent spotted does were so elegant! There were also mouse deer, wild bulls, boars, and wild dogs; I was impressed by all these creatures.

After we'd quenched our thirst, we remained there for a few moments to observe the other animals, and Manmath continued:

"Look at all these animals who are living in harmony with nature. Although this life may seem peaceful to you, extreme violence may also be concealed within it. Every creature must fight for its very survival, and life in the jungle is no easy matter. Freedom also has its price. And to return to our previous discussion, when you asked me if the gurukulam was afraid that the Gajahramans might escape to find freedom, you should know that we domesticated elephants have been groomed to be docile and subservient. This goes back a very long time. Too long, for that matter: four thousand years! Since then, we have been made to believe that it is better to live in captivity than in the jungle, and this notion has stripped us of any appetite for change. By exposing us to this life in the forest, the gurukulam strengthens our belief that our situation is in fact better than that of these animals who live in freedom. And so, effectively, for thousands of years, we have been living under the extreme illusion that our way of life is the best. As our ancestors never rebelled, this mode of existence became the norm for us. Our life in captivity, our caste system, our docility, and our acceptance of our condition: all of this became normality. We are scared to confront freedom. We think we're doing just fine, confined to our gilded cages! We are content to follow the path that has already been carved out for us, without giving a thought to what we really want. We are all just cowards. We lack courage. The courage to reinvent ourselves, to live our lives as we desire. And the worst thing is that this cowardice has now become hereditary. This grooming has killed off any desire for freedom and has stifled our ambition to be ourselves. We have become the product of a system in which it is difficult to escape from fate and caste. It's very rare for the elephants who attend the gurukulam to escape, because they wouldn't know what to do with their freedom. You see, to a certain extent, we're trapped in a vicious cycle. We are unhappy because we aren't free, but if we obtain freedom, we can't live like the other elephants, because we don't have a family; we don't belong to a group. So ultimately, we are condemned to falling in line with the established system."

Manmath had just provided an explanation of the issue that I had been pondering over from the start. This made sense to me, but I was no longer listening; all this made me weary. I hadn't even begun my battle, yet doubts had already started creeping into my mind. I had the impression that this would be an insurmountable task, and I was beginning to feel discouraged by Manmath's words on the complexity and difficulty of this life. But I didn't want to think of this; all I wanted was to savor this moment of happiness exploring the forest. My friend noticed my lack of interest in the discussion, stopped speaking, and continued to quench his thirst. All of a sudden, he prodded me with his trunk, and said:

"Look, Lakshmi, a herd of Gajavasis has just arrived."

Deep in thought, I hadn't noticed their arrival. There were around ten of them: five adult females with two young males and three calves. As I saw them arrive, calm and confident, I couldn't help but notice that this was a watering hole that they frequented. Of course, they hesitated a little when they saw us. The female adults gathered around the calves as if to protect them, and then they began to drink, without paying any attention to us.

Seeing them together like that as a family, I was overcome by joy.

"So that's what a family looks like: mothers, cousins, aunts, brothers, and sisters," I said to myself.

They all seemed happy. The calves were splashing themselves with water, playing with each other under the watchful gaze of the adults, while the two young elephants were engaged in a sort of playful fight, to measure up their strength. I was moved by this spectacle. But I couldn't explain the feeling it had aroused within me. It was as if I was happy and sad at the same time. Happy to sense their bliss, but at the same time sad, knowing that I would never have the opportunity to experience this joy myself. Perhaps it was melancholy. This melancholy that I had seen in my mother. It was visible in her eyes: this mix of joy and sadness. I now understood how she had felt all her life. I felt this was a moment of revelation: a realization of this melancholic feeling.

I felt like getting close to these elephants, smelling and feeling them; I felt like playing with the calves, sharing their happiness. But I remained there, transfixed, unable to move, and all I could do was observe them. After a while, Manmath told me that it was time to leave. In any case, the herd of Gajavasis was leaving thc watering hole, and I watched them set off. This final image would remain engraved in my memory forever: the calves in single file, holding on to one another's tails, followed by the older elephants, the family heading toward the setting sun.

Chapter Five

MY TRIPS INTO THE FOREST became increasingly more frequent. I'd got into the habit of breaking away from the gurukulam, or rather, escaping from this world. Manmath had noticed this change that was taking place within me, but he never said anything about it. I was often absent. I was quite sure that everyone knew, but strangely, I never felt as if anyone was going to prevent me from doing this. Sometimes, I would spend the whole day in the forest, and at dusk, I would return to the gurukulam. Several days passed by like this, until I had an astonishing experience, one that was strange, to say the least, an encounter that would change the course of my life.

■ ■ ■

As usual, I had left the gurukulam, heading toward the watering hole, where I would often encounter the herd of

Gajavasis. It was always the same elephants who would come here regularly, and I would spend my time watching them. But we would never communicate with each other. It was as if we belonged to two completely different species of animals. They never initiated any communication, and I never dared to take the first step. It seemed to me that even if I had, they would have turned me away; we were from two different worlds.

One day, I was a little weary of just looking at them without being able to get close to them, so I decided to go a little deeper into the forest, and I headed toward the hill overlooking the plain. Fueled by curiosity, I wanted to discover what lay behind it. Once I'd reached the foot of the hill, I paused to reflect a little: How much time would I need to climb it? Would I be back on time? I wasn't too sure of myself; perhaps I should postpone this trip? I was just about to leave when I turned around and found myself trunk to trunk with an elephant. This made me jump, and this in turn brought a smile to his face, and he said to me:

"Are you looking for something, or for someone?"

This surprised me a little.

"Well, I'm looking for something, I'm not sure what, but why someone? I don't know anyone here," I responded.

All the while, I was looking at him carefully to try to work out what he could be doing here. He didn't appear to be a Gajavasi, but I was also certain that he didn't belong to the gurukulam. I saw that he too was observing me in the same way, trying to work out where I'd come from, a smile permanently fixed on his face.

"That's what I thought: you must have lost your way. That's right, isn't it?"

There was something irritating about his smile; it was a bit like when someone asks you questions to which they clearly know the answer. He didn't seem to be dangerous, but Manmath had always told me to be wary of solitary males, and here was one of them. So I responded curtly:

"No, I'm not lost. I know exactly where I'm going. I want to go to the other side of the hill."

"Why's that?"

"What do you mean, why? I just want to go and see it. But maybe I don't have the right to do so?"

This time, his questions really irritated me. He must have sensed this, and as if he intended to hurt my feelings, he looked me in the eye and said:

"I hope you realize that you're in a forest? And that in a forest, each species has its own territory? But of course, I understand that a Gajahraman like you, coming from a gurukulam, doesn't know the rules."

He continued to sneer at me, which was getting on my nerves . . .

"You know what, I don't want to run into any trouble. I wanted to climb this hill just out of curiosity. But if it's your territory, you can have it all to yourself; I'm no longer interested, and—"

I stopped suddenly, mid-sentence; it had just occurred to me: How did he know that I was from the gurukulam? I had never met him before. Was he a spy? He couldn't be, otherwise Manmath would have forewarned me.

"How do you know I'm from the gurukulam?" I asked him suspiciously.

He burst into laughter. He seemed to be genuinely amused, as if he'd heard a good joke; this time, he wasn't mocking me.

"Well, it's glaringly obvious! The scars on your legs caused by chains . . . also, because you've been at the gurukulam, your skin smells of camphor and incense."

I then realized that the wretched chains had left scars on my hind legs. Scars that appeared as if they had been branded onto my legs, leaving behind a permanent wound. I felt most humiliated.

"Let me go," I said, confused.

He blocked my path.

"If I've nothing to do here, then I'd rather go."

Dodging him, I set off.

"Wait, don't leave!"

As he spoke, he took hold of my trunk with his, and held me back. I wanted to free myself from his grip, and I tried to extract myself, but it was impossible. I couldn't move; he was so strong! But I wasn't going to stay like that; that was out of the question. I also wanted to show him that I wasn't weak. I wanted to prove that I could match up to his strength, and I tugged even more forcefully. We remained like that for some time, measuring up our strength, but I sensed that he didn't want to fight, otherwise he would have charged at me. Moreover, he had large tusks. It was a tug of war, and I felt him gain ground. I felt my legs slide; he had a stronger grip, and he dragged me toward him. That's when I suddenly remembered a technique that my dear friend Manmath had taught me. With great difficulty, I pulled him toward me with all my strength, and when I felt his body tilt forward, I loosened my grip. He was taken by surprise, and, trunk in the air, he went flying into a tree, knocking branches and leaves onto his head. Normally, I'd have fled the scene in such a situation, but this one was so comical that I burst out laughing. I even went up to him.

"Are you OK? You haven't hurt yourself, have you?"

This time, I waited for him to charge at me. But he was a bit stunned by the branch that had struck his head, and as he shook his head and flapped his big ears to get rid of the leaves, he too laughed.

"You're a funny Gajahraman, you are! Usually, you lot don't like to fight; you prefer the sound of bells to the clashing of tusks. Where did you learn this technique?"

"My friend Manmath taught me; he's a Gajatrya. He has taught me many things." I felt very proud.

"That's good. In life, you need to know how to defend yourself! OK, let's call a truce? But in any case, I didn't want to fight with you. I only wanted to hold you back. I didn't want to prevent you from visiting the hill—in fact, I actually wanted to invite you there to see it."

He was looking at the hill, speaking in a very friendly tone.

"I didn't like your mocking tone and the way you were sneering at me," I said.

Just then, I noticed that his hind legs also bore light bruises caused by chains.

"By the way, I see that you too have chain marks. But I've never seen you at the gurukulam."

He turned around and looked at his hind legs.

"Yes, it's true, I also have scars, but they are old. I hope they will vanish one day. As for the wounds inflicted on my heart, they will never disappear."

"So, who are you? What are you doing here? Why are you here all alone? And how come you have chain marks but you're free?"

I bombarded him with questions.

"Whoa, whoa! Slow down! Firstly, it's a long story, and secondly, if you want to climb the hill, it's too late. So, come another time, and I'll tell you my story as we're climbing the hill; I'll show you around it."

Just then, I realized that the sun had already sunk behind the hills; twilight had fallen. This was the time of day I liked the most, when day and night come to greet each other. I was always enthralled by this pale shade of blue, streaked with hues of yellow, red, and orange, painted onto the canvas of the sky. This was the perfect time to experience the fragrance of the flowers, and the intoxicating profusion of colors and scents. This was the moment when the moon would enter the scene to chase away the sun, making way for the secretive and mysterious night. Once again, I sank into a deep rêverie.

"You like this time of the day, don't you? I'm here for the same reason: it's the best place to watch the sunset."

His words roused me from my daydream.

"Can I come back tomorrow?" I asked.

"Tomorrow? OK, I'll come and wait for you at the same place, but try to come earlier, because we need some time if you want to climb the hill."

"OK. See you tomorrow then! By the way, I'm called Lakshmi," I said, setting off for the gurukulam.

"I'm Veeran. See you tomorrow, Lakshmi the warrior," he replied, smiling.

And I disappeared into the night, an image of his friendly smile etched in my mind.

■ ■ ■

The following day, I waited impatiently for my chance to set off. Manmath noticed this and asked me why I was so restless. I kept quiet. It wasn't that I didn't want to tell him about my meeting with Veeran, but if he knew about this, he would lecture me endlessly, warning me about something or other. I knew it was only for my own good, but I was no longer the Lakshmi of the past. I felt more mature, more courageous, and ready to face life. At the end of the lessons and after the meals were served, I set off even before I'd finished eating, which worried Manmath even more.

"Tell me where you're heading. If you haven't come back by nightfall, at least I'll know where to find you," he told me.

His fatherly nature began to exasperate me.

"Don't worry, Manmath, I'll be back before nightfall, trust me. And you don't need to know where I'm going," I said, to put an end to any potential discussion.

He shook his head with a look of resignation and went back to his meal.

As I was on my way, I was riddled with doubt as usual. Who was this Veeran? What was he doing there all alone? It was common for a Gajavasi male to wander about alone looking for a companion if it was the mating season. But this wasn't the case with Veeran. Veeran wasn't a Gajavasi, and I didn't know which caste he belonged to, but he had chain marks on his legs. Was he one of those elephant touts who were sent out by hunters to capture others? Manmath had always told me to be wary of them. But now it was too late to turn back. Wracked with doubt, I was already at the foot of the hill when I spotted Veeran, who was waiting for me. He welcomed me cheerfully, and we set off together. As we walked, he told me his story.

■ ■ ■

"I'm like you, Lakshmi: I was born in captivity. But that's where our similarities end. My family are descendants of the Gajatryas of the Travancore kingdom; we once belonged to the court of the Varma kings, for several generations. In fact, our family lineage goes right back to the Raja Marthanda Varma, who was the founder of this kingdom. My ancestors participated in the conquest of the entire western coast, from Kanyakumarai right up to the kingdom of Cochin. They took part in the battles of Attingal, Kollam Kayakulam, Kotarakara, and Kottayam. These were the golden years for the Gajatryas of the south. However, history took its treacherous course: during the famous Battle of Colachel, which took place in 1741, our king Marthanda Varma defeated the Dutch East India Company, bringing Dutch supremacy to an end, and captured a soldier named Eustache de Lannoy. This would change the course of our destiny, because after his capture, this particular soldier was integrated into the king's army, owing to his knowledge of the latest military techniques. And that's how, from one day to the next, we found ourselves replaced by artillery, cannons, and weapons from Europe. The mission of this man, Eustache de Lannoy, was to modernize the kingdom's army, so that with the help of the British, cannons, vehicles, and other modern artillery would replace us.

"But that didn't mean that our status changed; we continued to enjoy the privileges accorded to the Gajatrya caste. In fact, Marthanda Varma even issued an order for the royal emblem to have two elephants, one on either side, guarding the sacred conch of Sri Padmanabha, which is encircled by a garland. Later on, this emblem was adopted once again by the modern state of Kerala. That gives you an idea as to how much the kingdom respected its elephants, regardless of caste.

"One day, in May 1824, our destiny changed because of the British invasion of Burma. It goes to show that events taking place in one part of the world can have repercussions elsewhere, with disastrous consequences. Tens of thousands of elephants were sent to Burma at the request of the British. The British scoured the whole of the western coast to recruit elephants, and when this was no longer possible, they resorted to force. Of course, the first to leave were the Gajasudras. It was like an exodus. Thousands of elephants were uprooted from their native land and were sent to work in unknown territories. And the more the British procured, the more they asked for; it was like feeding a great beast whose appetite could never be satiated.

"It wasn't that Burma lacked elephants; of course, it did have some, but they were not sufficient. And capturing new ones and taming them would have taken a lot of time. But the British were impatient; everything had to be done immediately, as fast as possible. When the supply of Gajasudras started to run low, they began to capture more and more Gajavasis. But this wasn't going fast enough, and they began to grow impatient. And so, one fine day, an envoy from the Crown made an appearance at the palace and asked the king to part with his prized Gajatryas. At first, the king refused, but the British were not the kind to accept any form of refusal. After hefty discussions, arguments, and threats, the king finally gave in. And that was the end of the golden era of the Gajatryas of the Travancore kingdom and the entire western coast. We were named Malayala Gajatryas, and our lifestyle was to be reduced to that of the Gajasudras. Even worse: we were to be condemned to slavery, with no hope of return."

■ ■ ■

Veeran paused at this point, and I realized that we had already reached the top of the hill. These Gajatryas had such a way of telling stories that I had lost all sense of time, and had also forgotten all my fatigue brought on by having just climbed the hill. Their stories were exciting; listening to them, you were transported to another world. Of course, I also experienced a sense of déjà vu. But compared to Manmath's story, Veeran's story was more detailed and enthralling, tinged with greater tones of tragedy and sadness. Manmath's life story had been more sketch-like. Geographically, I felt I could identify more with Veeran's story; I was particularly moved by it.

When we reached the top of the hill, Veeran suggested that we could take a break, so that we could catch our breath a little, and also admire the landscape. It was captivating, with a magnificent view looking out onto the Western Ghats in the distance and the three rivers, Kabini, Nagur, and Moyar, snaking their way through the valleys with their shimmering waters. The plain below was verdant and dense. This was the first time I'd reached such a high altitude; with his trunk, Veeran pointed to a mountain on his right.

"Do you see that mountain over there, far away in the distance? That's where my ancestors came from. That's where they were captured thousands of years ago, becoming Gajatryas. This region is called Anaimalai, which means 'Mountain of the Elephants.'"

He gazed for a few seconds at the mountain, then indicated that it was time to climb down. I couldn't wait to set off again to hear the rest of the story. After a few meters, Veeran continued.

"My ancestors were sent into the forests on the banks of the Irrawaddy River near Mandalay. More specifically, they worked in the teak and rubber plantations. Many died of exertion and exhaustion. Thousands of Gajatryas and Gajasudras were wiped out by anthrax, an illness that can finish off an animal in a matter of a few days. My family (by that, I mean my mother and aunts) were born in a teak plantation. For many years, they embraced this new way of life, unaware of their glorious past. Only the stories of the past lived on, passed down from generation to generation, so that we would not forget our origins; we lived in the hope that we might one day return to our roots.

"After I was born, things started to change. I was just a few years old, and I had already begun to work, when one day we heard strange noises coming not from the ground, but from the sky above. Those in the camp were gripped by a wave of panic. I saw that everyone was running about helter-skelter. The workers, supervisors, and oozies were all running to seek shelter, uncertain as to where they should go. Explosions followed. Strange objects fell from the sky, dropped down by peculiar creatures above, creating an unbearable racket. When they crashed into the ground, fire broke out. Everyone in the vicinity perished. We were paralyzed with fear, and didn't know what to do, when one of the members of our group trumpeted, warning us of danger. Everyone tried to find a place to hide as best as they could. We were scared, for we couldn't run like men; when we tried, we bumped into one another. Some elephants lost their lives in this scramble. I saw others who had been struck down in the attack losing a leg, trunk, or some other body part. It was a ghastly sight. My mother and I and about ten other elephants found shelter behind a large pile of logs. From our hiding place, we watched our brothers and sisters perish, and we saw others escaping into the forest. We remained there, hidden, powerless and unable to help them.

"After a while, silence pervaded the forest. No more sounds from above, no more explosions; instead, a deathly calm prevailed throughout the camp that became very apparent. Death, the deceased, and corpses were all around us. Flesh was scattered everywhere, blood was splattered on tree trunks, and human corpses lay alongside elephant legs, trunks, and ears. The camp was riddled with gaping holes, and uprooted trees lay on the ground, roots in the air. It was an apocalyptic vision, but we knew this wasn't a natural disaster, otherwise we would have sensed it. There was definitely something human about this. No, something inhuman.

"After a moment that seemed to last forever, we saw shadows emerging from behind the trees, and the silhouettes of humans leaving their shelters; they were our masters and the workers. Some were injured; they were bleeding heavily, and someone shouted: 'This is war! The Japanese are attacking us, we need to dismantle the camp and leave, we can't stay here any longer.' Discussions ensued, orders were issued . . . the men began to dismantle the huts and they loaded our backs with whatever they could salvage. They realized that not everything could be transported; about ten elephants lay dead in the camp, and perhaps about twenty had escaped during the attack.

"Once the camp had been dismantled, we set off through the forest, looking for another secure location. After two days of walking, we reached another camp, which was in a better state than our own. It had been heavily damaged, but the structure was still intact; compared to our camp, there were fewer injuries and fatalities here. Everyone was tired and hungry: we had been walking relentlessly for two days without eating, with only water to sustain us. A tense atmosphere prevailed, not only among the men, but also among the elephants. Everyone was frightened. The slightest sound of a vehicle being driven along the main path made us panic; the atmosphere was unbearable. There was no work to be done; we spent several days remaining idle, just waiting for a decision to be made.

"One night, we heard the sound of footsteps that the men couldn't hear. Initially, these footsteps were hesitant and timid, and as we heard them approach the camp, we could tell that they were the footsteps of elephants. Shadowy figures lurked behind the trees; the men continued to sleep. It was nighttime. As the forest was dense, the moonlight struggled to permeate the darkness. We had all gathered next to the main hut, and we were no longer attached to chains. Ever since the attack, the oozies no longer chained us up—they were afraid that if there was another attack, we wouldn't be able to escape.

"It took a few moments before we were able to recognize our friends who had fled from the previous camp. They had returned, but, strangely, they didn't seem to want to join us. It was as if they were trying to tell or communicate something to us. No one dared move; everyone stayed put, while my mother decided to go and meet them. She slipped softly among the trees, trying not to make too much noise as she treaded on the dry leaves, and vanished. After a while, which seemed to last an eternity, we saw her reappear, but she was alone. We looked to see if the other elephants were following her, but there were none. They had just evaporated into thin air, disappearing into the forest as if in a dream. On her return, my mother asked us to wait until dawn for her to tell us what had been said.

"The following day, when everyone in the camp woke up, we knew that it was going to be yet another day without work or travel, because the oozies were waiting for orders from their masters. No one seemed to be coming to any decision. In any case, there were only Burmese oozies, Tamil plantation workers, and one supervisor left, who was not British. They spent their days doing very little, sitting together around the hut, smoking their beedis and cheroots; they were indecisive and as frightened as we were. They could barely cook their meals, as they were afraid that the smoke might attract the attention of the Japanese. We were eagerly awaiting my mother's report. We distanced ourselves a little from the camp, pretending to search for our food. Once we were out of sight, my mother began to speak:

"'I've got something very important to tell you on behalf of our friends: the fact is that they no longer wish to join us. They have decided that from now on, they are going to choose freedom. Freedom, at last. They have chosen to liberate themselves from this life of slavery, set themselves free from chains, and no longer be subjected to blows and violence, inflicted by sticks and bullhooks. They no longer wish to work in these camps and die of fatigue and illness. They want to return to their native land, to our home, as free creatures. They no longer wish to be subjected to the domination of our masters, or to our caste system. And if we wish, we too can be like them; we can choose to be free. They are there to help us.'

"We listened to her with our large ears, in utter disbelief. This all seemed implausible. Who had put this idea into their heads? A revolution! We were going to revolt against our masters, setting ourselves free. We found it hard to believe . . . Some elderly elephants began to mutter that this was all impossible, that it was sheer madness, and that they didn't want to risk their lives. My mother turned toward the three or four uncooperative elephants and addressed them vehemently:

"'Ah yes! You would prefer to remain slaves for the rest of your lives, die from the blows inflicted by your master, or even worse, be bombed by the Japanese in this wretched camp! No, certainly not: I personally prefer to fight for my freedom; I prefer to die in pursuit of freedom than in captivity. I've made up my mind. You can each decide for yourself, but I won't die without putting up a fight. We know how to fight: the warrior traits of the Gajatryas still run in our blood. And it doesn't matter whether you are a Gajatrya, a Gajasudra, or from another caste, we're all united in our plight as slaves. We are all equal, and as equals, we will set ourselves free! And once we are free, we will all remain equal: it'll be the end of castes and hierarchy . . . Let those who desire a new way of life, a new status, a new system, join me, join us! Those who wish to remain subservient and weak as slaves can do so. But if by misfortune you should rise up against us, we will not hesitate to fight, and even kill you.'

"I was proud of my mother," said Veeran. "I had never seen her angry like that. But it was an anger that commanded respect. She was beautiful, like the enraged goddess Durga. Beautiful in her fury. I admired her decision, and I was one of the first to line up beside her. Others followed, though the elderly elephants were still hesitant. But we were convinced that our freedom was imminent, and my mother began to outline the plan that she had already devised with the escapees.

"'So, here's the plan: at nightfall, once the men are asleep, I'll send a signal to our friends, who will be hiding not far from here. They will attack the camp, and we will join them to ransack the hut, and trample all those who fight against us.

However, I think the men will try to escape, because they no longer have any weapons, and they continue to fear a Japanese attack. Their first reaction will be to flee, as they did previously. If all goes as planned, we shouldn't run into any problems; all we'll have to do is wait, and then we can leave the camp peacefully. And if for any reason we have to fight them, then so be it. For those who are still hesitant, you have been forewarned . . . See you this evening, let's get ready!'

"It began to rain heavily at the start of the evening; this helped us, because the men came back to the hut earlier than usual. We heard the rain drumming on the roof, and the wind howling through the trees. The ground under our feet turned to clay, becoming slippery; water puddles formed in the camp. This could be dangerous, but we had to take the risk; it was now or never. My mother made sure that the men were fast asleep, snoring heavily, and when we were ready, she sent out a signal. We waited in silence, a heavy, leaden silence, when suddenly we experienced something like an earthquake. It was as if the earth were shifting under our feet, and we saw our friends emerging from all directions, crushing everything in their path. Branches went flying, trees crashed down to the ground, and they charged at the hut.

"The camp was located in a hollow, with the hut in the middle; the attacker elephants had planned their assault well by surrounding the men, giving them very little chance of escaping. It was clear that their aim was to kill as many as possible, and our friends knocked down trees to block the path for potential escapees. When we saw that the attackers were approaching, we positioned ourselves in front of the door and began to demolish it, along with the walls of the hut. The men simply didn't have time to react. Confronted with this unknown sound, they began to flee, running about in all directions, not even attempting to locate the source of danger. It took them a few moments to realize that this wasn't a human attack, but an animal attack. The first to escape were the Tamil workers, whereas the oozies tried to fight us. But they had no weapons, not even bullhooks and sticks, which gave us the upper edge. This was my first battle, and I will never forget this image of war. The attackers fought with an incredible sangfroid; nothing could stop them. The oozies and some workers who had been surrounded were trampled, tossed into the air, and crushed against tree trunks. Some elephants armed themselves with branches and sent them crashing down onto the men. Those who tried to escape got trapped on the slippery slope; they were thrown into the air, and then trampled. The sound of the rain was drowned out by the cries, sobs, and curses of injured men, along with the cracking of bones and ribs. I couldn't say how long the battle lasted, but after a while, everything ground to a halt.

"Once again, the pitter-patter of the rain could be heard as we gathered at the spot where the hut once stood. From here, we were able to comprehend the extent of the damage. As in the Japanese attack, there were bodies scattered about everywhere: on the ground, under uprooted tree trunks, under the rubble of the demolished hut, and along the slope that led to the road. Not all were dead, but some were gravely injured: broken ribs, twisted ankles, arms wrenched out of sockets, shattered skulls . . . we could hear their gasps and groans of agony, and their sobs. We never found out how many had escaped—in any case, that didn't interest us—but we decided to leave this cursed place as quickly as possible, without waiting for dawn to break. There were no fatalities among us, just a few minor injuries. That was fortunate, as we had to depart quickly.

"And it was on this night, which reeked of blood, death, and rain, that we found freedom. A barren night that was moonless and starless, but filled with dark, rain-soaked clouds; a night that was bleak and macabre, but also lifesaving. We set off in silence, without any clear destination in mind, walking through the jungle, waiting for day to break to make a decision.

"The following day, at the crack of dawn, when the first rays of sunlight appeared, we stopped walking. We had already covered a good distance, and were far away from the camp; there was no longer any need to fear any potential retaliation. It had also stopped raining. The glowing sun was rising in the clear blue sky, thousands of rays emanating from it. A new life unfurled before us. A life without chains, masters, or forced labor: a life of freedom, without restrictions. No one would ride on our backs any longer, no one would give us orders anymore. Neither sticks nor hooks would touch our skin; from now on, our skin would only feel the caress of the forest breeze. And facing the Irrawaddy delta, we took this solemn vow: we would never be slaves again and we would live in harmony without any form of hierarchy or concept of caste, and we would all be equal. On this day, it was also decided that those who wished to stay in Burma would do so, and those who wished to return to India would undertake the long journey to our motherland.

"Lengthy, endless discussions followed, but at the end of the day, two groups were created. The first consisted of older elephants who would not be able to withstand the journey, along with some Burmese and Indian elephants who did not want to leave Burma. I was in the second group. The majority in this group were Indian, but there were also some Burmese elephants who longed for a new land. The farewells were painful. We were going to leave behind our brothers and sisters with whom we had shared all the suffering and pain of forced labor, the humiliation of being slaves, of being ill-treated . . . so many things that had united us! With heavy hearts, we went our separate ways. The first group had decided to head to Laos along the Mekong River. And for our group, the journey was going to be long. Very long indeed.

"From the very first day, my mother became the leader of the group by mutual consent. She decided that it would be easier to lead us southward, returning to India via Bangladesh. That's how our exodus toward the south began, along the Irrawaddy River, going via Chauk, Akyab, crossing the Chindwin River. The journey was tiring and dangerous, but no one ever complained or rebelled, and no one doubted my mother's decisions. On some occasions, we lost our way for several days, and we had to retrace our steps to try to get back on the right path, but I never saw my mother give up or even weaken. Her decisions were sensible and correct, and everyone felt safe under her guidance. Not once during this long trek did we feel unsafe, even if danger lurked.

"Finally, one fine day after weeks of walking, we found ourselves facing the Bay of Bengal. We were overcome with relief.

Although we hadn't yet reached the end of our journey, we had crossed the Indo-Burmese border. At this point, we had to decide where we were going to settle, but no one had the faintest idea as to where that might be. We had all been born in captivity; we had no ties to any location. The only place that had been mentioned to my mother by her ancestors was Anaimalai, our Promised Land. We therefore unanimously decided to settle there.

"Then began the second part of our trip toward our ancestral land, traversing India, from the northeast to the southwest. Here too there were numerous obstacles to overcome: we had to find our way, protect ourselves from predatory animals and hunters, and we had to fight against all kinds of things that could hinder our progress. Anaimalai: we kept dreaming about it. We became obsessed with the thought of this elephant mountain. Every kilometer we traveled and each day that passed took us closer to the Promised Land, even if we were unaware as to what awaited us there."

Veeran continued to narrate his tale:

"One morning, at that very spot where we were standing just now, my mother pointed toward Anaimalai, and announced, her voice breaking with emotion: 'Here we are, my friends, we have finally arrived! Our journey stops here. But only the journey will end here, not our struggle, as we still don't know how and where we are going to settle. This place seems to be a peaceful and perfect spot for us to recuperate, and it will give us a bit of time to explore our surroundings. As soon as we have rested, I'll set off with some scouts, and we will make a decision on our return.'

"The place that we had chosen was not unfamiliar to us. As a matter of fact, our new environment resembled the Burmese landscape; it had the same sort of vegetation, with bamboo, teak, and other trees. Two rivers, the Thamirabarani and the Vaigai, flowed between Anaimalai and this hill. It was an ideal location, with limited human activity and very few wild animals.

"My mother and some other elephants soon set off on an expedition toward Anaimalai, and we eagerly awaited their return. Some days later, they returned, worn out and a little downcast. As usual, my mother spoke up:

"'Our expedition went well, but I'm very sorry to report that it will be impossible to settle here in the place that we thought would be our Promised Land: this mountain, surrounded by enormous forests, is bustling with human activity, and it would be difficult for us to get past them unnoticed. There are numerous Gajavasis, and the men are in the process of setting up what they call national parks; this would make our lives difficult. We wouldn't be able to live in peace; we would be living in constant fear of being captured, as the presence of men nearby could be fatal for us. We have also seen that slavery is still rife in this forest: we noticed hundreds of our brothers and sisters chained up and working, just as we were in our camp. On our way back, we decided that we would set them free one day, just as we have set ourselves free. This freedom that has breathed new life into us must be shared! We will strive to set free as many elephants as possible, and this location that we have chosen for ourselves today will become a refuge for any elephant who decides to be free. Any elephant who has either managed to escape on their own, or who has been set free by our community, will be welcomed as a member of the family, and will enjoy the same freedom as us, regardless of caste or creed. From now on, we will be Gajarastas. We will liberate our brothers and sisters who are enslaved; we will not be afraid to fight. Death will be our companion, and freedom our life. This location seems ideal for launching attacks and then retreating. Here, we will be left in peace, hidden behind these hills.'

"My affection for my mother grew day by day," Veeran continued. "I was proud of her, and I admired the way in which she had skillfully led us through all these forests and jungles. She had delivered us safe and sound to our Promised Land, and now she was ready to fight for the plight of all elephants in slavery. As usual, she allowed those who didn't share her opinions to express their thoughts, but all were in agreement, and ever since that day, our community has been a land of refuge for all elephants who have rebelled against their situation and have abandoned it. Initially, we attacked the camps surrounding Anaimalai, and we liberated hundreds of elephants, but this came to an end when machines replaced elephants and there was no further need to risk our lives and peace. Having said that, we continue to welcome all those who wish to escape their fate."

This is how Veeran's story ended as we reached the foot of the hill. The location was well concealed. This part of the forest was blanketed by gigantic trees, and Veeran explained to me that we were standing on the right side of Anamudi, the highest peak of the Western Ghats; its enormous rocks formed a natural barrier against any invasion. I could now clearly understand why Veeran's mother had chosen this strategic location for establishing her community. Everything you needed could be found here: a river flowing nearby, thousands of fruit trees, bamboo trees in abundance, and a calm and serene atmosphere.

Veeran offered to take me to visit the community and introduce me to his friends. A good number of elephants were walking around peacefully, while others were lying down and resting. Some looked at me curiously, while others just ignored me. As we went past an elephant who was lying down, Veeran paused.

"I'll introduce you to one of the oldest elephants of the community; there are only four of them left. They are our comrades who have been with us right from the outset. There are only a few elephants remaining who can share memories of our journey to India."

The elephant looked at me, rose to his feet, and stretched; he greeted and welcomed me. He was old, very old indeed, and had trouble with his eyesight, and so he asked me to come close to him.

"What's your name?" he asked. His voice was barely audible.

"My name is Lakshmi."

"And where are you from?"

"I'm from the gurukulam," I responded.

His face lit up with a cryptic smile.

"Welcome, my dear Lakshmi. And whatever your reason for leaving the gurukulam, may peace be with you; you'll be safe here."

He then placed his trunk on my head to bless me. I was going to retort that I hadn't come to seek refuge, and that I'd come simply out of curiosity, but the old elephant was already lying down again, and had closed his eyes.

"Let him sleep," Veeran whispered to me. "It's his duty to welcome all the new elephants, but tomorrow he will already have forgotten you, and it's highly likely that he will ask you the same questions over and over again, until he gets used to your presence."

"Do you know why he smiled like that when I told him I was from the gurukulam?"

"No, I don't know, you'll have to ask him."

"Great idea! I mean, firstly, he's not going to recognize me, and if I ask him about his smile, the question will fall on deaf ears!" It was now my turn to smile.

We stepped away from the elderly elephant and headed toward the younger elephants. I noticed a cloud of dust rising from their midst. Veeran gave me a briefing as we drew closer.

"I must tell you that our community is a true refuge for wretched souls, a cour des miracles, you could say, but you'll see that for yourself. We have all kinds here: elephants who have escaped from forced labor, some from circuses, others from zoos, and then there are those who have worked in tourism . . . all sorts. Come, look over here: these are footballer elephants. And over there, you can see elephants who play polo. And look at this one."

He showed me an unusual-looking elephant with a very tiny hat perched on his large head, who was trying to balance on a tiny piece of wood.

"Do you see that elephant? Well, he escaped from the circus, but he never recovered from the experience. All these elephants are struggling to overcome their former trauma; they've undergone extreme suffering, and the scars remain. And there are other elephants who just can't shake off their former tics, like that elephant, standing at the foot of the tree, pulling on an invisible chain."

It was true; there he was, the poor elephant, moving his leg back and forth, trying to pull on an imaginary chain. This place, which had initially seemed calm and serene, was gradually proving to be more of a psychiatric hospital than a refuge for elephants fighting for the freedom of those who were enslaved. Further on, we walked past a group of elephants who looked particularly odd. There were four or five of them standing on their own, swaying from left to right. They were shaking their heads and ears more than usual.

"And what about them?" I asked Veeran, pointing my trunk at them.

"Them? They're just drunk!" He laughed heartily.

"What do you mean, drunk? What does that mean?"

"Drunk? That means being in a drunken state."

"OK. And what exactly does that mean?" I asked, dubiously.

"Come, let's leave them alone. They might get annoyed. Being drunk means being suspended in a state between consciousness and unconsciousness; it occurs when one ingests intoxicating substances, and for us, that means fermented fruits. Did you know that we elephants are among those rare animals who are aware of their own existence? And that by being conscious of our plight, we can experience sadness? And did you know that to forget our sorrow and distress, we have the ability to get drunk intentionally? That's what these elephants here are doing. They are elephants from the zoo; that's the worst thing that can happen to an animal. The zoo and the circus can finish off any animal mentally. It's the most violent and barbaric form of treatment that an animal can be subjected to. Working in the circus is the utmost form of subservience to man; we are groomed and made to do things that we are not designed to do naturally. And as for zoos, they completely brainwash you into believing that you're living in the wild, when you aren't. So sometimes we get drunk to forget our unhappiness."

"But aren't you happy?"

"Happiness is subjective. Not everyone has the same concept of happiness. Someone who gets drunk is as happy as me when they are under the influence of alcohol; that's their happiness, as ephemeral as it may be. That's why it becomes addictive: one looks for this ephemeral state, which tends to evaporate as soon as the effect disappears. Some elephants get drunk to forget their suffering, while others drink to kill boredom. It depends on their state of mind."

"But can I try it even if I'm not unhappy?"

"Of course! It will put you into a state of ecstasy, or a kind of jovial state, if you don't consume too much. But maybe you should try it another day, as it's beginning to get dark, and if you have to get home, you had better leave now."

The thought that I belonged to the gurukulam had not crossed my mind even once that day. This trip to the hill and Veeran's exciting story had made me forget all notions of reality. But it was true, I had to go back. Veeran offered to accompany me, and this time we took a shortcut that bypassed the hill. When we reached the edge of the river Moyar, I said to Veeran by way of farewell:

"Thank you, Veeran, that was an unforgettable day. I learned a lot. Could I come back and visit you again?"

"Of course, Lakshmi, you can come whenever you want, and even come for good if you're not happy at the gurukulam. But avoid taking this shortcut, because it's dangerous for someone who doesn't know this part of the forest. In any case, you know where to find me, don't you?"

We parted on these words, and I crossed the Moyar. It was good to feel the water on my skin; it had been a very hot day. As I sprayed my back with water, I listened to the realm of silence that had set into the night. The frogs and toads had begun their nocturnal chorus. Immersed in this river, I was comforted by the thought that freedom was within easy reach. Not all was lost; my life could take a new direction if I so wished. I had to make a decision, but I didn't have much time. Soon, I would be allocated an elephant keeper; after that, it would be too late. Telling myself that I would make a decision as quickly as possible, I got out of the water to set off toward the gurukulam. Water droplets glistened like a string of pearls along my back. In the moonlight, they resembled hundreds of shooting stars diving to the ground, where they would perish.

Chapter Six

OVER THE NEXT FEW DAYS, I remained at the gurukulam so as not to arouse too much suspicion. I took part in the training as if nothing had happened. The slightest faux pas would have raised alarm among the elephant keepers. As soon as I'd returned from my trip to the hill, I had told Manmath about my encounter with Veeran and the Gajarastas. This hadn't surprised him: he knew of this community. When I asked him why he had never spoken to me about them, it transpired that he didn't think much of them. To him, the Gajarastas were just a bunch of corrupt, lazy elephants who whiled away their time getting drunk. Even their concept of freedom was merely a utopian vision, he told me.

I didn't want to enter into a discussion with Manmath. I had quickly realized that he would never abandon his way of life, and so I didn't tell him about my plans, not because I was afraid that he would report me, but simply because I didn't want him to dissuade me from joining this community. But over the next few days, doubts were gnawing away at the back of my mind: What was I going to do? And if I escaped, would my life be confined to these hills alone? I would, of course, be free. But what next? Was freedom what I truly wanted? And what was I going to do with it? I went round in circles thinking about all of this, but I couldn't find an answer. Though I desperately wanted to be free, the fear of the unknown worried me, and, on an impulse, I decided to go and take another trip to the hill.

When I reached the hill, I found Veeran in the same place where we had seen each other for the first time. But he seemed to be behaving strangely. He was swaying from left to right like the other elephants I had previously seen. I instantly realized that he must have eaten fermented fruits, for as I came closer to him, I could smell a strong odor of mango and sugarcane. He greeted me jovially.

"Hello, Lakshmi. It's been a while since I last saw you. I was beginning to think that you were afraid of our community, and you no longer wanted to see me again."

"Of course not! I was busy; I wasn't scared of you. Why would I be scared?"

"Oh, you know, people say all sorts of things about us . . . We don't have a good reputation."

As he spoke, he picked up a mango that was lying at his feet. I hadn't initially noticed, but scattered around him were mangoes and pieces of sugarcane. He held the mango for a few moments in his trunk as if in contemplation, and then stuffed it into his mouth.

"Yes, it's true that you don't have a good reputation. I spoke to Manmath about it; he doesn't think much of you lot," I said, gazing at the fruits on the ground.

"Gosh, this Manmath . . . I must meet him! He seems to have a lot of influence on you. Must you really tell him everything?"

His broad grin gave way to that sneer I so hated. Oh no! He wasn't going to start that again!

"Listen, Veeran, I'm not in the mood to tolerate your sarcastic comments. I came here because I didn't feel good. But if you're going to make fun of me each time we meet, I'd prefer to put an end to our friendship. It's true that I'm younger than you, and that I have less life experience than you, but that doesn't mean I have to bear your sarcasm and ridicule!"

Veeran stopped swaying from side to side. His smile faded, and he looked at me apologetically.

"I'm sorry, Lakshmi, I was only teasing you."

Then, looking at the fruits around him, he said:

"You can join me if you want. In this kind of situation, getting drunk can help you. In fact, that's why I'm here: I didn't feel good either."

He pointed at the mangoes and pieces of sugarcane on the ground.

"Come, start by eating those. They are well fermented. Meanwhile, I'll go and look for more."

And he set off, staggering toward the mango trees. He looked comical with this swaying gait. I liked Veeran a lot. It felt good to be with him; it was like being with a big brother, even though I'd never had one. I could sense his fraternal presence and gaze, as if he was embracing me with his trunk. With him, I felt like I was with family; it was like being with someone whom you've known forever, someone with whom you've shared your joys and suffering. Of course, I liked Manmath a lot, but it wasn't quite the same. Manmath was a friend; Veeran was more than a friend. It was strange how you could become attached to someone in such a short period of time without really getting to know them . . . without really wanting to get to know them, or really wanting to know everything about them. His presence alone was enough.

Meanwhile, I had already ingested a good quantity of the fruits on the ground, and I began to feel the first signs of intoxication. All of a sudden, I felt lightheaded; my body no longer seemed to feel as heavy as it usually did. It felt as if someone was inside my head, slowly stirring my brain with a large ladle. My muscles relaxed, and I saw double. The trees had multiplied, each with thousands of branches. The sun looked like an enormous ball of fire. In the distance, I spotted a herd of speckled doe that were gradually increasing in number as I observed them. The river Moyar split into two, accompanied by a din that grew louder. But the noise had shifted from my ears to inside my head. Yes, I could hear the river Moyar in my head! The calm and soft murmur had transformed into a torrent . . . a downpour . . . a waterfall—as if I had the Jog Falls roaring inside my head.

Nevertheless, it did me good. By the time Veeran had returned with more fruits, I had already finished the ones around me, and I felt like eating more. Veeran deposited the fruits he had gathered in front of me; this time, there were also bananas and pineapples. We began to eat in silence. Once he was full, Veeran went to lie down under a tree, leaving me on my own with the rest of the fruit. My head began to spin again, and I found it increasingly difficult to stand. I decided to copy Veeran, but I struggled to walk, and my legs refused to obey me; I couldn't move forward. As soon as I took a step, I lost my balance, and felt as if I was going to fall down; it was a most unpleasant sensation. Much as I had liked this feeling of lightness in my body and head, I hated this sensation of not being able to move. But somehow or other, I found a tree, and collapsed at its foot.

It was an enormous banyan tree; its aerial roots dangled down, and also reached upward toward the sky. Its branches stretched out toward the horizon like gnarled arms. I wedged my head between the roots that were well anchored into the ground and I closed my eyes for a few seconds. This did me good; my body relaxed. I waited for my heart to stop pounding, for I felt my pulse racing, and I opened my eyes. That was a mistake, as from below, this banyan tree resembled Lord Shiva with his tangled locks, furiously dancing his eternal Tandava. And his head swayed to the rhythm of the powerful gusts of wind. I felt as if the entire tree, which made up his body, was about to break into a dance. A dance into which I would be drawn by Shiva, who would hold me captive in his strong and twisted arms. I could sense thousands of creepers seizing me, lifting and carrying me to an unknown land; I was afraid, and closed my eyes.

The darkness and emptiness morphed into a black void. A black hole from which something emerged. I couldn't say what.

A beast, perhaps. Yes, a beast. Not a big beast. In fact, he was tiny compared to me. A kind of reptile. But it was impossible to say what kind of reptile. A yellow head appeared, followed by a vibrant blue body covered in scales. And his body stopped there. Something was missing. I wasn't sure what was missing, but he seemed to be incomplete. He wasn't a pleasant sight. He climbed down the tree, and after every two or three small, rapid steps, he would stop, his yellow head bobbing up and down. He moved his head like this repeatedly, and his eyes darted back and forth, as if he were afraid of something, as if he were being pursued. He paused at the foot of the tree and looked at me with his globular eyes.

"Hey there, e-e-elephant! Can you h-h-help me?"

"What do you want? But first of all, who are you?"

"A-a-actually, I don't know wh-wh-who I am, or at least I don't know any more. C-c-can you tell me who I am?"

"What do you mean? You don't know who you are? Are you making fun of me?"

"No, e-e-elephant, I'm being serious," he said, his eyes darting back and forth.

I then noticed he had another tic: apart from shaking his head, he kept flicking his tongue out all the time. My goodness, he really was unsightly. And on top of all this, he kept changing color! He was truly bizarre . . .

"Listen, I've never seen a creature like you before. So I can't help you. But look here, you funny thing, what I find strange is that you know who I am, but you don't know who *you* are," I said, surprised.

"That's . . . b-b-be-cause of my tail," he replied, his head bobbing up and down.

I really wanted to take him by the scruff of the neck and put a stop to this involuntary movement; it was tiring!

"What do you mean, your tail?"

"Well, ever s-s-since I lost my tail, I don't know who I am."

"And how did you lose your tail?" I asked.

I was beginning to find him truly amusing, and his manner of speech was even more entertaining. It was as if his words were initially reluctant to emerge from his mouth, and then all of a sudden, they gushed out in a torrent.

"A-a-a frog ate it."

"And what were you doing with this frog?"

"I-I wanted to eat the frog; I was really hungry. W-w-we got into a fight, and she ate my tail."

"Right, but how is the fact that you lost your tail related to your lost identity?"

"Well, as it happens, ever since I lost my tail, no one recognizes me anymore."

"And do you remember what you were before?"

"I b-b-b-elieve that I was a ch-ch-chameleon," he said, not very sure of himself.

"Well, you're still a chameleon, then. You haven't stopped being a chameleon just because you lost your tail."

"I-I-don't know anymore. I'm confused. E-e-veryone is ignoring me. I-i-it's as if I no longer exist. N-n-no one is paying any attention to me. I've become i-i-invisible to everyone in the f-f-forest. N-n-no one talks to m-me anymore!"

"S-s-since (I was beginning to talk like him; his tic was contagious!) when do chameleons eat frogs? Well, that's your problem. But your story is quite comical; you lost your identity because you lost your tail, and that means you've stopped existing?"

"I tell you, th-th-the world is brutal. From one d-d-day to the next, you can find yourself nonexistent in the eyes of others because you have l-l-lost a tiny part of yourself. It was as i-i-if my tail was the most important part of my b-b-body. The world is more interested in what you don't possess than in what you do."

Suddenly, I realized that this chameleon was magnificent, despite his handicap. Not because I felt sorry for him, but this quirk he was endowed with, his tic, his constant color transitions, and his globular eyes, which could view the world in a thousand different ways . . . I liked all of this, so much so that I didn't even notice that his tail was missing.

"Tell me, chameleon, how can I help you?"

His face broke into a big grin; he seemed joyous and relieved, and his yellow head bobbed up and down even more.

"No need, el-el-elephant. Y-y-you called me 'chameleon.' That is sufficient for me. You recognized me. That's all I w-w-wanted. Th-th-thanks a lot."

And he began to climb the tree, giving me one last wink.

I opened my eyes, and there was no one about. Where had the chameleon gone? Had I been dreaming? I got back on my feet: my head was no longer spinning. Had I fallen asleep? I wasn't sure. What had happened? The last image I could recollect was that of Veeran returning with more fruits. After that, nothing. Speaking of which, where was Veeran? He was no longer there. He must have left. I looked around me: the fruits we had not eaten still lay on the ground. I was puzzled and began to walk toward the gurukulam. This time, my legs obeyed me; I no longer stumbled. I had recovered my usual gait, and on the way back, I became aware of the effect of the fermented fruits. It wasn't that bad, except that I had lost control of my movements and thoughts. But I liked this hallucinatory sensation, which allowed me to enter a world that I couldn't normally access. Intoxication took me to a different place, an intangible world suspended between dream and reality.

Over the next few weeks, I frequently returned to meet Veeran, and we would indulge in this ephemeral pleasure. He would take me to a magnificent location, a clearing not far from the river, where these magic fruits were growing. Like me, Veeran was a great dreamer. Once he had entered into his world, he would become meditative and melancholic. And sometimes, he could also be poetic.

One day, he made me laugh by recounting his adventure with the moon—the story in which he tried to devour her. In disbelief, I teased him, but he insisted on telling his story.

"Yes, Lakshmi, I assure you," he told me, devouring a piece of sugarcane, "that for a long time now, I've been trying to swallow her, yet each time, she escapes. I don't know how to keep hold of her. However, I can feel her within my trunk when she enters, but then, just like that, *whoosh!* she escapes as quickly as she came."

"You're talking nonsense, Veeran! No one can devour the moon, she's too high up in the sky. But to start with, why do you want to swallow her?" I laughed, mocking his silliness.

"I'm telling you the truth, Lakshmi. I'm able to swallow her, but I can't keep hold of her. Why do I want to swallow her? Because she's beautiful! Especially when she is a full moon. I'll even admit that I'm in love with her. In fact, I was trying to kiss her, and that's when I noticed that I could swallow her. But I sense that she doesn't love me, otherwise she'd stay within me," he explained, his voice tinged with sadness. "If you don't believe me, I can show you, if you like."

We had practically finished our first portion of fruits. The night was clear, and the sky was studded with stars. Although the moon was large, she wasn't a full moon. I was eager to see how Veeran was going to go about his mission.

He headed toward the river. I had difficulty following him, for my legs had become wobbly and kept knocking together with every step I took. I made a lot of noise as I walked, and I kept bumping into branches and tree trunks.

"Tread softly, don't make too much noise; you're going to scare her," breathed Veeran.

"Scare whom?" I asked.

I didn't know whom he was talking about; I had already forgotten his story.

"The moon, of course! Now keep quiet. First of all, you need to hide behind this tree. And most importantly, don't come out of your hiding place. The moon is very bashful, and she could well hide behind the clouds if she spots you. I took a long time to persuade her to let me kiss her, and I don't want you to come and spoil everything."

I leaned against the designated tree and watched him set off toward the river. I could no longer stand, and my head began to spin. As I leaned against the tree, I must have roused a slumbering owl perched on a branch. With her large eyes, she looked at me threateningly, then glanced at me in irritation and took flight, emitting a screech that pierced the silence of the night.

■ ■ ■

Once he had reached the edge of the river, Veeran stood still and waited, observing the surface of the flowing water.

"But what's he waiting for?" I wondered, concealed in my hiding place a few meters away.

After a few minutes, Veeran entered the river. He waded into the water, treading gingerly, taking small steps, so as not to make ripples around him. I understood why when I spotted the moon's reflection on the river's surface.

As Veeran drew close to the reflection, the moon was playing with the ripples he had created. She was bobbing up and down to the rhythm of these ripples. Veeran came even closer to the moon. Now he was right in the middle of the river. And then he paused. I could clearly see the reflection of the moon, for the current was not strong. She most certainly was stunning. Veeran treaded carefully around the reflection, creating even smaller ripples.

Suddenly, I witnessed the most beautiful spectacle I'd ever seen. The entire forest was transformed into an open-air theater. The moon performed a hauntingly beautiful dance, swaying to the pulse of the ripples Veeran had created. And then he led her into the dance, and the elephant and the moon danced together. I'd have never thought that such a spectacle could exist; it was simply breathtaking. They both danced to the melody of the water lapping at the shores of the river; they danced to the rustling of the trees. Flower buds about to burst into bloom quivered at the sight of this spectacle. Silvery fish leaped around them. And they danced on, oblivious to the jealous murmur of the stars. This spectacle was so dazzling that I closed my eyes to capture the image in my mind, enclosing it in my drawer of memories.

When I opened my eyes, Veeran and the moon had stopped dancing. The moon had frozen upon the river's surface, and I saw her tremble as her lover approached. Veeran gazed at her for a long time, raised his trunk, then placed it most gently on the surface of the water, and kissed the moon.

"You see, Lakshmi, the same thing happens each time. There she is, waiting for me, but as soon as I kiss her and take her in, she disappears. She escapes and hides behind her veil of clouds," said Veeran, joining me near the tree.

He seemed upset and couldn't take his eyes off the spot where the moon had just vanished. I didn't know what to say. I was still spellbound by the beauty of the magical scene I'd just witnessed. My eyes were still fixed on the water's surface, where Veeran had tried to capture the moon after he had kissed her. Yes, I had certainly seen her disappear into his trunk. But she had reappeared the very next moment on the river beneath the ripples that Veeran had created as he took her in. Then she had vanished, plunging the forest into darkness. I was perplexed. Could Veeran have really swallowed the moon? So why, then, was it dark? Where had she gone? I couldn't think straight.

"Are you sure you don't still have her in your trunk, Veeran?"

I walked around him to see if I could spot her through his tough hide.

"Sneeze, to see if she's there!" I said.

"But look, Lakshmi, I'd be able to feel her if she were inside me! She isn't there. In any case, let me tell you something; as beautiful as the moon may be, she is also odd."

"Oh really, why's that?"

"You saw what just happened, didn't you? Well, it's been like that since I fell in love with her. I'll tell you about it as we walk back. Come on, I feel like eating more fruits."

We set back on the path leading to the clearing, and I couldn't help but glance back to see if the moon had reappeared. Veeran carried on without even looking back; he must have got used to this. He was planning to drown his sadness in an avalanche of fruit, and perhaps fly away to the clouds in search of his beloved.

"Yes," Veeran continued, "this moon is certainly strange. Well, I don't know . . . our love story is quite strange and unusual. Our love is very fleeting, and only lasts for a few days," he said, gathering a bunch of bananas, which he divided into two portions.

He began to eat one of the portions and passed me the other. I took it and placed it at my feet: I didn't want to eat it immediately. I wanted to hear and understand Veeran's story first.

Getting drunk was out of the question until I got to the bottom of the mystery of the devoured moon.

"The first time I kissed her . . . well, the first time she let me kiss her, I should say, as she kept playing hide-and-seek with me; this game lasted for a while. So, the first time, it was an evening like this one. She was round and resplendent. You know that she diminishes in size gradually, don't you?"

Without even waiting for me to answer, he carried on.

"The first time, I just kissed her. The idea of swallowing her only came to me much later, when she refused to recognize me."

Veeran stopped and looked at me to see if I was following his story, but I was confused.

"You don't seem to be following me," he said. "You look dazed."

Then, seeing the bunch of bananas at my feet, he inquired:

"Why don't you eat your bananas?"

I was muddled. I didn't really understand his story.

"I just wanted to wait until the end of the story before eating," I replied.

"Go on, eat them. In any case, with or without bananas, you won't understand anything. It's an absurd story. So, I told you that the idea of swallowing her only came to me much later. After the second or third encounter. But I will always remember the first time I kissed her. One evening, I was on my way back, and I'd reached the foot of the hill, when I saw her emerge from the other side of the slope. The sun had just set, leaving behind red and orange streaks upon the canvas of the sky. And by the time the moon appeared, an invisible hand had drawn tiny stars onto the bluish backdrop of the sky, which grew bigger as I observed them. She was a large, yellow moon. She strode through the sky like a goddess cloaked in a blue robe, dotted with clouds. It was love at first sight. I had never seen her so radiant. I couldn't take my eyes off her. I began to follow her as she moved. Keeping one eye on her, and the other on the path, I ran among the trees and plants until I reached the river. And when I paused to catch my breath, and saw her settle upon the water's surface, I realized that she was mine. Like today, I entered the water and kissed her. And I sensed that she was also in love with me, for she let me kiss her without pushing me away.

"But our love story only lasted for a few days. Thereafter, she began to hide more frequently behind the clouds. She refused to appear, and even worse, she grew smaller. She was wearing a halo of light and remained distant and remote; her beauty diminished by the day. Was she hiding for fear of not being beautiful enough? I have no idea. In any case, one evening, she disappeared, plunging the forest into gloom. This was the first time I had experienced the sorrow of love. My heart bled. I pined for her. Her absence became unbearable. Every so often, when I spotted her through a curtain of clouds, I'd sink into depression. In distress, I would walk round and round in circles in this clearing, for I couldn't get close to her. When I waited for her at the river's edge, all I could see was a dark stain of clouds floating upon the water's surface. I wandered through the forest like a soulless imbecile.

"I had lost all hope of seeing her again, when suddenly, one evening, she reappeared. Just like the first time, she was stunning, and round. Spontaneously, I ran toward the river. I knew she would come there. My heart was pounding as I awaited her. And then she arrived. I saw her come close to the river, accompanied by thousands of fireflies, which illuminated her path.

"There wasn't a moment to lose. I had already waded back into the water, waiting for her to settle on the surface. But when she saw me, she stopped at the river's edge; she seemed hesitant to enter the water.

"'Good evening, my beautiful moon,' I said to her in my most melodious voice. 'I'm so happy to see you! I missed you, you know. I was so sad not to have seen you these past few days.'

"She looked at me wide-eyed in surprise, and smiled at me, saying:

"'Who are you, elephant? I don't know you. I've never seen you before.'

"This was the first time I had heard her speak. Her voice was as gentle as the breeze.

"'It's me, beautiful moon. Don't you remember? I met you a few days ago, we danced in this river, and I even kissed you.'

"Upon hearing these words, the moon blushed, caught hold of a cloud that was sailing by, and hid behind it.

"'Oh no! My beautiful moon, I beg of you, don't hide! Show yourself, show me your face . . . Without you, my life has become hell. I love you, my beautiful moon! Don't make me suffer.'

"I pleaded with her. Heeding my words, the moon came out from behind the cloud and revealed herself.

"'You see, elephant," she said, "I believe I'm also in love with you. I like you a lot, but I assure you that I've never seen you before.'

"'But you're the same moon I kissed last time. Don't you remember?'

"'Ah, no, I'm the new moon.'

"'What do you mean, the new moon?' I said, slightly irritated.

"I began to grow impatient, and I wondered if this moon had gone mad, or if she was just mocking me. I was completely lost. All I wanted was to be able to love this moon, kiss her, and dance with her. And now she was telling me that she was the new moon, that she didn't recognize me, that she had never seen me, and all kinds of things . . . However, she was the moon I'd previously kissed. If it weren't her, then where had the other moon gone? My thoughts were jumbled; I couldn't make sense of it all.

"Seeing me in this state, the moon took pity on me.

"'You know, elephant, you look confused and mournful. But as I've said, I like you a lot and I'd like you to kiss me.'

"And she came into the river. I felt a surge of joy when I finally saw her reflection on the water's surface.

"The breeze picked up, small ripples appeared on the water's surface, accompanied by the shimmering fish, and we were in love again, just like the first time."

At this point in the story, Veeran paused. I hastened to question him.

"And so everything has been OK since then? I still don't understand why you want to swallow her if you can kiss her."

By nature, I'd always been impatient when it came to listening to stories, especially when I didn't understand them . . .

"No, that's exactly the problem. After our second meeting, she disappeared again after a few days; it was exactly like the first time. And of course, she then reappeared . . ."

"Wait, let me guess," I said, interrupting him. "When she reappeared, she no longer recognized you, because it was a new moon. That's it, isn't it?" I concluded, laughing at him mockingly.

"Exactly, you've understood the whole thing. Even today, I don't know if she does it on purpose or if she actually is a new moon each time. That's why I try to devour her: that way, I would keep her inside me. But that doesn't work either. So, I accepted our relationship as it is. I came to terms with an impossible and ephemeral kind of love. I no longer seek to devour her, but I'm content just kissing her, all the while cherishing the sweet hope that one day, she might stay within me and light up my heart, which is sinking into the depths of despair."

As much as I had laughed mockingly earlier, I was also overcome by a deep sense of despair as Veeran's final words melted into the silence of the night. I didn't know how to comfort him; I was at a loss for words. An uncomfortable silence set in between us. Without entering into any further discussion, Veeran turned around and headed toward the hill.

Thereafter, I began to leave him alone as soon as I sensed he was becoming melancholic and nostalgic. I had quickly understood that, like his love, he didn't want to share his suffering. His state of mind was contagious though, and his sadness rubbed off onto me. But I didn't want to drown in his sorrow! So I would drift into my surreal world, becoming blind to everything around me, and I would drink myself into oblivion.

I met Alphonse during one of these periods of delirium. It was a strange encounter. Even today, I couldn't say if Alphonse really exists, or if he is a figment of my imagination, because I still see him: every so often, he comes to visit me at the Eswaran Kovil.

■ ■ ■

Our first encounter took place during the final days I was to spend at the gurukulam. During this period, I had to make a decision: either to escape or accept my fate. And this decision was a difficult one. For even though every inch of my body yearned for freedom, an element of doubt nevertheless still lingered in my mind. I was waiting for something, but I didn't know what: a signal, perhaps. And the drunken stupor into which I had sunk hardly helped me. This state of semiconsciousness helped me more to forget my sorrows than to make a decision. It felt as if my thoughts were refusing to emerge from the fog where they had taken refuge, as if my mind were afraid of thinking in even the slightest rational manner. This was my state of mind when Alphonse appeared.

As usual, I was lying under my banyan tree that had a head like Shiva's when I sensed something moving overhead. I opened my eyes partially, and spotted a creature flying among the creepers. It was playfully zigzagging between the gnarled arms of the banyan tree, but it wasn't a bird. It had a strange shape that I'd seen before—a shape that I had seen elsewhere, but not in the air. I opened my eyes wide so as to identify it, but it was weaving in and out of the creepers, which made the task harder. I waited for a few seconds . . . but there was nothing there. It had disappeared. Or perhaps it was hiding? I had got used to seeing strange creatures when I was drunk, and ever since my first encounter with the chameleon, I knew more or less how to differentiate between the real and the imaginary. This was because whatever appeared in my mind would disappear once the effect of alcohol had worn off. But there were some creatures, like the chameleon, who actually existed in the flesh, with whom I had had strange encounters. But when it came to this creature, I wasn't sure. It appeared as soon as I closed my eyes, and disappeared when I opened them, as if it was trying to play a trick on me. It truly exasperated me. This game carried on for a while, until I pretended to close my eyes and waited for it to appear behind the creepers so I could grab it midflight. It then crashed into my trunk and tumbled onto the large roots of the banyan tree. I abandoned my resting position and sat up on my hind legs to discover that it was a quivering fish. He was lying on his side, struggling to get up. My first reaction was to open my eyes fully to be certain of what I saw, and when I was sure that he was indeed a fish, I helped him up. *Whoosh!* Off he soared into the air; he brushed off the dust sticking to his skin and began to fly above my head. A flying fish! Now I really had seen everything! I wanted to make sure that he was well and truly real, so I asked him:

"Tell me, who are you, flying fish?"

He carried on flying without answering me, as if he hadn't heard the question. Or maybe he was just ignoring me.

"Hey there, do you hear me? Or do you want me to knock you down to the ground again?"

"Don't bother, elephant; I just wanted to play with you. Don't take it badly, I've been observing you for some time now, and I'd like to get to know you. Something tells me that I might be able to help you," he said, continuing to fly around me.

"Oh really? And how could a flying fish help me? But first of all, since when do fish fly? It's utterly absurd!"

"Exactly! I am the absurd. I belong neither to the real world nor to the imaginary world. My existence oscillates between being and nonbeing; well, when I talk about existence, I am not even sure if I exist. I am the nonsensical. But what do I know about it? You say that it's absurd. Of course: What isn't absurd? Your life is absurd, and mine is too. An elephant who refuses to accept her destiny, an elephant on a quest for freedom who believes she can find a solution through intoxication, that's absurd! And what's most absurd is your belief that by fleeing from your current situation, you'd be free. Lakshmi, I know what you're like! Your freedom should neither be a choice, nor should it be a reaction to your situation, because your aspiration for freedom is physical, based on the experience of others. Freedom should involve observation, without any restrictions. So, you'll never be free unless you are rid of your anguish, doubts, and all the other feelings that are only obstacles in your quest for freedom. But at the same time, your anguish is a consequence of freedom; you don't know what to do with it, and that makes you anxious. That's what the absurd is!"

But what was this fish telling me? All I'd said was that it was absurd to see a flying fish, and here he was, spouting out words I didn't understand. I knew that he was talking to me about freedom, but his own freedom was quite different to mine, and I wasn't able to grasp his point. I willed him to disappear, and I automatically closed my eyes. But he was still there when I opened them. So, he was well and truly real; he wasn't one of those creatures who frequently haunted my mind.

This fish, an angel fish, was impressive. In the sunlight, he gleamed with dazzling tones of silver. He had red eyes and three black vertical stripes on his side. The strangest thing was that he only had dorsal and pelvic fins. So how could he fly? He had an imposing presence, and his gestures were majestic. And though I was seduced by his beauty, his incomprehensible speech irritated me. But that didn't prevent me from wanting to know who he was, and what he was doing there. And how could it be that he knew my name, even though I had never met him before? I certainly seemed to stumble on the strangest of creatures. The chameleon with an identity crisis, followed by this creature with his existential problem: there was never a dull moment in my life!

"All right, wise fish. I don't understand a thing you're telling me, but your words must have a deeper meaning that eludes me. Can't we start with something simpler? How about you tell me where you're from?"

The fish gave me a resigned look, as if he was sad that his philosophical outburst was cut short, and he replied without looking at me.

"You're more interested in me than in yourself. I wanted to talk about you, and about your state of mind, but if you're more interested in trivial matters, well then, I'll tell you my story."

■ ■ ■

"My name is Alphonse, and I was born in Pondichéry. It's a small, beautiful, and tranquil town on the shores of the Bay of Bengal; it's a nice place to live. I was born in the Ariyankuppam River, which is located to the south of the town. Even as a young fish, I felt very cramped there. I dreamed of vast stretches of water, the sea, and the oceans. One of the arms of the Ariyankuppam River that flows into the sea would always fascinate me. But I was born with the handicap of being a freshwater fish, so I was condemned to the fate of never being able to discover the vastness of the ocean and its creatures.

"Suddenly, my life was transformed by love. Yes, love, for I was madly in love with a kingfisher.

"Our first encounter was quite strange, and also dangerous for me. My father had always prohibited me from straying away and venturing close to the river's edge, where danger lurked in the form of fishermen and kingfishers. But like all children who disobey their parents, I couldn't resist the temptation, and I often swam about at the river's edge. There, along the riverbank, I could see the fishermen with their nets and fishing rods along the riverbank, waist-deep in water. I enjoyed darting in and out between their legs. I got a thrill from brushing with danger like this.

"One day, without realizing, I had come close to the trees upon which kingfishers had perched. Suddenly, I heard the flapping of wings, and I saw a bird plunge into the water; he grasped me with his orange beak. And all of a sudden, I found myself out of water, in the beak of this kingfisher. In normal circumstances, I would have been scared, but oddly, on this occasion, I felt joyous. I felt happy to be out of the water, viewing the river from above. I was struck by the beauty of the river and everything around it. The majestic coconut palms towered over the riverbank, some standing tall, others bowing down, their trunks and palm leaves skimming the water's surface. Mango and jackfruit trees bearing luscious fruits were home to a myriad of brilliantly colored birds. The bird embarked on a long flight, before settling in the hollow of his tree. While I was writhing in his beak, I managed to catch a glimpse of the Ariyankuppam bridge, and the church in the distance. I saw people crossing the bridge in bullock carts. I saw buses, pedestrians, and people on bicycles and motorcycles. A whole new world opened up to me, one that was boisterous, bustling with activity.

"But I still wasn't afraid," Alphonse continued, "because I knew that there was some leeway for escape: I wasn't positioned correctly for the kingfisher to be able to swallow me! For the kingfisher can only swallow you in the direction of your scales; to set you in this position, he tosses you into the air, and then catches you again. I knew all this, as ever since I was little, my father had taught me how to execute what he called 'the pirouette of death.' This involves 'playing dead' until the bird throws you into the air, and then, just before falling into his beak, you do a pirouette, and dive back into the water to escape.

"I was already excited at the prospect of executing my father's technique, and also playing a trick on this bird. I felt confident. Once the kingfisher had perched on his tree and was getting ready to eat me, I glanced down, and saw that the tree was only a few meters away from the water. I waited for him to toss me into the air, and when I felt that I was no longer in his beak, I performed my pirouette. I only needed a few milliseconds to get back into the water, and I dived as deep down as I could. And when I emerged after some time, I spotted the kingfisher, who was still perched on his branch. I could see him through the water. His silhouette was swaying, as if he was moving to the lilt of the ripples. He clearly hadn't seen it coming. It wasn't every day that a fish escaped your clutches doing a pirouette! He looked surprised and was scanning the water's surface to see if I was floating about somewhere. I was hiding under a floating banyan leaf so as to observe him. He was handsome. Very handsome indeed. His feathers were a vivid blue, a different shade to that of the sky. The turquoise blue stood out among his scintillating hues, and his chest was red. I was instantly attracted to this bird. I'd even say that I was in love with him. I couldn't take my eyes off him. His beauty dazzled me, but even more than his beauty, his skill of flying fascinated me.

"Suddenly, the banyan leaf under which I was hiding moved because of the ripples created by an object that had been thrown into the river. As they grew bigger, these ripples drew the leaf into their circular dance, and the kingfisher spotted me. He didn't stir; we both froze, observing each other. Not one movement, not one gesture. Silence reigned over the river's edge; only the sound of the water lapping against the riverbank could be heard. The hustle and bustle of the Ariyankuppam bridge was now far in the distance. There I was, being rocked back and forth by the motion of the ripples; I no longer wished to hide or escape. I wanted to remain there, watching him. I even wished he would catch me again. I wanted him to dive in, and come and fetch me. I wanted to sense his beak on my body; I wanted him to lift me up high, very high, toward unknown lands. I wanted to soar above the clouds, be scorched by the sun's rays, and feel the raindrops on my skin.

"I had always liked the rain," Alphonse continued, "but I had never felt a drop of rain on my body. Because once the drops have fallen into the river, they lose their form, merging with the river. I wanted to fly once more with this bird, even if it meant that I might perish upon touching the sky. I felt the ripples subside after they had reached the roots of the trees at the river's edge and the sandbank. These ripples returned, but they were no longer the same. They no longer had the same shape or energy, yet it was the same water. The ripples returned to the point of impact, and then vanished, giving way to the natural flow of the river. I then experienced something of a revelation; it dawned on me that from this moment onward, my life would never be the same again. I could now cross the entire length of this river, live in its depths, swim close to the river's mouth, which opened out into the sea, and lose myself in the vastness of the ocean; my life would no longer be the same after having experienced this flight in the company of the kingfisher.

"For a moment that seemed to last an eternity, to my great sadness, the bird didn't stir from his branch. Then, eventually, he took flight and disappeared into the sky. This was the saddest moment of my life. I spent the rest of my day in tears, but no one spotted this; it is, after all, difficult to notice a fish weeping in the water. I spent days on end waiting, returning to the location where I had met the bird for the first time. But it was empty; the branch was bare, and there was no trace of my kingfisher.

"A few days passed before I saw him again. On this day, early in the morning, I came and positioned myself as close as possible to the riverbank. After a few minutes, I spotted a flash of turquoise on the water's surface. I knew it was him. It was a reflection of my kingfisher, who was flying peacefully over the river. I began to quiver and tremble to signal my presence to him. My silvery tones glinted in the sunshine; our colors blended at the water's surface to form a rainbow. His gaze settled on me, and I began to quiver even more. I saw him soar above my head, but he completely ignored me. 'My word!' I said, floating on my side, pretending I was dead. 'This bird is mad! Can't he see that I'm giving myself over to him?' But nothing could be done, he didn't want me. It was as if he no longer wanted to have anything to do with me; he did not want to risk being humiliated again . . . but what could I do? I didn't know how to catch his attention, but then I had the idea of getting washed up on the bank. If I got caught by the fishermen, too bad; I'd end up in an aquarium for the rest of my life. Having made my decision, I darted toward the riverbank. The bird saw me head toward the fishermen, and as if he had understood how determined I was, he dived toward me at a great speed. He had been flying quite high in the sky, and the impact of his body on the water made a tremendous splash. I closed my eyes.

"The very next moment, I was up in the sky. Yet again, I felt a sense of exhilaration being in the clutches of the kingfisher. This time, his beak did not grip me as tightly as the first time. He held me gently, as if he didn't mean to hurt me. And instead of carrying me to the tree upon which he would usually perch, he carried me far, far away; well, what seemed to be far away. We flew over the bridge and the paddy fields of Murungapakkam; we continued flying toward Villianur, passing through Kombakkam and other small villages on the way. I saw many temples and enormous tamarind trees flanking the road to Villianur. Emerald-green paddy fields stretched out as far as the eye could see, dotted with casuarina plantations.

"We reached the temple of Villianur. He then paused and dropped me into the temple pond. The contact with the water did me good; it was the first time I had spent so much time out of the water. The bird must have sensed that my skin was becoming dry, and that I needed moisture. It seemed that he no longer wanted to devour me, or at least, not immediately. I could still savor some moments of happiness, flying once more before dying. He waited patiently on the steps of the pond, and when he knew that I had bathed long enough, he took me into his beak with the same gentle grasp, and set off again. Once we had reached the river, I waited for him to go and perch on his branch to eat me in peace. But to my great surprise, he dropped me into the water and continued his flight in silence.

It took me a few seconds to recover from this incredible journey. I didn't understand his behavior. 'Well, this certainly is an extraordinary bird,' I said to myself, happy to still be alive. Why was he acting like this? What was his plan? I was eager to see him again to get to know him better. Would he ever return? My mind was flooded by all these questions, but I was tired, and with the vision of the verdant paddy fields engraved in my mind, I drifted off to sleep.

"From then onward, we got into the habit of seeing each other every day. As soon as I heard the *kik-kik-kik* of the kingfisher, I would go close to the tree where he was sitting, and we would set off on our flight. These were moments of ecstasy: traversing the sky, cutting through the air, seeing the town from above. I felt happy in his beak, content to feel his strong wings flapping in the air, and I never grew weary of seeing the splendor of his feathers glowing in the sunlight. Sometimes he would take me far, far, away, to a place where I'd completely lose my sense of time and space, but he would always take me back to the river. Very often, he would take me to a temple located near the railway line of Villianur in the village of Arumanthapuram. He would drop me into the pond, and go and perch on a branch of a thorny and aromatic bael tree. All this seemed odd to me. One day, I could no longer contain my curiosity, and I asked him why he was taking me on these journeys, and when he was planning to devour me. This was the first time we spoke to each other.

"'You must have realized that I'm no ordinary bird,' he began. 'I don't act like other kingfishers and I don't intend to eat you. I am a soul. The soul of Paradesi Swamigal. I am the reincarnation of Saint Siddha, whose temple is located here. You don't understand what I'm saying, do you?

"'First of all, you should know that this part of Pondichéry, which is called Villianur, is a unique location. In fact, this town used to be called Vilvanallur, which means 'the beautiful town of Vilva.' Vilva is the name we give to the bael tree, this sacred tree on which I have perched. It's also the sacred tree of Shiva. Legend has it that Lakshmi worshipped Shiva by offering him a thousand lotus flowers every day. One night, she was taken by surprise, because lotus flowers close in the evening, and she noticed that two were missing. She remembered the comparison that her husband Vishnu had made: he had said that her breasts resembled lotus flowers, and so she decided to offer them to Shiva in place of flowers. She began by removing one of her breasts, placing it on the altar of the Lord. Shiva saw all this and stopped her before she had removed her other breast. He admired Lakshmi's devotion so much that he transformed the breast into a bael fruit and dropped it onto the ground; that's why the bael tree flourishes near Shiva temples.

"'Before the construction of the Shiva temple by Raja Dharmabala of the Chola dynasty, Vilvanallur was a forest of bael trees. Over time, it became known as Villianur. More than two hundred years ago, a siddha who was sitting at the foot of this tree decided to retreat into Jeeva Samadhi, which means "entombed life" in Sanskrit. He remained in this state for a long time, and no one disturbed him.

"'Around the year 1868, during the occupation of Pondichéry, the French had decided to construct a railway line linking the town to Villianur. One day, when the workers were digging to build the track, they saw blood appear upon a clump of soil. They took fright and informed their supervisors; once they had arrived at the scene, they asked the workers to dig deeper. That's when they discovered this holy man who was sitting in a lotus position. A doctor was called to give a diagnosis. He checked whether his blood circulation and pulse were normal; everything was as it should be. It was as if the holy man was still alive. But he could not be roused. The villagers then decided to bury him again and build a temple at that very location. And it was during this period that the holy man began the process of transmigrating souls.

"'This is how the *Bhagavad Gita* describes transmigration: "Just as a man casts off his worn-out garments and adopts new ones, the soul rejects its spent body and enters others that are new." You see, it seems complicated, but it's very easy to understand. And now I have reached the end of my life as a bird. I now need to transfer my soul to someone else, and for this purpose, I have chosen you.'

"And that's how the kingfisher ended his story.

"I remained dubious," admitted Alphonse. "I understood more or less what he meant, but I found it hard to believe. A holy man decides to bury himself, but remains alive . . . and one fine day, he leaves his former body and starts living through others? But even if all this seemed improbable, I felt that this location was certainly special. You could sense an indescribable buzz of energy. A kind of magnetic energy, brimming with spirituality.'

"The bird continued:

"'You see, there are two siddhas buried in Arumanthapuram alone. And throughout the whole of Pondichéry, there are twenty-nine of us, scattered across the four corners of the town. This is what has always made Pondichéry special, since the dawn of time. It's a sacred and mystical land, steeped in spirituality, bearing the tapasya of all these siddhas. I see that you are skeptical. I was myself, when I inherited this soul from the deer of the Villianur temple. But when I felt it enter me, I could do nothing but accept it. This moment of peace and joy rivals any other emotion. You'll see when it's your turn. Of course, you can always refuse being the next body to carry the soul, but it would be your loss. Being chosen is a blessing. Why you, and not someone else? Because, dear fish, you are already a pure soul by birth, and receiving the soul of this siddha could only be beneficial to you. In any case, I cannot transfer this beautiful soul to an evil being. And now . . .'

"He paused for a moment and began to chant:

"'Tridalam Trigunakaram / Trinetrancha Triyaayudham / Trijanma Paapa Samharam / Eka Bilvam Shivarpanam . . .'

"His voice was melodious. I didn't know if this was a song or a prayer, but the atmosphere was suddenly filled with a sense of serenity and peace. I became deaf to the hustle and bustle of life around me; I could hear nothing but his chant, which resonated in my mind. The setting sun was a fiery shade of scarlet. The birds, who were returning to their nests, had fallen silent. It was as if the world stood still for the duration of the chant. The kingfisher then took a bael leaf and threw it into the pond. As it fell, it touched and enveloped me. A shiver ran down my spine; a strange sensation ran through my body as it came into contact with this sacred leaf. Everything spun before my eyes, and I thought I was going to become unconscious and faint. I felt my scaly body soften, and I began to slowly sink to the bottom of the pond. The bird let me sink for a few seconds, and then, just as I was going to touch the bottom, he caught me and lifted me out of the water. On the way back, the kingfisher and I remained silent.

"I didn't have the energy to ask him anything; the day had left me deeply unsettled.

"Over the next few days, the bird took me to visit different temples where the tombs of the twenty-nine siddhas in Pondichéry were located. It gave me the opportunity to discover this town, which I barely knew. I discovered the temples of Siddhananda at Karuvadikuppam, Acka Swamigal at V.O.C. Nagar, Nagalinga Swamigal in the center of the town, Thollakadu Swamigal near the temple of Ganesh, and so on. At each temple, the kingfisher told me the story of these holy men who had walked upon this sacred land. I didn't know what to make of this spiritual experience that had come my way; until then, I had lived under water, oblivious as to what surrounded me.

"Shortly afterward, the kingfisher perished, leaving the soul of Paradesi Swamigal to me. My life thereafter was completely transformed. I left my family and river, and I began to travel the world.

"Strangely, everything that I had longed for with all my heart when I was small—the ability to cross seas and oceans—was granted to me by this soul. Thanks to its yogic powers, not only can I fly, but I can also swim in the deepest oceans. Time and space have no control over me. Ever since this soul has entered my body, I have ceased to exist; my body is nothing but a shell. I am simultaneously within it and outside it. I am still Alphonse the fish, but my conscience has become universal. I am everything and nothing at the same time. When the reflection of the soul encounters ignorance, it comes into existence with a body and intuition. And each being feels as if it has its own unique and distinct soul, called the individual soul. This concept of existence is only true on a practical level. At a transcendental level, there is only one soul, and that's the universal soul."

These final words from Alphonse echoed in my mind as if they were coming from afar, for I had fallen asleep. His story had kept me awake up until the point when the kingfisher died, but, my goodness, when he started to spout his incomprehensible words again, my head felt heavy because of this whole story of siddhas, the soul, and the bird who wasn't a bird; I was lost. Conquered by fatigue, I drifted off to sleep. And of course, when I woke up to return to the gurukulam, Alphonse the fish was no longer there! Yet again, I was confused: Was he real, or merely an apparition? With a weary mind, I went home. On my way back to the gurukulam, my memory of the fish came back to me. Everything he had told me about freedom kept haunting my mind. Was this a sign that I was supposed to decipher? Was the appearance of the fish going to change the course of my life? I didn't dare speak of this meeting to either Veeran or Manmath; they would have thought I was mad. The best thing to do was to wait and see if he would appear one day when I hadn't consumed these cursed fermented fruits that kept playing tricks on me.

But the day of the allocation of elephant keepers was approaching; I had to make a decision as quickly as possible. Leave or stay: this question had arisen in my mind thousands of times, and I hadn't yet been able to find an answer. Finally, on the eve of the fateful day, I decided to escape. I didn't share my intentions with Manmath, as I was afraid that he might make my decision even more difficult. I knew that he would try to dissuade me; I knew his point of view. Having a discussion with him would have made my task difficult. So I left the gurukulam without saying farewell to him. However, I thought highly of Manmath, and I was grateful to him for having helped me when I had started out at the gurukulam. Thanks to him, not only had my life been easy, but I had also learned a lot.

Just after our last training session at the temple of the gurukulam, I set off toward the hill. My intention was to seek refuge with Veeran and his lot. As I arrived at the foot of the hill, I had hoped to find Veeran, but he wasn't there. I waited for a few moments, and then I began to climb the hill. Throughout the journey, thousands of questions plagued my mind. But wasn't I supposed to be savoring my freedom? This freedom that I had so longed for, this freedom I had so desired ever since I had felt the icy shackles around my legs. Shouldn't I have been gamboling among these kritamalas, named "golden-shower trees" owing to their cascade of magnificent yellow ochre blooms? Shouldn't I have been savoring the scent of sandalwood that flooded this forest? No, nothing of the sort; instead, my legs felt leaden, and my mind was elsewhere. This wretched fish was certainly right: freedom was worrying. Unless I was liberated from my fears, doubts, and anguish, I couldn't be truly free.

I really had to find this fish again. He alone could help me find peace. Veeran was of no use for this kind of thing; all he could do was give me an illusion of peace. But I couldn't blame him for it either.

I eventually reached the community of the Gajarastas, where I was welcomed with great cheers of delight when they learned that I had decided to leave the gurukulam to join them. The patriarch asked me to come close to him, asked me the same questions as the first day, smiled and blessed me just as he had the first time, and then he lay down again, sinking into a slumber. I saw the circus elephant again, with his mini hat perched on his head. He was wearing a clown's smile and trying to make a herd of elephant calves laugh. The sight of this spectacle and the warm welcome of the Gajarastas made me forget all the worries that had troubled me during my journey. As for Veeran, he was the happiest of all; he went from one elephant to another, telling them how we had met. He then went up to some other elephants who seemed quite withdrawn, and asked them to organize a party in my honor. These elephants then slipped away, swaying clumsily from side to side, murmuring and jostling one another.

Once these introductions were over, Veeran led me toward the river. When we were near the banyan tree, we saw that thousands of fruits of all kinds had already been collected, and some elephants were continuing to pick more. A joyous and lighthearted atmosphere prevailed. It was my first party, and I was the center of attention. I felt as if I was part of a large family, among brothers, sisters, and cousins. This did me a lot of good. And once the first fruits had been consumed, everything changed. My anguish and worries evaporated, and the joy and gaiety of my friends rubbed off on me. Veeran ensured that the atmosphere was relaxed, and he introduced me to a rather odd-looking group of elephants, who lived somewhat at the fringes of the community.

"Look at those over there," he said, devouring a large quantity of bananas. "They are more or less like you; they have all chosen freedom. But unlike you, they have had a painful past, both physically and mentally. Some have been tortured and physically abused; others have been imprisoned in cages and zoos for such a long time that their suffering is part of them, and they struggle to overcome it. Why am I explaining this to you? Because you shouldn't get the impression that all they do is while away their time getting drunk. Their suffering is too profound to be forgotten easily. Here, take the case of Patti . . ."

He pointed at the elephant with the mini hat and the clown's smile.

"Well, Patti was a member of the Bharat Circus. From a very young age, he was the butt of everyone's jokes. Since childhood, he was forced to wear this ridiculous hat and trained to stand upright on a tiny stool, playing the clown. Mocked and humiliated for decades, he never recovered. Rambo, whom you see over there, was born in captivity in a zoo. He'd only ever experienced the bars of his cage, and ever since he was liberated, all he does is just stand in front of rows of trees, unable to move. And so on. Each elephant has their own wounds that they try to heal as best as they can. The community does all it can so that these elephants can regain a semblance of normal life. Some recover, others don't. You'll see; you'll come to know us, and realize that despite all these unfortunate experiences, we remain disobedient and rebellious. But enough about the others; we are all very happy to welcome you among us and we hope that you will like it here," he concluded, ushering me toward a pile of sugarcane.

It took me some time to realize that I was well and truly free, but to go from there to the realization that I had escaped my fate . . . this seemed odd. Could life be as simple as that? Had I escaped my fate as a temple elephant by fleeing from the gurukulam, seeking refuge with the Gajarastas? And what was I going to do for the rest of my life? I was conflicted about the matter. I had chosen freedom, but the freedom I had yearned for was one that enabled me to choose a life different to the one I was destined for. Was this really what I wanted? Maybe I had simply wanted to try out another career other than that of a temple elephant? Had I been stupid enough to confuse a change of career with a change of fate? I could no longer make sense of anything, and I tortured myself with all these questions. Oddly, I felt trapped by my own freedom. As if my life had ceased to have meaning. As if my status as a Gajahraman had defined my life. Had I got carried away by Veeran's ideas of revolution and freedom, without weighing up their consequences? I imagined Manmath mocking me if he saw me like this. I hadn't even said farewell to him, and this thought saddened me.

I was in the midst of all these thoughts when Alphonse appeared. Alphonse! My savior! It was a great relief to see him. My doubts about his existence dissolved; so, this flying fish truly existed. He wasn't a just a consequence of my hallucinations.

Alphonse seemed happy, but I believe he had always been happy. He landed next to me.

"So, Lakshmi, how are you?"

"Life could be better; I don't feel good, and . . ."

"I know, Lakshmi," he interrupted me. "I know you are going through a period of doubt. But you've always been like this, haven't you? Ever since you were little, you haven't stopped asking yourself questions. Doubt is a good thing. It's certainly an unsettling feeling that constantly competes with certainty. But this battle is necessary for our evolution. And I understand that this sudden freedom bothers you. As much as you had wanted it, it now troubles you, because you aren't at peace with yourself. You are, as men say, 'putting the cart before the horse.' Find your inner peace; then, you will be able to appreciate freedom."

"And how will I find my inner peace, Alphonse?"

"Well, in this matter, Lakshmi, unfortunately I can't help you. The kind of peace I'm talking about can only be sought, sensed, and experienced by you. I could give you some tips, but they will not be of any help to you. Inner peace must be and is a personal experience. All I can tell you is that you're on the right track. Your doubts, questions, and uncertainties will lead you to this peace. But now I must dash—I'm late. See you soon, Lakshmi!"

Alphonse came to visit me often. He was most certainly a funny fish. He always made me laugh with his stories. For instance, he told me that he had gone to attend a jazz concert by David Rothenberg with humpback whales (concert, jazz . . . I had no idea what these were, but I listened to him nonetheless). Another day, he told me that he had gone to attend a conference given by carps on silence, and that he had been to an exhibition of sand sculptures on the beaches in Puri, or a ballet of octopi in the depths of the ocean, goodness knows where. I didn't know if he was inventing all this to impress me, or if it was actually the truth. In any case, time always flew when I was in his company.

■ ■ ■

One day, as I was wandering about in search of food, I realized that I wasn't far from the gurukulam. I thought of Manmath. Maybe I should take advantage of this opportunity to say goodbye to him? The idea seemed both stupid and dangerous. But fueled by this desire, I ventured toward the river Moyar, where he had shown me the first herd of Gajavasis. I had hoped to meet him, or even just catch a glimpse of him. But when I reached the watering hole where I'd previously seen this family of Gajavasis, I could see only some does and stags who were drinking water; there was no sign of Manmath.

I decided to wait for some time at the edge of the river Moyar, and then I suddenly noticed that the does had stopped drinking and were glancing in all directions as if they had sensed danger. And sure enough, as I pricked up my ears, I could hear the sound of footsteps, and I detected the presence of men, and then elephants. I began to panic. I didn't know who these elephants were, and what they were doing with these men. At any rate, they were coming toward me. I could hear them draw nearer; I could hear their voices, and finally, I could see them through the trees. The other animals had already fled upon their arrival. But I remained rooted to the spot, paralyzed, not knowing what to do . . . When I realized that these men wanted to capture me, I attempted to escape. I began to run along the river, trumpeting to alert the Gajarastas. But in my confusion, I went the wrong way. Instead of running toward the hill, I set off in the opposite direction and I soon saw two elephants suddenly appear, mounted by their keepers. I felt trapped and wanted to turn left, but there were two more elephants there. And to my right was the river. In the space of a few seconds, I was surrounded by six elephants. I didn't know what to do; I had never prepared myself for the eventuality of being captured one day. As I stood there, immobile, I felt a first lasso around my head, then others around my legs and neck. The two elephants on my left tightened their grip, and those in front of me turned to face me so that I didn't make a run for it. Those behind me split up; one stood to my right, and the other behind my tail.

My freedom was suspended at the end of the lassos. Feeling them on my body was more humiliating than wearing the chains I was used to, because the chains were only attached to my legs, whereas these lassos had taken possession of my entire body, preventing me from making even the slightest movement. I wondered which was more humiliating? Was it the moment of capture—the sensation of being hounded, trapped, and powerless—or being subjected to domestication and treated as a slave? Both were terrible. Either way, no one could come to my rescue . . . Where was Manmath, who had warned me from the start about the risks of freedom? Where was Veeran, who had sown the seeds of rebellion and freedom in my mind? Where was Alphonse, who had spoken to me about inner peace and mysticism? That's exactly when I realized that none of my three friends were to blame; it was I who had wanted freedom, who had wanted to change the course of my destiny, and I had to shoulder my responsibilities.

■ ■ ■

I was led along the river Moyar by my captors through the Bandipur Forest, where I had found meaning to my life. A life that had now become riddled with uncertainty, the future unknown. At the sight of the branches bending down onto my path and the trees shedding tears of sap as they witnessed my fate, I realized I had to say farewell to my former life.

Chapter Seven

"BUT THIS ISN'T A WILD ELEPHANT!" the man exclaimed.

These were the first words I heard when I woke up. I looked around. I found myself in a large clearing surrounded by trees, with a small lake in the middle. This clearing was in the outskirts of a small village. In the distance, smoke was rising from thatched houses; one could detect the presence of other men, who had come to look for wood. It didn't take me long to work out that I was in a training camp for captured elephants; Veeran had told me about this kind of place, which he had seen in Burma. It was a place destined to break any sign of resistance an animal might display, forcing them to accept man's domination.

"And what's more," shouted the man who seemed to be the boss, "you've captured a Gajahraman, you good-for-nothing idiots!"

He spat out saliva stained bloodred with betel nut, scratching his head. Crouching with his feet spread out, he held a stick in his hand and tapped the ground with it, as if he sought to appease his anger. The men who had taken part in my capture stood in front of him, arms folded, heads bowed, so as to avoid the boss's angry gaze. He got up, sighed, and called over to one of the men, who was the youngest in the group.

"How many times must I tell you to look carefully at an elephant before capturing it?"

He raised his stick at the same time as he delivered these words and brought it down on the young man's side; he howled in pain. The boss delivered a second blow to the same spot with the same force, and, as the young man received the third blow, he opened up his folded arms to try to shield himself. This aroused even more anger from the man, who yelled as he dealt even more blows.

"Keep your arms folded, don't behave like a woman! When will I make a true man of you, my only son? And now, flee, before I kill you!" he concluded, throwing down his stick.

The young man folded his arms again, took two steps back, and withdrew from the group, his head still lowered. The boss paced back and forth in front of the others as he muttered to himself; then he suddenly stopped in front of the man who appeared to be the oldest in the group, and grabbed him by the collar.

"And as for you: you're supposed to be the most experienced of all my men. I have entrusted my son's education to you; don't you know that capturing a Gajahraman brings bad luck? How can you be so careless?"

Loosening his grip and spitting out a spurt of betel nut juice for the umpteenth time, he ordered his men to leave. He remained standing there, deep in thought. Eventually, he came up to me.

He was a tall man, strong and sturdy like a tree. His torso was bare and very dark, unlike the other men, who had a lighter complexion. He had a large mustache, which curled up at the ends, and it reminded me of millipedes coiling up into spirals. He looked tough, but his caresses were gentle. His voice also mellowed when he talked to me.

"Om Muruga, Muruga! Don't worry, elephant, no harm will come to you," he said, stroking my trunk. "You will not be ill-treated; you won't stay here for long, this isn't the right place for you."

His words calmed me down, but I still didn't know what was to become of me. This place reeked of violence; I had just seen proof of it, witnessing the father punishing his son. But over the following days, I was to experience scenes that were even more violent.

Some days after my arrival, the men returned with a new elephant. This time, there were neither blows nor reprimands; the boss was visibly happy. He even kissed his son on his forehead and patted him on the back. This elephant was led by another elephant, who had been groomed to become docile. The new captive was tethered between two tree trunks, such that he could not move. And when, mad with rage, he tried to pull on the rope and push against the trees, the boss came over and began to beat him, sinking a hook into his side in several places. The elephant yelled in pain and fury, and as the boss continued to beat him, he simultaneously spoke gentle words to calm him down. I was horrified to see such a spectacle; my eyes welled up with tears. The pain of this elephant penetrated my soul; his roar became unbearable.

It echoed in my mind even while I was sleeping. After a while, the boss stopped this torture, but the elephant was given nothing to eat or drink. He stood there between the tree trunks, tired, famished, and thirsty, for several days. And every day, the boss would return and resume his training, using the same method. I could no longer bear to watch this spectacle. But I was kept tethered in the training area, which made me fully aware of how men tamed us elephants, and made me realize that, as a Gajahraman, I should be grateful not to be subjected to the same fate. It was cruel. Four or five days later, the Gajavasi no longer showed any signs of resistance. The pain, hunger, and torture had weakened him, and he ended up accepting man's domination. Weeks passed by like this, with new captives and new torture sessions, until one morning we were loaded into several vans. A few hours later, we all found ourselves, along with other elephants, in a location that turned out to be a market. The elephant market of Kovalam. We were going to be sold.

"The first person to breathe a word about this elephant will have his skull smashed open," said the boss, pointing at me.

We were unloaded from the vans and lined up. I found myself in the midst of all this, but I still didn't understand why everyone was acting so mysteriously and secretively when it came to my background. The sale began. Elephant keepers paced back and forth in front of us; they touched us, scrutinized us, lifted up our legs and our trunks, and looked behind our ears, making comments. Some of them retreated a distance to observe us better from afar, and then came up close to look at the finer details. There were endless discussions on our backgrounds, skills, docility, and abilities, and so many other points were considered before a price was agreed upon.

Over the course of the day, my friends left me one by one, and still no one was interested in me. At the end of the day, there were just two of us remaining. The capricious boss, whose mood had changed like a chameleon all day long, became increasingly annoyed seeing that I had still not been sold. At times, when he obtained a good price, he had been happy with the sale; when he obtained a bad price, he had become furious, and had begun to shout at everyone. A torrent of insults gushed out from his reddened, betel nut–stained mouth, insults that would have made even a foul-mouthed autorickshaw driver blush, and his spurts of saliva formed a red line in front of our feet. A line not to be crossed unless you were interested. It seemed as if everyone in the market knew him. Some came to tease him; others avoided him like the plague, unwilling to negotiate with him.

Toward the end of the day, a man came up to the boss.

"So, Nagalingam, how is your sale going? I see that you still have two more elephants left."

"May lightning strike me! If I don't manage to sell these two last elephants, I'm ruined. Who will pay my men? How am I going to feed my family? And my daughter whom I am going to marry off soon! How will I pay her dowry? And her blasted husband, who wants a scooter!"

"What's the problem with those two elephants?"

Nagalingam was squatting as he had done previously, tapping his stick on the ground in the same way. This must have been his own unique way of pondering whenever he had a problem. The other man circled around us; he made us raise our legs, mounted us, looked behind our ears, examined our toes . . .

"This one, this female, you didn't train her, did you?" he said eventually.

Nagalingam sprung to his feet.

"What do you mean, I didn't train her? I swear to you on my community, I swear upon my mother's head! Let smallpox take away my children if I'm lying. I personally trained her; you have my word on that!"

"Nagalingam, I wasn't born yesterday, and we have known each other since the birth of your first boy. I was the one who slaughtered the sheep when your daughter entered maturity. So don't put on an act! I know you're a great actor. Tell me the truth."

"But this is the truth, dear brother-in-law! You're like a brother to my wife, you're like an uncle to my children. My entire family is grateful to you for the seven lives that are yet to come. We worship you like our community's deity. Come, ask my eldest. Hey, you over there, come here! Which photo is next to our idol of Murugan?"

The boy, arms folded, looked at the man and said to his father:

"The photo of Uncle."

"You see?" said Nagalingam, looking proudly at the man, while patting his son on the back.

"Come," he added, addressing his son, "go and fetch two teas for your uncle and me. And tell Nayar to put lots of milk in it, and not too much sugar for your uncle."

Then, turning to the man, he said:

"So, brother-in-law, would you be interested in this beautiful female elephant? Look how beautiful she is! Look at these white spots that cover her trunk and even her ears! Do you see this white spot on her forehead? It's a natural tilak, like that worn by most Hindus on their forehead; it represents the third eye of Shiva. This elephant has the sacred character of the goddess Lakshmi. You'll see, you will not regret buying her."

The man looked at me for a long time, and then turned to Nagalingam.

"You see, Nagalingam, the sad thing about you is that you'd be capable of selling your entire family for an elephant. You can never be trusted. You're a very good hunter and a very good trainer, there's no question about that, but when it comes to sales, everyone here knows that you are a crook, as cunning as a fox. Everyone avoids doing business with you, because you are capable of selling a mouse, saying that it's an elephant. Like now, for instance. I see that this elephant does not have a single fresh wound. In fact, she practically has no wounds at all. But the chains have left deep marks on her legs, so she's an elephant born in captivity. The way she stands, motionless and calm, indicates that she is used to this position. Look: she hardly moves her head and ears! And what does that mean? That this elephant must be a Gajahraman or a Gajasya. Tell me the truth!"

Meanwhile, Nagalingam's son had returned with the tea. The two men sat down and began to slurp their tea while lighting up their beedis. So I'd done it! I no longer belonged to any caste. By fleeing the gurukulam, I'd also escaped from the caste system! Wasn't that what I'd always wanted? To escape my fate, and not be labeled as one caste or another? To avoid having to conform to this social structure, having the freedom to choose my way of life? But having made this choice, I found myself in a situation where I could become anything. At this point in my life, I could well end up in a circus, a building site, and, with a bit of luck, I could have an easy life. I could already picture myself like Patti, a hat on my head, playing the clown, or working in a building site, killing myself lifting tons of logs. At worst, I could end up in a zoo, amid the macaws and chimpanzees. My God! What had I done? Having obtained freedom, I was going to end up in a different caste to my original one.

Nagalingam knew that I was a Gajahraman, but he couldn't sell me as such, because the elephant keepers' code of ethics prohibits the capture and sale of Gajahramans. He would therefore do everything to conceal my identity. My future was being decided upon, here, now, before my very eyes, by these two men.

Having finished his beedi, Nagalingam spat out a stream of betel nut–stained saliva and spoke to the other man.

"All right, brother-in-law, I'm going to tell you the truth, because you're a benefactor of our family. Without you, I wouldn't be able to marry off your sister's daughter. Once we've finalized this deal, come home; your sister will prepare the mutton curry that you're so fond of, with some dosas so hot that you'll burn your tongue."

"Stop trying to work your charms on me. You think I'm going to fall into your trap? Also, since when has your wife cooked meat? She doesn't eat meat!"

"Ah yes, you don't know about that! I have a second wife," he said, winking. "She cooks like a queen! We'll buy a bottle of rum and she will make us a curry and some tripe. You'll see, she's very beautiful. Her complexion is very fair. So fair that when you pinch her, her skin goes bright red," he said, smiling, his gaping mouth also a bright shade of crimson.

"Your family affairs don't interest me; let's get back to business."

"Yes, I'm going to tell you the truth, because you're my brother-in-law. So here it is: a few weeks ago, these idiots captured this female elephant not far from the gurukulam. You know the one in Bandipur, don't you? Well, that's where they found her! But I assure you, this elephant is not a Gajahraman. Close to the gurukulam, there is a community of good-for-nothing Gajarastas. Well, that's where we found her. In fact, she was totally drunk. My men didn't have much difficulty in capturing her; she could barely stand. Why am I certain she's not a Gajahraman? No Gajahraman would risk their life and status by fleeing the gurukulam to go and visit these Gajarasta rascals. I'd bet my life on it! In all my life as a hunter and an elephant vendor, I've never seen a Gajahraman flee from or leave the gurukulam. You'd have to be really stupid to do that kind of thing. And this elephant doesn't seem to be so foolish! I'm telling you: she has the sacred character of the goddess Lakshmi. She'll bring you fortune! You can trust me, brother-in-law.

You know that I respect my profession; I wouldn't do anything against the rules of my community."

"You're right on one count, Nagalingam; this elephant has something sacred about her. But if by misfortune you've lied to me, your family would be wiped out by a disease, and you would end up without any offspring. All right, I'll take this female elephant, because I've just had a request from a film producer. He needs elephants, several elephants! And this one seems to be very beautiful and docile. Deal done! Go and buy me the bottle and the mutton you promised me, and meanwhile I'll get the money sorted for you."

The jubilant Nagalingam sent his men to the market. He placed a rolled-up betel leaf in his mouth, untied me, and led me to another van, into which I was loaded. In the van, he patted my trunk.

"You see, elephant, you're very lucky. You must have been born under a lucky star! All the elephants who come on this market have different fates. An elephant without a caste like you could have a very cruel fate. But you see, the gods are with you; you're going to act in films! Maybe one day, I'll see you on a poster. Then I'll recognize you and I'll be proud that I was the one who sold you. Good luck, elephant!"

He then got out of the van, put his arm around the new owner, and they began to walk toward his vehicle, where his men were standing with plastic bags, mutton protruding out of them.

■ ■ ■

My film career got off to a good start, despite an initial hiccup.

A few weeks after my arrival in Madras, I was taken to Kodambakkam, where all the film studios and production companies were located. Muthu, my new owner, was a reputable elephant supplier for Indian cinema, just as his father had been before him. He was well acquainted with all the producers and production companies, from the north to the south of India. My first job was with Devar Films.

The business was run by a former actor who had become a producer, called Sando Chinnappa Devar. He was a very pious man who was always bare chested, with streaks of vibhuti smeared on his body and forehead; he would utter the name Muruga, the brother of Lord Ganesha, every two minutes. In the cinema world, he was renowned for being very strict, making no compromises, and he had a very good knowledge of animals. Devar was getting started on making his first color film with his favorite actor, MGR, the superstar of Tamil cinema. MGR was more than an actor; he was essentially worshipped like a god. Before the casting, Muthu had told me that it would be a great honor for me to feature in his film. I had absolutely no experience of acting, unlike the Gajasyas, who had been trained for this purpose since their birth, but Muthu had decided to try his luck.

On the day of the casting, there were around ten of us, and Devar wanted four; three had already been selected, and I was to be the fourth. We had a meeting in the Vahini studio. From the morning, my new owner prepared me for the event with great care. After he reached the studio, he applied the finishing touches to my makeup. But at the time of the casting session, his hands were trembling, for he knew that I was not ready for the movies. He was relying entirely on my beauty and docility. He also knew that if Devar were to discover this, his cinema career would be over.

Devar arrived a few hours later, and immediately came toward us. He reviewed all the elephants, paced back and forth in front of us, and each time, his footsteps became hesitant when he passed in front of me. Muthu took this to be an encouraging sign. So did I, for that matter. I could already picture myself in the film: MGR climbing onto my back and singing songs; MGR and I fighting the baddies . . . who would have thought! I, a temple elephant from the darkest depths of Kerala, was going to act in the movies. And not just in any old film. I was going to star alongside MGR! So, my gamble had been successful: I was going to become what I had always wanted to be. I remembered my dreams at the edge of the Varkala cliff. So, if you can dream it, you can do it! Dreams are achievable provided that you really want them, and work for them. I felt proud, beautiful, and confident in myself. Devar paced one last time in front of me, stroking the rudraksha beads he was wearing around his neck, and he uttered the words "Muruga, Muruga!" before taking Muthu aside.

"Muthu, I know you, and I knew your father. You have always been loyal, and honest with me. But something tells me that this elephant is not made for the movies. In any case, not for this kind of film. She has something sacred about her. I'm even wondering if she is a Gajahraman. But equally, I know you wouldn't do this kind of thing for the money. But if by misfortune we make a Gajahraman act in a film, this sin would not be cleansed for many generations to come . . . Give me some time to reflect, and I'll give you my verdict after a while. Meanwhile, you can take the others for the trials."

I found myself all alone in sadness, watching the others leave. All my dreams had been wiped out in just a few seconds. And all this because I had been born in the wrong caste . . . But surely I couldn't fail so close to the goal! No, that just wouldn't be fair. There I was, right in the midst of the projectors, cameras, trailers, and cinema posters. There was a real commotion: people were scurrying about from left to right with their scripts, fans, chairs, and makeup. Everyone seemed to be in a hurry, busy doing something or other . . . whereas I just stood there, frozen, awaiting the verdict, watching my chances slipping away.

I sensed I was being watched from afar. Devar was sitting at his desk, observing me through his window. He glanced at me furtively while issuing orders to his assistants from time to time.

Time seemed to stand still. Eventually, Muthu came back. He stood beside me. He too seemed to be sad. He stroked my trunk as if to reassure me, to tell me that all would go well, then he went off to fetch me a bucket of water. That was when Devar came out of his office. He began to pace up and down, scrutinized me for a long time, and then finally came up close to me. He walked around me as he waited for Muthu. Then, when Muthu came back with the bucket, he took it from his hands and gave me a drink. When the bucket was empty, he put it down.

"You see," he said to Muthu, "this animal has something unique about it. I can't work out what it is. But something tells me that it isn't a Gajasya. At the same time, it would be a shame to miss out on such a beauty. What I can suggest to you is that this elephant only acts in religious films. That way, not only would she not lose this sacred character with her caste is endowed with, but she could also have the life for which she is destined."

One of his assistants brought him a tray of camphor and vibhuti, and, uttering his famous mantra "Muruga, Muruga," he smeared three horizontal streaks on my forehead, wishing me a long life.

And that's how my cinema career began, with Devar's blessing. A week later, Muthu was contacted by a producer who knew Devar regarding a film called *The Temple Elephant*. It couldn't have worked out better; I was to play my own role! Life truly is full of twists and turns; here I was, being offered the very role that I had wanted to escape from!

The film was a great success; my presence and beauty left an impression on the audience and on other producers. In the space of a few months, I was inundated with requests. I was in great demand, and Muthu filled in more call sheets; we traveled across the whole of India, from Madras to Bombay, from Bombay to Andhra, and from Andhra to Bengal. There wasn't a single religious film in which I didn't feature. I was admired, pampered, and idolized like a great star. I had a personal stable at my disposal, and a personal van for my travels. I was served the best sugarcane and the best sweets. The producers were even ready to postpone shooting days in case I was tired, or if I wasn't in the right mood. For as my career progressed and advanced at a dizzying speed, my tantrums and mood swings escalated, becoming more frequent. I only wanted to act in religious films. If a producer offered me a role in a commercial film, which was soon to happen, I would refuse. I refused to act alongside actors who resembled plump pink sweets, mustaches penciled on their faces, who would burst into song every five minutes with actresses who were as large as me. I had carved out a reputation for myself as an elephant who only played sacred roles. But I didn't realize that all this attention and adulation were altering my character. The euphoria of all this popularity and praise was making me stubborn and temperamental. I was letting myself get sucked into this whirlwind of media. Each of my public appearances would draw a crowd, everyone jostling to catch a glimpse of me, touch me, and receive my blessing. I was well and truly considered to be a sacred elephant. And each time I passed through a town, I would see myself on giant posters, alongside other famous movie stars.

At the time, it never occurred to me that all this could not last forever. I felt as if I was flying on a cloud that no one could reach, a cloud from which I would never descend. I was the most beautiful and most worshipped elephant. The other Gajasyas must have been jealous of my fame. Nothing mattered to me. I was the best, and I was the one who had conquered her destiny. I had triumphed! I had the arrogance of a winner. In my eyes, the others were worthless beings who had considered it beneath them to confront their fate. I wanted to show these other elephants who were subjected to the caste system that I, Lakshmi, born as a temple elephant, was now the most cherished and adored film star. Curiously, this name Lakshmi, which Chacko Chattan had given me, had remained; when Muthu had to give me a name, he had named me Lakshmi without any hesitation. I had truly been born to bear this name.

Years passed like this, until one day, the wind changed direction in the world of Indian cinema. As soon as the film *Eenadu* (This land) was released, everything changed: no one wanted to produce sacred films anymore. Everyone became more interested in societal issues. As if India was suddenly discovering the injustices ravaging society, producers, directors, and screenwriters rushed to these kinds of topics. It was as if a blind person had regained their sight, and the cinema world was experiencing an enlightenment after years of darkness. This was the end of gods and miracles, the end of Shiva dancing on the Kailash, the end of Murugan flying on his peacock, and the end of elephants representing Ganesh . . . All the gods were put away into the closet. On film posters, the trishul was replaced by the hammer and sickle. The clean-shaven face of Murugan was replaced by the bearded Karl Marx. Shiva's tangled jatas were replaced by the bald-headed Lenin. The communist wave swept away the final debris of all things sacred. Indian cinema had discovered a new religion, where there was no place for animals. All that mattered now were the workers, the poor, the working class, the outcasts, and the masses with their raised fists.

Muthu began to get rid of his first few elephants; I watched them leave us, one by one. Not a single day went by without us receiving visitors who were potential buyers, and each time, I saw them look at me longingly. But Muthu refused to sell me. I was his Lakshmi, who had helped him make his fortune. But when his Adyar house was sold, he had no choice other than to part with me.

On the day of my departure, he came to see me with his tray of camphor and vibhuti, performed a final puja, smeared horizontal marks on my forehead, and pressed his face to my trunk. Hot tears flowed down his cheeks, and I also wept.

"Farewell, my beautiful Lakshmi," he said to me, in a strangled voice. "Farewell. Please forgive me for selling you off; sadly, I don't have a choice. I don't want to let you die of hunger and thirst with me, and I have no more money to keep you. All I can give you is the certainty that you will not be unhappy. I haven't sold you to a circus, a zoo, or a building site. You will be what you have always been: a Gajahraman. Yes, henceforth, you'll be a temple elephant. You've come full circle. You did what you could. It isn't what you wanted, but life had other plans for you. Having said that, don't have any regrets; at least you tried. And you've seen a different life compared to that of your peers; you have had experiences that no elephant of your caste has ever had. You now know it all, and have experienced everything: freedom, life in the wild, captivity, domestication . . . all these experiences will only bring you peace. This inner peace you were seeking, the peace of having experienced and known the unknown."

His gentle voice and words continued to resound in my ears as I left the large garden that surrounded the house, accompanied by my new owner. A van awaited me outside on the street, where people were toing and froing. No one paid any attention to me, Lakshmi, the superstar, who, just a few years ago, had attracted thousands of people each time she had made an appearance. Some young boys on their way to school stopped in front of the van, but not to see me; no, what amused them was seeing an elephant climb into a van. As the van set off, I spotted a placid cow on the opposite pavement, where there was a tea stall, who was munching a film poster. The van did a U-turn and drove past it; the poster was none other than that for my first film: *The Temple Elephant.*

Chapter Eight

WHEN I ARRIVED in Pondichéry, I knew I was embarking on the final phase of my life. I no longer wished to escape from or revolt against my situation; I was resigned to spending the rest of my life in peace. The circumstances around me made me just as angry as before, but my youthful energy had now diminished. This didn't mean that I would accept my fate; certainly not. But it meant that I had experienced what I'd wanted to.

Sometime after my arrival at the Ganesh temple, I received a visit from Alphonse. I had not seen my flying fish since my time with the Gajarastas. He had let me lead my life, and I was overjoyed to meet him again at the Shiva temple on the corner of rue Eswaran Kovil and rue Gandhi, where I live. I stay in a room at the back of the temple. It isn't big; I have just enough room to stand up. And everything is done in this room: I eat, sleep, and am bathed there. My days are all alike. In the morning, Tokuram washes me and applies my makeup. Then he gives me something to eat, and we head toward the temple. We always take the same route every day: I walk along rue Eswaran Kovil toward the beach, then I reach rue Manakulla Vinayagar, and turn right, carrying on until I get to the temple. There have been no changes to our routine since my arrival, no unnecessary or extravagant activities . . .

One evening, after a long day at work, I'd finished my meal, and I was tired and had closed my eyes when Alphonse appeared.

"Lakshmi! Finally, you're here! I've been waiting for you for a long time."

"Did you know that I was going to come here?"

"Of course, Lakshmi, ever since that first day when I saw you under the tree, I knew you'd come. I knew I'd find you in Pondichéry."

Of course, this fish knew everything, with his magical powers. But why hadn't he told me this earlier? That would have saved me a lot of trouble!

"And why didn't you tell me this earlier, Alphonse?"

"If I had unveiled your future to you, you wouldn't have had all these wonderful experiences."

"But at the end of the day, the outcome is the same, Alphonse; I've ended up as I began: as a temple elephant."

Alphonse flew around me for a few seconds, then faced me and looked me straight in the eye.

"You know, Lakshmi, on a journey, it isn't the destination that matters, it's the journey itself. Anyone can go from one point to another. What matters most is how you undertake this journey."

"For you, maybe. For me, it's the destination that counts; to me, it doesn't matter how you get there."

Alphonse remained silent, and then looked at me, a smile on his face.

"It's all a question of perspective. I see that you've matured. You no longer ask yourself questions, and your doubts have vanished. You see things from a different angle. That's what life is all about. You weren't destined to lead just any ordinary life, nor were you destined to become something else; you were destined to discover the secret of life, of *your* life. Don't think that by becoming a temple elephant again, you've failed in your gamble. No, instead, you have been able to rip apart the veil of illusion to penetrate the truth. And this truth is peace. Peace with yourself. Your inner peace."

Alphonse was right. Since my arrival in Pondichéry, this ancient, sacred land, upon which so many saints and siddhas had set foot, I felt calm. This magical town had given me the inner peace I had yearned for all my life. This is the mystical land of which the greatest Tamil poet Subramania Bharati once sang. Born in 1882, Bharati was an independence activist who fled from British India to seek refuge in Pondichéry. He met his death in Madras in 1921 owing to injuries inflicted by a temple elephant. He used to live on the street that I cross every day.

I was tired, but happy to meet Alphonse. He was the only link with my eventful past, which now seemed to be a distant memory. Curiously, I no longer thought of it. That period of my life resembled a poem written upon a seashore: washed away by the waves, it had made way for the sand dunes, which, in turn, were swept away by the swirling wind. Chacko Chattan, Manmath, Bandipur, Veeran, Nagalingam, Muthu, Devar: names and words that rang hollow in my mind. The only creatures I was now left with were Alphonse and this stupid Tripod Dog Baba.

Incidentally, thinking of him, I felt compelled to ask Alphonse if he knew him.

"Tell me, Alphonse, as you know everything and everyone, do you know Tripod Dog Baba?"

"Tripod Dog Baba? Who's that?"

"You don't know Tripod Dog Baba? But the entire town knows him. He's the dog who is always beside me."

"Ah yes! Tripod. Of course I know him. But why do you call him Tripod Dog Baba?"

"Well, because ever since he returned from Rameswaram, everyone calls him Tripod Dog Baba. In any case, that's what he likes to be called."

"Since he returned from Rameswaram? What do you mean? He's never set a paw in Rameswaram! Ah, this rascal, this dog from the gutter . . . he's deceiving everyone! This stray dog has never gone to this holy location; besides, he'd have been chased away if he had. And how do you suppose he got there with his three and half legs, and being blind on top of that?"

"I don't know, but the dogs of the town treat him with a particular degree of respect and admiration. Some men respect him too."

"Men are stupid. As for the dogs of the town, one can't hope for any better. But beware of this dog; he's a crook. He's capable of doing anything when it comes to saving his skin. Beneath his disabled appearance and pleasant demeanor, he's a trickster who deceives everyone in the name of spirituality. And the female dog is no better; she's even worse than Tripod Dog Baba. Watch out for the disciple too. Those three are to be avoided like the plague! You'll see for yourself when you get to know them. But don't worry, I'm here to watch over you. I'll come and visit you often. See you soon, Lakshmi!"

After Alphonse left, I took a long time to fall asleep. The next day, as I was getting ready, I couldn't stop thinking of this dog. Why was he behaving like this? Why was he telling lies?

At around nine o'clock, Tokuram and I set off for the temple. As usual, as we went past Bharati's former house on rue Eswaran Kovil, I was overcome with remorse at the thought that he had been killed by one of my kind. The country had lost one of its greatest poets because of an elephant! As we arrived at the temple, the priest welcomed us as he did every day, performed his puja, and smeared three horizontal lines on my forehead. I then went to take up my position between the two pillars to the right of the temple, and my day began.

Tripod Dog Baba was still not there, but the shops were already open. Sacred chants were blaring out from a radio mast; the blended perfumes of camphor and flowers began to fill the air. The first coconut was cracked open in front of the temple, and the beggars tried to collect the pieces of coconut that were scattered about everywhere. Lemons were placed on the ground, and brand-new cars were driven over them by their owners, crushing them, such that they resembled yellow frogs. Yet another absurd custom, which involves placing lemons under the wheels of new vehicles as a symbol of sacrifice. Perhaps this act foreshadowed all the victims who were to get run over on the roads by the drunken and unlicensed drivers. The priest's bell competed with the honking of cars.

A couple then came toward me. The man was carrying a child in his arms. Their heads were freshly shaven, and the sandalwood paste that had been smeared on their shaven heads had not yet dried. This was to be the first blessing of the day. The man slipped a filthy, creased rupee note into my trunk, which I passed to Tokuram. When I raised my trunk to place it on the child's head, it wailed so much that the father stepped back. He came toward me a second time, so I turned to Tokuram, for each blessing had to be paid for. This is how I'd been trained; each time I raised my trunk, a note or coin had to be slipped into my trunk. But sometimes, like in this case, the blessing would be unsuccessful. So Tokuram indicated that I should try again. But this child refused to accept his blessing. Each time he saw me raise my trunk, he would let out a piercing scream, and so his father would retreat, and then come back again; he wouldn't leave without a blessing. After a while, his wife asked him to stop. She wanted to take the child into her arms. But the man refused; he wanted my trunk to be placed on his offspring at all costs. I began to grow impatient. I just wanted to knock him unconscious! Noticing my irritation, Tokuram asked the man to leave. But he wanted to attempt a final time, and when Tokuram refused, he asked to be reimbursed. An argument then broke out between the two men. The shaven pilgrim became increasingly threatening; after passing the child to the mother, he virtually came to blows with

Tokuram. The shopkeepers emerged from their shops to come to the rescue of my keeper. And that's when I saw Tripod Dog Baba enter the scene. I don't know where he had been hiding all this while. But as soon as he saw Tokuram being attacked, he pounced on the man, barking and tugging on his dhoti. The man hadn't expected this. Taken by surprise by this three-and-a-half-legged dog who was attacking him, he didn't ask for his refund, and left the temple, glowering at Tokuram.

Tripod Dog Baba chased him right up to the corner of the road, and then, once he was convinced that the man was well and truly gone, he came back to us. Et voilà! He had performed his trick yet again! Tokuram patted him on his head.

"You're a very good dog, Tripod Dog Baba! You're the guardian of this temple, and everyone will be safe as long as you are here."

Tripod Dog Baba looked at him proudly, nuzzled against his leg, and began to do a victory lap among the shopkeepers and the beggars, who were praising him for his bravery.

Tokuram bought him two soft, white idlis, which he placed on a banana leaf next to him. Tripod Dog Baba eating idlis! Now I'd really seen it all . . . he sat in front of the banana leaf, sniffed the idlis, but didn't touch anything. He glanced from left to right and spotted a dog near the autorickshaw stand; he gave a short bark to invite him over. This dog rushed toward the guru as soon as he heard the call. Tripod Dog Baba then nodded, pointing at the idlis, and placed his half leg onto the head of the dog, who yapped gratefully, bowed his head to receive his blessing, and set off again with the banana leaf. After this blessing was given, Tripod Dog Baba lay down on his side again, and went to sleep, as if all this effort had tired him out. I then heard Tokuram say to the coconut seller:

"You see, Ram, this dog is the perfect example of sanctity. He doesn't expect anything from anyone; he shares everything that you give him with the others. He has very unusual qualities. You see, he defended me, and when I gave him something to eat, he chose to give it to another dog so that he could go and meditate. A true sadhu!"

But no, he wasn't meditating! He was sleeping, the lazy dog! I even heard him snore! This dog was certainly good at his craft. He deceived more than one person. The rest of the day was uneventful, and at around one in the afternoon, Tokuram and I set off on the path of the Eswaran temple for our daily break, leaving behind our fake guru, who was pretending to meditate. All he was waiting for was for the street to fall silent, and for everyone to go for their siesta so he could indulge in his meat and curry orgy. When I reached the junction between rue Vysial and rue Manakulla Vinayagar, I spotted the female dog and the disciple roaming about, waiting for everyone to leave; I knew the rest of the story.

During my break, the image of this dog kept haunting my mind. Who was he? What was his story? I was so consumed by curiosity that I couldn't rest. Was he really an imposter? I just had to know. At around four in the afternoon, when I returned to the temple, I found him asleep under the power generator. At the sound of the bell that I was wearing around my neck, he woke up, and waited for me to settle between my two pillars. He wagged his tail to show that he was happy to see us again, and he then came to sit down next to me. These first hours of the afternoon were always calm; visitors wouldn't come to the temple until after sunset. I wanted to take advantage of this to get to know his story. So I observed him out of the corner of my eye. He looked very fresh after his siesta; he was sitting on his hind legs, wearing the jasmine garland and tilak that the flower seller put on him every day. Now I'd really seen it all! For without this garland and tilak, no one would have paid any attention to this disabled dog! But this idiotic flower seller called Maha would take it upon herself to fashion a garland for him, and would decorate him with a red tilak every day, ever since Tripod had become Tripod Dog Baba. On the hottest of days, I suspected he would go and cool off in the canal, where dirty water flowed. He would return reeking of urine and mud. And at the end of the day, as the scent of the jasmine faded, a cocktail of smells would waft through the air, rivaling those produced by Senteur Gilles, the perfumery division of the ashram.

A group of students from the ashram, wearing khaki shorts and white shirts, passed by on their way to the sports hall. Tripod Dog Baba looked at them and began to yawn, his tongue hanging out. He was getting bored already! But I was certainly not going to let him fall asleep.

"Tell me, Tripod Dog Baba, what's Rameswaram like?"

"What? Rameswaram? Which Rameswaram? Who's Rameswaram? I don't know him," he said, coming to his senses, without even looking at me.

"But . . . Rameswaram! The town where you became Dog Baba, isn't that Rameswaram?"

He turned to me, pretending to delve deep inside his memory. He remained silent for a few seconds. Then he composed himself, and said:

"Ah yes, Rameswaram! Of course! And what about it?"

"Well, tell me something about it. What's it like?"

"Why do you want to know? Are you planning to go there? No. Don't annoy me with such questions, just because you're bored. Actually, I feel like you've been quizzing me with strange questions for some time now. Like the other day. I can't remember exactly . . . ah yes! You asked me why does the word 'why' exist! You're a funny elephant, Lakshmi."

"Of course not, Tripod Dog Baba, I just want to get to know you better. We've been around each other for a while now, but I don't know your story. I don't know who you are, nor do I know about your past. Mine is simple; I'm just a temple elephant, there's nothing extraordinary about me. I've been working in temples all my life, and I don't know anything beyond that. But I'm sure you've had an eventful life, Tripod Dog Baba. You must have seen many things! There must be a reason as to why you are adored and respected. To have reached this level of holiness, you must have led an extraordinary life, and that's what I want to know about. Like everyone else, I admire you a lot."

I knew what he was like, this dog, full of pride and vanity; if I'd started to get as confrontational as him, I wouldn't have got anything out of him. Whereas if I flattered him, I'd get him to open up. He was scratching his ear and listening, but not looking at me, sitting on his two hind legs. This was his unique way of scratching himself; because he only had three and a half legs, he had to sit on his hind legs, as his half leg could not support him. But by sitting like this, he resembled a kangaroo more than a dog. I thought he looked ridiculous.

There was a pregnant pause. Then Tripod Dog Baba began his story, glancing over at the beggars who were settling down for the day. They were returning from their siesta, squabbling as usual. Why were they squabbling? This was a real mystery, but their corner has always been noisy.

■ ■ ■

"I was born on a pavement. Yes, that's right, a pavement on the corner between rue des Missions Etrangères and rue Kamatchi Amman Kovil. A stone's throw away from the Collège Calvé. The family of a rickshaw driver once lived there. My mother didn't belong to them, but she lived there too, because they fed her. And like all stray dogs, I had never known my father. Unlike you, I was never given a name at birth. I was called 'dog.' My mother didn't have a name either, for she was a stray dog. She was doomed to live under the stars, without a roof over her head, in a lawless world. Actually, the street did have laws; these were brutal, violent, and unfair laws, which I was to experience very early on in my youth.

"Originally, we were a family of four: two brothers, one sister, and me. We got split up very early on. One of my brothers was adopted by the family of another rickshaw driver in rue Muthu Mariamman Kovil, and the other was adopted by the family of a retired soldier who had served in the French army in rue Perumal Kovil. My sister and I remained with our mother.

No one wanted us. Understandably, no one wanted my sister, as she was a female. Being a female in our society is a disadvantage; our society is very discriminatory, and only males have the right to live in it. Females have no function apart from reproduction, and they are considered to be worthless creatures, additional mouths to be fed. And it's often the case that females who are born to pet dogs are also abandoned on the streets, increasing the stray dog population. Regardless of whether we're talking about guard dogs or pet dogs, society prefers males. Society is selective, and it only respects beauty and strength; strong, big, and muscular dogs are favored. The only dogs that are favorably looked upon are the Rajapalayam, Kanni, Chippiparai, or Kombai dogs. But Pondichéry didn't have many pedigree dogs during this period. There were a few German shepherds and two or three bulldogs; the rest were of mixed breeds. The discrimination in society was therefore particularly severe. But fate hadn't worked in my favor; I was small, white, and speckled with yellow spots, ears folded back, and so I was abandoned on the streets.

"The only memories I have of my brothers and sister are from the first few months after my birth, when we were spoiled by the rickshaw driver's children. They would spend the whole day playing with us. Even the students of the Collège Calvé would find us adorable and would bring us biscuits and cakes from the Chettiar's stall, where they would gather at break time.

"After my two brothers left, we still enjoyed the attention of this small group. In particular, I remember a young boy who was very fond of me. At break time, at ten in the morning, he would always buy me a bowl of milk and a biscuit; he would play with me for a few minutes and then go back to class. My sister was jealous of this. We had a happy childhood, even if we didn't have much to eat. But three mouths to feed was too much for the family of this poor rickshaw driver, who himself was dependent on a paltry salary. We overheard them say that they had to get rid of us as soon as possible. The threat of separation loomed over us. And this happened earlier than expected when our mother was killed, run over by the Fatima school bus, which would hurtle past us every day at great speed on rue des Missions Etrangères.

"A few days later, my sister disappeared," the dog continued. "I never found out what actually happened. One morning when I woke up, I just noticed that she was no longer there. From one day to the next, I found myself all alone, without a family. The only family I had left was the rickshaw driver's family.

"As time passed by and I grew up, I noticed that all the attention I had enjoyed as a puppy began to diminish. As the days went by, I lost my cute puppy features and I became just any old dog, ordinary, and almost invisible. My ears were drooping, and my tail had adopted an awkward position; it was neither curled upward, nor was it drooping, but it was in between the two. I wasn't big, and my fur was turning a somewhat dirty off-white color. The children would no longer play with me; the school students would ignore me. Even the young boy who used to offer me milk no longer paid any attention to me. When I went up to him wagging my tail, he barely looked at me, and instead he shouted at me while smoking his cigarette: 'Hey, clear off, dog!' I had to get used to this new world. Until then, I'd only known love and kindness, but now I was confronted with violence and abuse. I'll always remember the first time I was kicked . . .

"The days after my mother's death were very tough. Until then, I had never experienced hunger. So when I felt these pangs of hunger for the first time, it took me a while to work out what was happening. I began to run around in circles to find something to eat. I no longer had any milk from my mother or from this student, who was now hidden behind a cloud of cigarette smoke, nor did I have any biscuits or cakes . . . I sniffed about for food everywhere. Running around in circles on an empty stomach, I began to feel dizzy; and then, all of a sudden, I caught a whiff of food. The rickshaw driver's wife was heating up yesterday's fish curry for her husband, who was about to leave for work. The sight of the smoke and the scents that were emanating from the terracotta pot comforted me. I saw the rickshaw driver sit down in front of his plate, and I went and sat beside him. At first, I waited patiently and calmly, hoping that he would give me a handful of rice. But when I saw that his hand was intent only on moving from plate to mouth, and that the rice was rapidly disappearing, I began to despair. My mouth was watering, my tongue was hanging out, and I was drooling . . . the rickshaw driver noticed this, and he repeated a phrase several times, one I would hear for the rest of my life: 'Hey, clear off, dog!' But the hunger that tormented me made me deaf and blind. So when the man got up to go and fetch some water, I immediately stuck my snout into his plate. I had barely swallowed a bit of rice and fish when I heard the words 'Filthy dog!' And even before I had the time to react, I got kicked on my right side.

"The very next moment, I found myself far away from the plate, crushed against the front wheel of the rickshaw. Just as I got back on my feet, a stone came flying toward me. As I'd never previously experienced violence and blows, I didn't know how to react. When the stone struck me right on my forehead, I experienced pain for the first time. I howled and barked at the same time. I had no option but to flee; I wanted to be out of there. More stones were flung toward me. I saw the rickshaw driver running behind me, cursing me. I had never run so fast all my life! I weaved my way in and out between the cycles and motorcycles that were passing by. Uncertain as to where to go, I carried on running straight down rue des Missions Etrangères.

"I was out of breath when I stopped, and I realized that I was in front of a wall. I had reached the end of the road, and I'd ended up on boulevard Nord. I had to take a right or a left. But I didn't need to make that decision, because the rickshaw driver had stopped chasing me. I paused, breathing a sigh of relief. Relief that then turned to shame when I noticed that my tail was between my legs.

"It was a day I'll never forget all my life," said the dog, "as this was a day of revelation. The realization of hunger, pain, fear, and shame. All these emotions in just one day, in one instance alone, just because I stuck my snout into a plate. I was scared of going back home. Well, when I say home, it wasn't exactly a house. Just three jute bags fastened directly to the pavement alongside the wall of the last house on the street, which was on the corner of rue des Missions Etrangères.

"That was where the two rickshaw driver brothers lived with their wives and children. They shared the pavement. In those days, each street corner had its own rickshaw stand, and the driver's family also lived there. As a general rule, all rickshaw drivers had children, and they were scattered throughout the district. And so right from rue Nehru up to boulevard Nord, and along rue des Missions Etrangères, all drivers belonged to the same family. But they only got together during the major festivals. They spent the rest of the time fighting among themselves. Not a single day went by without a fight. After a hard day of work, the men would return to the pavement completely drunk, and they would indulge in their favorite sport: beating their wives. And when they weren't doing this, they would fight among themselves. At nightfall, each street corner was transformed into a boxing ring. The men against their wives, the men against one another, the wives against the men, and the wives against one another. They fought every evening, insulted one another, and went to bed with tufts of hair in the palms of their hands. The insults and the language of the rickshaw drivers were so foul and incomprehensible that they would have made even the pope forget his Latin. Incidentally, that's what the people of Pondichéry called the language of the rickshaw drivers: Latin.

"By nightfall, I realized I had spent my entire day roaming about. It was the first time I had wandered this far out. Until this day, I had never gone beyond rue Kamatchi Amman Kovil. I had been confined to the area between rue des Missions Etrangères on one side and quai d'Ambour on the other side. But on this day, the fear of being attacked again haunted me, and so I set off to explore the town. I stumbled upon the boulevard, and paused there for a while, disorientated, unsure as to which direction I should take. Then, glancing to my right, I realized that this side of town was calmer than the left, where the hustle and bustle of the town, along with the blaring of bus and car horns, could be heard. I therefore decided to go up boulevard Nord again.

"This was the first time I had walked down such a long road," the dog continued. "It was never-ending. It was also broader than the one I was living on and was flanked by large houses. There was more traffic, and it was more densely populated. As it so happened, I was going past a rickshaw stand on the corner of quai d'Ambour and the boulevard when some dogs, who were sitting there, looked at me curiously and began to bark. I didn't know what to do, so I stopped, and I barked in return to say hello. One of them got up, began to bark louder, and bared his teeth; I understood that I wasn't welcome there. When I saw him come up to me, my tail slunk between my legs again, and without thinking, I began to run. As it was, the day had already been quite eventful, involving pain, humiliation, and hunger . . . I wasn't prepared to face a fight on top of that. I'd save that for another day. In any case, I didn't know how to fight.

■ ■ ■

"While I was running, I suddenly caught a whiff of fish, and the farther I ran, the stronger the scent became. I had reached a point where the boulevard bore right, leading onto an avenue that was even broader and longer than the one I had just taken. The smell of fish came from the left. I decided to follow it, because I was still hungry; I hadn't eaten anything all day. The road led to a cluster of houses, a type that I had never seen before. They were small, you could even say minuscule, and they were thatched with coconut palm leaves and had tiny entrances. Some houses didn't even have a door; a jute cloth served the purpose. Men were sitting in front of these houses, going about various tasks. Some were picking their teeth using twigs, some were busy repairing fishing nets, while others were simply chatting. Thin wisps of smoke emanated from each house, and an aroma of fish curry wafted through the air. In fact, the whole road smelled of fish. I set off in pursuit of this aroma, when I noticed a big stretch of water to my right. I'd never seen so much water, and water that roared too! It was only later that I came to realize that it was the sea, and that I had reached a fishing village known as Kurusukuppam.

"I went from house to house, sniffing about, trying to find at least one piece of fish. It wasn't my favorite food, but I would have been very content with even just one tiny piece. Eventually, I stopped in front of a house where some children were eating. They were sitting by the doorway, their plates piled high with rice and fish curry. I went up to the door, which was ajar, and I wagged my tail. One of the children turned to me and yelled: 'Hey, clear off, dog!,' raising his hand as if to hit me. I retreated, but I didn't want to leave. I even sat down to indicate that I had no intention of leaving this place without eating. He then turned around, and shouted through the door:

"'Amma, there's a dog outside!'

"'Chase it away!' came a voice from inside.

"'I tried, but it won't leave,' the child retorted, threatening to hit me again.

"I looked at him with my tongue hanging out and continued to wag my tail. After a while, the voice from inside inquired:

"'Is the dog still there?'

"The voice belonged to a woman who emerged with a plate of rice and fish. She placed the plate in front of the door, next to me. A heavily dented aluminum plate that had a dubious smell. But I wasn't going to be difficult; this was the first time I was being served food on a plate.

"'Poor dog, he must be really hungry to come to the fishermen community for food,' she told the child. And pushing the plate toward me, she said: 'Eat, dog, eat.'

"I didn't need any persuasion; I pounced on the plate and began to devour this unexpected meal. The mother and children stood there, watching me. When I had finished, the mother came back with a little water, which she poured onto my dented plate. I licked it clean, looking at her gratefully. She went back inside, but the child stayed until I'd finished my plate, which he pushed aside with his feet before going inside, closing the door behind him.

"With great trepidation, I decided to go back home, because I had to sleep somewhere. As I approached my street, I was relieved that the rickshaw driver was nowhere to be seen. His vehicle was there; this meant that the man had left to go for a drink. When I reached the pavement, I saw that the women were busy cooking. One of them spoke to me:

"'Ah, here you are, you filthy dog! You have the nerve to come back, after what you did this morning! Wait till my husband comes back; you're in for it. Because of you, he hasn't even eaten and is in a foul mood. And who's going to take the beating? Me, of course! Clear off, you scum!'

"As she uttered these words, she threw a burning splinter of wood at me. I narrowly dodged it, surprised to have been attacked by the woman too. I set off to lie down on the pavement opposite. I was tired, but I dreaded the wrath of the rickshaw driver. It wasn't long before he came home, staggering and squabbling with his brother. When he noticed me, he bent down, and picked something up. I was still lying down, watching him out of the corner of my eye. I noticed that he had tucked his arms behind his back as he continued to walk. My sixth sense told me that he was hiding something behind his back . . . Cautiously, I wagged my tail to show the rickshaw driver that I was happy to see him.

"'You filthy mongrel! You're still here? After what you did this morning, I didn't think I'd ever see you again!'

"A stone flew toward me, just as he uttered his final word. But the man's aim was no longer as precise as it had been in the morning; the stone flew straight past me, striking the main door of the Collège Calvé. The very next second, I was out of there. A single stone had just knocked my life into the precarious realm of the unknown."

Chapter Nine

"MY NOMADIC LIFE HAD JUST BEGUN," Tripod Dog Baba continued. "I had nowhere to go and I wasn't mature enough to face the future. The first weeks were very difficult. As I didn't know the town, I didn't want to venture too far beyond my district. I avoided rue Kamatchi Amman Kovil and decided to set up my home two roads farther down. To my surprise, I noticed that this part of the town wasn't home to a single dog: neither to pet dogs, nor to stray dogs. But I very quickly realized that living in this district was going to be difficult. When I had lived with the rickshaw driver's family, I had never been worried about food. I would eat the family's leftovers: fresh fish, dried fish, and beef. On two or three occasions, I even got to eat mutton. Eating meat was a luxury for rickshaw drivers, and that meant it was for me, too. But when I discovered which part of town I was in, I was most dismayed . . . from now on, I'd be living among the Chettiars and upper-caste Hindus! This meant no meat, no fish, and only vegetables. I now understood why there were no dogs here . . . What idiot would choose to live in this vegetarian district? And these people didn't have pet dogs either, since they were not allowed to cook or eat meat.

"During the first few weeks, I spent my time wandering about, looking for a bone. But I had no success! No one gave me anything to eat either; when I rummaged in the trash cans, I only found gourds, eggplants, and dhal, which stuck to my snout, and other vegetables that I hadn't even known existed.

"From rue Ambalatadayar up to rue Perumal Kovil, each main road had its own temple, around which the entire Hindu community congregated. The zone was also dotted with some retired soldiers' houses; the people of Pondichéry called these soldiers by their French name, soldats. And these soldats ate meat. Once in a while, I caught a whiff of a good beef or mutton curry as I walked—or, rather, wandered about on an empty stomach—through the district. But for one reason or another, even the trash cans of these soldiers didn't contain any leftovers; anyone would think that they threw away their bones elsewhere so as not to offend their Hindu neighbors!

"Once, and once only, for the first time since my exile, I was lucky enough to taste this dish they call biriyani. This colorful, highly fragrant dish was enough to attract a pack of dogs; this rice dish mixed with pieces of mutton or chicken was so exquisitely cooked that it could tempt and persuade any vegetarian to sink their teeth into this tender, spiced meat . . . It was a moment of pure bliss. After I'd eaten this biriyani, I no longer wished to leave the pavement in front of this house. I lay down, feeling satisfied and content after my meal. I had barely closed my eyes to sink into a siesta when I heard a dog bark. It came from inside, and when the door opened, a big German shepherd appeared who dutifully chased me away, pronto.

"Hunger drove me back to the fishing village from time to time, until the day when I realized that it was infested with cats. It was their kingdom!

▪ ▪ ▪

"One evening, after I'd eaten in the house of this good and generous woman, who would feed me each time I came (maybe she didn't like cats?), I found myself surrounded by half a dozen cats who were trying to attack me. They must have planned this ambush, as it took place after my meal, when I had decided to go and drink water from the small canal that ran through the district. This foul, colorful water came from the paper factory of the ashram on boulevard Nord and it flowed into the sea. Depending on the kind of paper being printed, the paper factory discharged water of various colors into the sea. So, after I had had a drink, I found that my tongue was either blue, yellow, red, or green, depending on what was being produced that day.

"A cat sitting on the wall of this tiny bridge pounced on me; this was the first one. I hadn't noticed him; I still had pangs of hunger, as the woman had served me only very little rice, and so I wasn't very alert. This attack took me by surprise, and what's more, the coward attacked me from behind! I successfully dodged him, but as I turned around, I found myself face to face with a big, striped cat, who was beginning to bare his claws, arching his back. His tail was curled over, fur standing on end. I had never fought until then, let alone with a cat! So all I did was bare my teeth to frighten him; my mouth was the color of blood after I'd drunk the red water from the canal. But that wasn't enough; the cat started hissing, ears pointing outward. He came up to me and swiped at me with his paw. I felt his claws scratch my snout, and so, instinctively, I leaped onto his throat. Some fur stuck to my mouth; I'd got him. The cat was surprised, and so was I; I was surprised by my ability to fight. I had been successful in this first attack, but I was still angry; this cat was going to pay for absolutely everything. All my frustration and fury were going to be unleashed on this unfortunate creature who had had the misfortune of attacking me . . . I was preparing for my second attack when other cats entered the scene. They just appeared out of the blue. In the space of a few minutes, I found myself surrounded by them. But fleeing was out of the question: even if I were to die at the claws of these cursed cats, I was going to fight. The humiliating memories of these past few days fueled my courage. I sank my teeth into the cat's flesh; I got clawed all over, and this pain further reinforced my strength and intensified my rage. But these blasted cats (having spent time with the rickshaw drivers, I had adopted their language) began to get the upper hand. I felt myself weaken; fighting against six enemies who were pouncing on me from all sides was no easy thing. At the same time, I was trying to draw this battle to a triumphant close. Looking around me, I saw that we were only a few meters away from the sea. I had to lead them to the water. Here, I'd have the upper hand. And it worked. I could sense they were abandoning ship the closer I came to the waves.

"I felt relieved, and then, suddenly, I heard a dog barking. And in an instant, the fight came to a standstill. Everyone was distracted by this sound, and I saw a dog emerge from the shadows. He came to my rescue, running on the beach alongside the distillery. The cats took fright and began to bolt. The two of us set off, chasing them, and since they struggled to run on the sand, I managed to catch one. This was the cat who had attacked me initially. Holding him in my mouth, I shook him as if he were a cuddly toy before throwing him to the waves. The others fled.

"And that's how the evening of my first victory ended. As we walked back up rue Goudronnée, I saw a ball of striped fur that rocked back and forth to the motion of the waves."

■ ■ ■

"'I'm called Jimmy,' said the other dog, once we were back on firm ground.

"We were sitting on the corner of boulevard Nord and cours Chabrol, just in front of the distillery entrance, in the light of the streetlamp. I was a fine mess, with scratch marks all over my snout, but I was happy to have found someone whom I could talk to, to whom I could recount my misfortune. At first sight, he looked older than me and seemed to be well fed. He must be a pet dog, as he had a collar. Tall and slender, he resembled a German shepherd, or at least, he was of the same color. Whatever could he be doing here, at such an hour, in a fishing village? But he beat me to it, asking:

"'What were you doing there? Don't you belong to a household?'

"'I was hungry, and there's a fisherman's wife who gives me food from time to time. No, I have no home; I'm a stray dog.'

"'You're lucky!' he murmured.

"Was he making fun of me or what, this dog? Here I was telling him that I was a stray dog, and he was telling me that I was lucky!

"'Oh really? In what way am I lucky?' I retorted, trying to conceal my bad mood.

"'Because you don't have a master. You can do what you want, you can go wherever you like, and you don't have any restrictions. You're free!'

"'Well then, you have to live only one day on the street and you'll see that it's no easy thing. You'll die of hunger in a few days. You think I'm lucky? Try to survive on the street, you'll see if you feel lucky . . . You're totally mad, you are!'

"He looked at me, appearing to be amused.

"'You're the one who's mad. No, you must be a fool! If you can't manage to find anything to eat, it's either because you don't know the town, or you're an idiot. I personally think it's because you don't know the town. What dog would come and venture into a fishing village? But to start with, which district are you from?'

"'From the area around the Collège Calvé.'

"'You unfortunate creature, what are you doing in the Hindu district?'

"'It's not my fault, that's where I was born.'

"And I told him my story.

"He listened to me patiently amid the dazzling headlights of the cars driving past us along cours Chabrol.

"'Now I understand your situation better. If you want, you can come with me. I know the town better than anyone, and I also have many acquaintances. You have nothing to fear.'"

■ ■ ■

"And that's how I discovered a whole new world," Tripod Dog Baba continued. "Jimmy introduced me to the Creole district in the ville blanche; that was where he came from. He lived in a big yellow house on rue Suffren. This district was nothing like what I'd experienced before. If someone had told me that heaven existed on the other side of the canal, I wouldn't have believed them.

"The district consisted of enormous houses, painted in attractive colors. The fragrance of meat, cooked in a thousand and one different ways, emanated from these houses. The roads were broad and well shaded, and there was less traffic here. The garbage cans were full of bones. Pieces of beef neck and shoulder joints, beef shanks, rib steak, rump steak: you name it. Every part of the cow was there. . . . and there wasn't just beef! I was to discover a whole range of meats: chicken, pork, duck, lamb, mutton . . . everything a dog could ever dream of. This district was inhabited by the white and Creole population, who would joyfully indulge in a meat orgy. As soon as you crossed the canal, the contrast was immediately palpable; the other side was characterized by a sense of austerity and fervent acts of devotion, whereas this side had a sense of nonchalance about it, and a lighthearted atmosphere prevailed. The sari was replaced by skirts, the dhoti by trousers, the temples by churches, and what was most striking was the scent of vindaloo, which replaced that of ghee.

■ ■ ■

"It was easy for me to get used to this new world. I found myself a spot on the pavement on rue du Bazar Saint-Laurent, next to some small shops on the corner of rue Romain Rolland. There were two cobblers, a shop that sold school textbooks, and another where you could buy various assorted items. A few meters away on rue Romain Rolland was the École de Saint Joseph de Cluny. My first territory extended from the corner of rue Suffren up to rue du Bazar Saint-Laurent, culminating on cours Chabrol. There were very few stray dogs here, because practically every household had its own pet dog. At the other end of rue du Bazar Saint-Laurent, just before the canal, there lived a family of pousseurs—that's what the rickshaw drivers were called in this part of the town—with two dogs, who left me in peace and quiet. Henceforth, my life promised to be calm and happy.

"I began to get to know Jimmy better. He seemed to be somewhat unhappy with life. He was certainly spoiled, fed, and looked after by his owners, but he had a thirst for freedom and vagabondage. Moreover, he was not the only dog of the house; there were four of them, and they whiled away their time squabbling. Jimmy needed space. He felt stifled between his four walls, so he would escape for his nocturnal strolls, which didn't bother anyone. When his master noticed that Jimmy had a new friend, this didn't bother him either. I even had an aluminum bowl placed on the pavement, close to the entrance door, where I was served food. My first bowl!

"For the first time in my life, I no longer had to worry about food. No need to go and poke my snout into trash cans; no need to run around in circles on an empty stomach, looking distressed with my tongue hanging out. I now had something to eat. I even began to gain weight. Those around me were kind. From time to time, pedestrians stroked me. And when evening fell, Jimmy and I would wander through the town. Jimmy knew the entire town and all the dogs. He was also respected, and no one picked a fight with him, for he was tough, and must have been a fighter in his youth—confirmed by a large wound on his left ear. And it wasn't just a wound; the tip of his ear was clearly missing. One day, he explained to me that this was a token of his conquest of the La Centrale district, which I would discover later. And this is how I earned respect without having to fight even once: by being Jimmy's protégé. My territory grew bigger; from now on, I could walk through the entire district, from quai de Gingy up to cours Chabrol, without fear of being attacked.

"One evening, while we were walking, Jimmy offered to take me to the La Centrale district. I asked him why he didn't like to stay at home like the other dogs, whereas I, for example, only dreamed of one thing: that someone would put a collar around my neck and tie me to a chain in front of a sign with the words 'Watch out, vicious dog.' The ultimate aim of my life was to get adopted. But what I really yearned for, and would have truly given my life for, was to have a name! All the dogs in this district had one, even the pousseurs' dogs! Jimmy, Bobby, Médor, Asky, Iris, Misty, Missie: they all had a name. I wanted one too, but who was going to give me one? I was always just known as 'dog.' As we walked past the houses, Jimmy would say to me: 'Look at Médor: he's a good guard dog. And look at Laika: at one point in time, she was so beautiful that all the dogs were in love with her. And you see Zébulon over there? He's so stupid.' And so on, and so forth. I knew all their names, but I suffered in silence, because I didn't have one."

■ ■ ■

"'You see, dog, it's true that being a pet comes with the advantage of being loved, having something to eat, and having a roof over your head . . .'

"'Having a name, too!' I interrupted him.

"'What do you mean, a name?' he said, in surprise. 'Ah yes, it's true that you don't have one . . . but that's not the most important thing. The most important thing is freedom. I envy you, you know. Of course, your life hasn't always been easy; but you don't have a master, nor do you have a collar that ties you to a place. You're free!'

"'You're also free, in your own way. You needn't complain. You have the best of both worlds, which not everyone has.'

"'You're right, dog,' Jimmy acknowledged, indicating that I should turn right at the end of Quai d'Ambour.

"We had just crossed the canal for the first time in several weeks. Now we were in the southern part of the town. After a few meters, we turned left, and we found ourselves on rue Bussy, and with the sea behind us, we headed toward La Centrale.

"'You're right,' he continued, 'but there are times, you know, when I just want to leave; I just want to let go of everything. My house, my home comforts, my district, my master . . . everything. Leave, and set forth without a destination, roam about, and see the world from a different perspective. I don't just want to live anymore, I want to live life on the edge; I want to live in fear of what tomorrow may bring, be it hunger or thirst. I want to fight. Yes, fight! But not with other dogs; no, I want to fight for survival in this brutal world. My life is too secure; it's too monotonous, without any surprises or challenges. But now I am too old for that. That's why I envy you: I envy your youth and your freedom. You're exactly what I would have wanted to be in my youth. A dog without a name, a master, or a collar; a dog who belongs to the road and the world.'

"We had reached rue des Missions Etrangères. Rue des Missions Etrangères! It was here on this very road, but at the other end, where my life had begun, and my destiny had taken a turn for the worse. God alone knew what was going to happen next.

"'So, here you are, dog. This is the La Centrale district. If my district is the Franco-Creole paradise of vindaloo, ham, and roast chicken, this district is the kingdom of the Franco-Indian Catholics. Fragrant coconut-milk korma with free-range chicken and white pepper, duck curry with cumin, liver fricassée, delicate sheep brain pâtés, spicy Koujambounote sauce with veal blanquette. Here, you'll find dishes that a dog could only ever dream of tasting. Trust me, I know a thing or two about it. The Indian Catholic district extends from rue Bussy right up to the cathedral, and all the dogs know me. You have nothing to fear.'

"He had hardly finished his sentence when we noticed a pack of dogs on the corner of rue Laporte who were relishing a midnight feast. We joined them, and Jimmy dived most joyfully into the garbage bin, looking for the best leftovers.

"This dog was extraordinary; he preferred to live a life of vagabondage and homelessness. And I wanted the exact opposite; the situation was truly absurd. How could he enjoy a life of being kicked, being attacked by stones, and yelled at: 'Hey, clear off, dog!'? How could he prefer this eternal fight for survival to his world of comfort and luxury? I found it hard to understand, but I followed him through the maze of this town, which I was discovering bit by bit. And at dawn, as we left La Centrale, we were accompanied by the cacophony of the first strokes of the coffin makers' hammers, along with the honks from the milkmen's vehicles, which resounded along the petit canal behind rue Savarirayalu."

■ ■ ■

At this point in his story, Tripod Dog Baba paused. The visitors were beginning to flock toward the temple, and it was difficult for me, as the temple elephant, to follow his story between blessings. I had never seen him awake for such a long time.

Predictably, as soon as he stopped talking, he sank into a deep slumber.

In the evening, the temple became animated. The pujari rang his little bell more and more frantically, and the scents of incense and camphor engulfed the whole district. It was fascinating to think that just a few meters away from this chaotic world, where disciples pushed and shoved one another to catch a glimpse of the sanctum sanctorum, the sober silence of the ashram prevailed. Two different worlds, side by side, each with their own notion of the sacred. But for the moment, I was eager to know the rest of Tripod Dog Baba's story. Realizing that I would have to wait until tomorrow, I went back to my temple, haunted by images of cats and dogs fighting around garbage cans full of bones and scraps of fish . . .

■ ■ ■

"By the time Jimmy disappeared, I was familiar with the whole town," Tripod Dog Baba continued, without being asked. "He had shown me everything and had introduced me to everyone in all the districts. The Muslim district no longer held any secrets from me; I knew its famous biriyanis, the big and small bazaars, extending right up to boulevard Sud. Jimmy had even introduced me to the Kauravas, who had settled along the railway track. This community of hunters would treat us to good game meat. I could never thank Jimmy enough for having taught me, and for having revealed everything to me, as if I'd been his own son.

"His disappearance affected me profoundly. For several days, I ate nothing, lying in front of the door of the yellow house without touching my bowl. However, I have never been sentimental; having been conditioned to the harsh reality of life, my heart didn't lend itself to any tender or nostalgic sentiments. I also wasn't a romantic dreamer like Jimmy, who would have liked to experience a life of vagabondage under the moonlight and stars, listening to the murmur of the waves, sitting on the parapet of cours Chabrol, or chasing butterflies in Parc du Gouverneur . . . but I missed Jimmy.

"In the final days that preceded his death, he seemed to be behaving strangely. He must have sensed the imminence of his departure, and he took me on a full tour of the town to explain to the dogs of all the districts that I would be his successor, and that they owed me the same token of respect and friendliness. On the final evening, he took me to the Vietnamese restaurant on rue Romain Roland. The owner knew him well. She served us two decent bowls of sautéed beef with mushrooms. After the meal, we went to wait for Jimmy's master, who was watching a film in the Salle Jeanne d'Arc on the same street. He was very surprised to see us there; he knew that at this time, Jimmy would normally wander the streets. But he didn't say anything. Upon our return, Jimmy followed his master into the house, and I never saw him again.

"I could have stayed in this yellow house, spending the rest of my life in peace, with a collar and a sign with the words 'Watch out, vicious dog.' But as a homage to Jimmy, I decided otherwise.

"Some days after Jimmy's death, my bowl disappeared. I searched for it everywhere, but was unable to find it. I then noticed that the front door, which was normally always closed, was partially open. Was this an invitation? My curiosity and hunger led me to push open the door with my snout. Lakshmi, this was the first time I was entering a house; previously, I had only known streets and pavements.

"The house was enormous. At its entrance was a large garden with plants and exquisite flowers, and in the middle, there was a path that led to the main house. My steps became hesitant as I began to walk down this pathway. On the right, tucked away under the bougainvillea trees, there was even a tiny shrine dedicated to some Hindu god. How strange! Hadn't Jimmy told me that everyone who lived in this district was Catholic? Yet these people were eating meat! It wasn't until later that I came to understand the kind, tolerant nature of the owner of the premises.

"At this point, I wondered whether I should continue or return to the pavement, when I saw two dogs emerge from a small hut at the end of the path. They rushed toward me, barking, and stopped two steps away, baring their teeth. Instinctively, I became defensive and waited for them to attack first. But I didn't have to wait for long; a gate opened to the left of the path and a voice emerged, urging them to calm down. The two dogs barked for a few seconds longer, then lay down, wagging their tails in silence. The master of the house then invited the two dogs to enter the house, closed the gate, and indicated that I should follow. This reassured me. At the end of the path, he opened another gate, which gave access to the back of the kitchen, and here, I noticed my bowl. Four or five people were busy doing different household tasks. The master asked the woman who was doing the dishes to serve me something to eat.

She turned toward me, and said to her master in Pondicherrian Creole, a form of French spoken with a Tamil accent:

"'But, Monsieur, it's a stray dog. Don't tell me you're going to let him into the house! It's a dog off the streets!'

"'Shut up and do what I tell you,' answered the master, authoritatively. 'And keep your voice down: I don't want Madame to hear.'

"The housemaid murmured something and returned with a hot dish of meatballs and rice, followed by another woman.

"'Oh no, Étienne, you're not going to start this again! I've had enough of your dogs! We've only just lost Jimmy, and now you're bringing me another dog, and a mongrel at that—a stray dog! Enough is enough!'

"The master, scorched by the maid's angry gaze, grabbed the bowl from her hands and carried on down the path, without responding. The woman followed us, yelling at the man and glancing at me, her eyes full of hatred. In the middle of the garden, to the right of the path, there was a veranda sheltered by a thatched coconut palm roof. The man put my bowl down on the floor and went to sit down on a Pondicherienne; traditionally used by plantation owners, these chairs are commonly seen throughout the town. He invited me to eat, lit up his pipe, opened a newspaper, and began to read without bothering about the woman. She was standing there, glaring at us, hands on hips.

"'OK, Étienne. As usual, you do what you like without ever consulting me. But I warn you, this stray dog won't be allowed inside the house. And if I ever see it there, I'll break its legs,' she said, going back into the house."

"Is that how you lost half of your leg?" I interrupted Tripod Dog Baba.

At this point, I was beginning to lose interest in the story. All these details about the house, the master, their conversations, the district of La Centrale . . . I, Lakshmi, didn't care! All I wanted to know was how he had lost his leg, how he had become Tripod Dog Baba, and when and where his life as a fake guru had begun. Tripod Dog Baba must have sensed my impatience, for he turned to me angrily, saying:

"Listen, Lakshmi, you're the one who wanted to hear my life story, and now that I've begun, you're going to listen until the very end without interrupting me!"

The dog continued: "So, for the very first time, I lived in a house and I had a master. I spent my days lying beside him; he spent his time on the veranda reading and meeting his friends. He only stepped away for meals and his siesta. The rest of the time, we kept each other company. He was kind to me, although he never talked to me. I probably reminded him of Jimmy, who must have been his favorite dog; he was content just gazing at me, before immersing himself in his books again. And since I wasn't used to being stroked or hearing kind words, I was perfectly content like this. The silence didn't bother me at all.

"But over time, I began to feel the same as Jimmy; this inertia, laziness, and inaction made me sink into a state of depression. I missed the street; I longed for the sounds of the town and the traffic, the company of other stray dogs and challenges. I realized that I was still too young to become trapped within this monotonous way of life, luxurious though it was.

"One day, just as the man had previously opened the door to let me in, he now opened it to let me out. He must have sensed that, like Jimmy, I was suffering from being in confinement. I looked at him gratefully, then glanced at my bowl a final time, and set off.

"A new period of nomadism began," continued Tripod Dog Baba. "But this time, I was better armed. I knew every nook and cranny of the town. I knew all the dogs of the different districts; I knew exactly where to obtain the foods that I desired. The town revealed another facet to me. I began to regain my appetite for life, wandering through the big bazaar in search of the best bones in the butchers' lane; strolling through La Centrale, especially on Sundays; here, mouthwatering scents of curry would waft through the air; the Muslim district, where I would rush every Friday as soon as I heard the call of the muezzin; here, I would enjoy the famous biriyani after the prayer. I also went from time to time to the quartier blanc to taste the roast chicken and other Creole dishes. That's where I developed my taste for fine cuisine.

"Whereas the other dogs had claimed their respective districts, I refused to settle in a specific area for good. This gave me the feeling that the whole town belonged to me, and the other dogs grew used to seeing me wander about, without disturbing them or claiming ownership of any particular territory. That's how I forged a reputation as a nomadic dog, without any ties. I never fought or quarreled with the other dogs. Whenever I felt that a fight was going to break out, I would leave the scene. Not because I was scared, but because I was simply drawn to the principles of peace and nonviolence. This attitude laid the foundation for my reputation as a Baba, an honorary title given to ascetics," added Tripod Dog Baba.

■ ■ ■

"Lakshmi, years slipped by like this, quite uneventfully, when one day, a rumor spread through the town that the council was going to capture all the dogs without collars in order to shoot them. A good number of dog owners rushed to the shops to buy collars. Until then, only the pedigree dogs had remained on a leash, so they didn't go and mix with the other dogs and lose the purity of their pedigree or catch diseases. The other pet dogs didn't have collars.

"Rumor had it that the two sons of a minister had just set up a business. One manufactured dog collars and the other manufactured tennis balls made of dog skin. These two had decided to make money and get rich at our expense. This was a most bizarre and absurd period, as the operation began with dogs and ended up targeting human beings.

"After this initial step was taken to eradicate the stray dogs, the next phase of town enhancement began. This consisted of evicting all unemployed people, beggars, and families of rickshaw drivers beyond the boulevards. They then progressed to the most absurd act in the entire history of the country: the forced sterilization of young males. And when I say males, I'm not talking about dogs, but men! Everyone began to panic.

"But as I told you earlier, Lakshmi, since this society is so discriminatory and elitist, this policy targeted only the poor, the illiterate, and the farmers. The elite living in town, the educated, and the rich were spared this madness. And so, the entire population of dogs, rickshaw drivers, poor people, and farmers would run and hide at the slightest glimpse of a uniform. The dog catchers were dressed in dirty khaki shorts and shirts. They always walked with their hands behind their backs to hide their lassos, and they reeked of alcohol, which could be smelled ten meters away. The people who caught men for sterilization wore white coats like doctors. And those who evicted the rickshaw drivers and the poor were the local policemen, who wore khaki and colonial képis on their heads. This whole official squad in uniform was bent on eradicating all traces of 'non-civilization.'"

■ ■ ■

"When these measures initially came into force, the roads became desolate. Hundreds of dogs were captured; the beggars and the homeless were deported outside of the town. The families of the rickshaw drivers were forced to evacuate the pavements and to find accommodation beyond the boulevard, and they left in droves to seek refuge in the region of Kurusukuppam and beyond. Pondichéry resembled a ghost town where only the so-called good people wandered about like shadows; they themselves were unaware as to what was happening. From one day to the next, they found themselves with all this newfound space. They no longer had to zigzag their bicycles between stray dogs. There were no longer any beggars to whom they could give their leftovers. The servants, rickshaw drivers, laundry men, barbers, and all the illiterate people who would normally perform the menial tasks no longer came to the town for fear of getting caught by the sterilization squad. The garbage piled up like mountains on each street corner, because the road sweepers who normally collected it were also in charge of capturing dogs. Without realizing it, Pondi had just shot itself in the foot! This was a state of emergency."

■ ■ ■

"It was during this period of confusion that I lost my paw," Tripod Dog Baba continued. (Finally, he'd got to the point! I secretly breathed a sigh of relief). "Whereas a good number of dogs got caught or fled beyond the town, I decided not to flee, but to play hide-and-seek with these men in khaki. I found it exciting to brave dangerous situations. I traveled from one district to another, as if the whole town belonged to me, without encountering any problems. And then suddenly, it occurred to me that I could seek refuge in the district where I was born. The men in khaki rarely visited this district, because it was a well-known fact that few dogs sought shelter there. As I remarked earlier, what dog would go and eat gourds and potatoes in the Hindu district? So, I returned to the street where I was born.

"I noticed that the spot where the rickshaw driver's family had previously lived was now vacant, and so I set up home on the pavement. The jute bags that had served as a wall were still there; in some way, this made for an ideal hiding place. I was happy to have returned to my birthplace, even if it had not always been kind to me. The sweet nostalgia of having shared this part of the pavement with my mother, sister, and brothers comforted me to an extent.

"But, Lakshmi, my happiness did not last long, for I soon spotted the rickshaw driver. The very same one. The one who had chased after me some years ago. He came here every day, because this was his workplace, where his rickshaw stand was. He had the right to work here, as long as he didn't settle here with his family. When he saw me, he gazed at me for a while; I don't know if he recognized me. We both stood there staring at each other, and he then uttered the phrase that I hadn't heard for a long time: 'Hey, clear off, dog! Clear off!' He had barely finished his sentence when I saw him bend down to pick up a stone. Painful memories flooded my mind. This time, I wasn't going to just let things be! I emerged from my jute shelter and pounced on him, trying to bite him. He ran around his rickshaw with his stone in his hand, yelling: 'Hey, clear off, dog! Clear off!' But I had noticed the fear on his face, and the more fearful he became, the more I chased after him, barking. Not knowing how to react, he mounted his rickshaw and cleared off. I followed him for a few meters, and then, feeling triumphant, my tail in the air, I returned to my hiding place. The wheel of fortune had turned: I was the one who had chased him away this time.

"But despite all this, he didn't abandon the area; he would return every day. Without disturbing me, he would sit on his rickshaw and smoke his beedi, waiting for his customers. From time to time, he glowered at me, and I sensed that he was agitated. He kept glancing from left to right, as if he feared something."

■ ■ ■

"One day, while I was sitting down, I saw him clap his hands and gesticulate wildly, as if he was trying to attract someone's attention. He got up, went to speak to someone, and came back to sit down calmly in his rickshaw, grinning. Even if I didn't sense any danger, I was wary of him, especially as he turned to me several times, constantly smiling, as if he was going to play a dirty trick on me. I was so preoccupied keeping a close eye on him that I didn't notice two men in khaki approach me. They emerged from either side of the pavement, with their hands behind their backs. I eventually noticed the tip of the lasso sticking out; it was the dog squad! There was only one way out for me, but my hopes faded when I saw the rickshaw driver blocking the exit of my hiding place with his vehicle, still grinning. I was well and truly cornered. I succeeded in dodging the first lasso, but the second one got me and tightened around my neck. I struggled with all my might, but nothing could be done; I watched the council cart approach, dragged along by a third man, with four or five dogs who had already been captured crouching inside. Was my life going to end like that, in such a ridiculous way? Was I to end up as a tennis ball, spending the rest of my life bouncing back and forth off the wall of the tennis court of the Cercle de Pondichéry? That would be so unfair!

"Just as he was about to toss me into the vehicle, the man in khaki paused, as if an idea had suddenly occurred to him. He beckoned to the second man to come close to him, and whispered something in his ear. The two men returned to the rickshaw driver, who was standing next to the vehicle with his devilish grin, already relishing the prospect of my capture, and one of the men in khaki asked him:

"'Tell me, rickshaw driver, how come you're still here? Aren't you afraid of the sterilization campaign?'

"'Yes, but I still need to work. Who is going to feed my family? But don't worry, I'm too shrewd for them. I know how to recognize the sterilization squad from afar, and I go and hide,' answered the rickshaw driver, his evil smile breaking into a wink.

"The two men exchanged glances, a smug look on their faces. The man who was holding the lasso suddenly caught hold of the rickshaw driver by the scruff of his neck. The rickshaw driver began to thrash about, trying to release himself from the man's grip, and started to yell:

"'But what's got into you? Why are you doing this? Let me go, I haven't done anything!'

"The man who was gripping me with the lasso came to assist the first man.

"'You see, thambi,' he said, 'we get paid one rupee per dog. But if we catch a guy for sterilization, we get fifty rupees!'

"'But you aren't from the sterilization campaign! You've no right to do this to me! Let me go!' said the rickshaw driver, struggling like a madman.

"This time, his grin faded, and he rolled his eyes; his face became paralyzed with fear.

"The man who was holding me captive laughed, and replied:

"'Exactly, ever since you lot became so crafty, the council gave us the right to capture men along with dogs; what's more, we're better paid for it. Come, rickshaw driver, don't make a fuss. It'll work out better for you. You'll stop having children, and that way, you won't need to feed them!'

"Hearing this, the rickshaw driver began to struggle even more. The man who was holding him began to lose his grip, and he requested the man who was holding me in the lasso to help him. In the punch-up that followed, I felt my own lasso loosen. It was now or never! By the time the two men had managed to get the rickshaw driver under control, my head had already slipped out of the noose and I was out of there.

"I was joyous and elated to have escaped death; this was the life I loved!" Tripod Dog Baba continued. "This life that fluctuated between life and death, with all its dangers and uncertainties. Like a tightrope walker, I didn't mind whether I slipped to the left or the right, because it was all the same to me; the main thing, Lakshmi, was to stay on the rope."

Chapter Ten

"**IF KARNA HAD KNOWN** that he was the son of Kunti and Surya, my life would have taken a different turn," Tripod Dog Baba began to narrate a tale. "If Krishna had revealed his identity to Draupadi, who secretly loved Karna, I wouldn't be sitting here next to you, Lakshmi. If Kunti, who was not fully aware of the situation, hadn't told the Pandava brothers to share Draupadi among themselves, I would still have my fourth leg intact."

What was wrong with this dog? Had he lost his head? What did the *Mahābhārata* have to do with him? He genuinely believed that the whole world revolved around him. As if everything happening in the universe was somehow linked to him!

"But what on earth are you saying, Tripod Dog Baba? What do the Pandavas and Draupadi have to do with your story?"

Tripod Dog Baba looked at his stump in sadness and paused briefly before continuing his tale.

"It's a long story, Lakshmi. Look, I'll tell you another one. Arjuna, one of the Pandava brothers, was happy to have won Draupadi's hand by winning a competition. But he didn't know that Yudhishthira, one of his brothers, was in love with her, and that he secretly desired her. As they went home, knowing perfectly well what he was doing, Yudhishthira spoke to Kunti:

"'Mother, we have received a wonderful gift today.'

"His mother, who was busy doing some housework, answered, without even giving a thought to what it was they had brought home.

"'Well then, all you have to do is share it, as usual.'

"'But mother, I'm talking about Draupadi. How can we share a wife between us?'

"Realizing her error, Kunti was distraught, but she could no longer take back her words. King Drupada, Draupadi's father, was also dismayed to learn that his daughter was becoming the wife to five brothers. He then asked the great sage Vyasa to come and help him. He came to the kingdom and explained to the king that the situation wasn't so terrible. Draupadi had asked Shiva to find her a husband with five holy qualities. But Shiva, who had been too drunk that day, had granted five different husbands to her, each with one quality, instead of one husband with five qualities. And inevitably, that's what happened.

"On their return from exile, the Pandavas took possession of their magnificent palace, built by the goddess Maya. But soon they were faced with the dilemma as to how they were going to share Draupadi. They settled on the plan that each time Draupadi was with one of the brothers, a pair of shoes would be placed at the door of her room. And everything went smoothly, as planned, until the day when the palace dog did the most foolish thing ever.

"You know, Lakshmi, we dogs love playing with shoes. Don't ask me why, I couldn't tell you. Well, when I say us, I'm mainly talking about pet dogs. Because we stray dogs don't have time to play. But those idiots can spend days on end chewing shoes. Sometimes they even entertain themselves by hiding them.

"And that's what happened. One day when Draupadi was in the bedroom with Yudhishthira, his dog, who was playing with his shoes, took them away. Arjuna, who was passing by, entered the bedroom, as he hadn't seen any shoes in front of the door. Draupadi felt humiliated and ordered the two brothers to leave. They were confused and wondered what could have happened. When, later on, they offered an explanation to Draupadi, she asked for the dog to be sent away from the palace, but this was impossible, for it was Yudhishthira's favorite dog. Her self-esteem wounded, Draupadi was resolved to seek revenge, and cursed the dog:

"'From today onward, I condemn you and your descendants to no longer have any privacy. Just as Arjuna took me by surprise because of you, you and your descendants will be condemned to a similar fate. The shame I'm now experiencing is what you'll face each time.'"

I listened to Tripod Dog Baba, fascinated by his knowledge of the *Mahābhārata*. He knew rather a lot after all, this dog. But I still couldn't see how the *Mahābhārata* was linked to his story . . . Noticing that I was perplexed, he continued:

"I see that you've still got many questions on your mind, Lakshmi. You must be wondering what Draupadi's curse has to do with me . . . Well, let me tell you. My period of exile in rue Kamatchi Amman Kovil lasted longer than expected. Things had, however, calmed down in Pondichéry. The crazy enterprise of town enhancement ended just as suddenly as it had begun. The rickshaw drivers returned to their pavements, the stray dogs went back to their trash cans, and the road sweepers to their shovels and brooms. The dogs who had previously lived there had fled, but new dogs had come to populate the street. And the members of the sterilization squad had now become lottery ticket sellers; after the state of emergency, the government had decided to act in an even more cunning manner, and lottery tickets were offered to anyone who agreed to get sterilized.

"Normality had resumed, and life carried on as usual. The rickshaw driver's family had returned to his jute cloth house. The sterilized rickshaw driver no longer paid any attention to me. This seemed strange, but my mind was otherwise preoccupied. In fact, I could have left this district if I hadn't been in love with a female dog. That's right; during my period of exile, I had fallen in love with a pet dog . . . How beautiful she was! She was completely white, as white as a snowflake. She lived in the same street in a large house that was visible through its large gate. This house belonged to a rich lawyer.

"The first time I saw her, she was playing with a plastic toy that squeaked. I was going past the gate when I heard a sound coming from underneath a car in the driveway. Intrigued, I stopped and stood on my hind legs, supporting myself on the gates to get a better view. The noise continued, but I couldn't see who was making it. So I decided to yap a little to draw attention to myself. A few seconds later, she came out. When I saw her, I couldn't help but snort with laughter. She looked at me with her large black eyes, wondering, no doubt, why I was laughing. She had actually rubbed her snout on an exhaust pipe while playing under the car, and it had become coated in black. She looked very funny like that! Regardless, she was breathtakingly beautiful. She was neither big nor small, but of average size; her fur was entirely white but for a few orange spots on her snout, forehead, and back. Her pointed ears and tail curled over her back made her look like a princess. I had fallen under her spell. Wagging her tail, she came up to the gate, and began to sniff me. I immediately knew that there was chemistry between us. But our love story was thwarted by this gate, for she only ever came out under the supervision of a servant, who would take her for a walk every evening along cours Chabrol.

"I pined for her," Tripod Dog Baba continued. "As soon as she set off, I would follow her at a distance during her walk. And she would keep glancing at me furtively, encouraging me to follow her. But I didn't know how to get close to her . . . The servant held a stick at all times to chase away overzealous dogs. Saddened, I spent entire days waiting for her in front of the gate, sitting on the pavement opposite, listening to the sound of her plastic toy. The gate only ever opened to allow the lawyer's car to enter; the rest of the time, it remained closed. I observed her through it; her sorrowful gaze expressed the suffering of solitude. I wanted to set her free from her prison, show her the true meaning of life, share with her a bone stolen from the butcher's in the big bazaar, show her the Creole paradise on the other side of the canal, and I wanted to show all these Zébulons and

Missys, who had previously snubbed me, that I was, in fact, a desirable dog . . .

"One evening at nightfall, while I was sitting on my pavement, I saw the lawyer's car arrive. Ever since the rickshaw driver's family had returned, I had changed pavements; I was on the same road, but a few houses further down. So, the car appeared, and the lawyer waited for the servant to open the gate. I got up to catch a glimpse of my beauty. The gate swung open, and there she was . . . I saw her standing on the front steps, waiting for her master. She noticed me too, and I heard her whining and wagging her tail to express her joy. For some unknown reason, at this point, the gate remained open longer than usual. It was only later that I realized that there was a problem with the car, and that it couldn't get started. The servant, who was standing near the gate, went over to give his master a hand; he went behind the car and tried to push it inside. The gate was open, the car was outside, and the two men were busy; the very next moment, my love was outside!

"I relished the happiest moment of my life. This life, which until then had only been one of suffering and solitude, was to experience the warmth of companionship, of being with a partner. And not just any partner! My partner wasn't just any ordinary stray dog . . . no, she was a grande dame, raised in the lap of luxury! Even if I knew that our fleeting romance wasn't going to last, I wanted to make the most of it.

"The two men, who were busy trying to get the car to enter the gate, hadn't noticed anything. As for my love, as soon as she found herself on the street, she came up to me directly. I instantly knew that we had to leave this place. And so, without any further delay, we fled.

"Initially, my love followed me willingly, but when we reached the end of rue Kamatchi Amman, she hesitated. She didn't want to cross over to the other side of the canal. She must have felt that if she crossed it, her world was going to change dramatically. I beckoned to her to follow me, and we remained there for a while, rooted to the spot, just looking at each other, I on quai de Gingy, and she on quai d'Ambour. I didn't know if it was the buses and three-wheelers hurtling by at great speed that scared her, or if it was simply the fear of leaving her street and the comfort of her home that held her back.

"My heart was beating furiously when I saw her eventually cross the road. I could no longer contain my happiness. I barked and yapped with joy; I could no longer control my tail, which had begun to wag uncontrollably . . . I led her into my world and took her to Parc du Gouverneur. I wanted her to experience all that I'd dreamed of.

"We walked around a small pond full of water lilies, in which tiny fish in a myriad of colors were swimming under the strict gaze of Nandi, the sacred bull. I took her to the bottom of the park, where we had fun tobogganing. I wanted her to taste the Vietnamese cuisine in the restaurant on rue Romain Rolland, the same restaurant to which Jimmy had taken me that final day. I often went back there: the owner, remembering Jimmy, would gladly serve me some decent leftovers. My partner was undoubtedly impressed by my company; she followed me without hesitation, gazed at me lovingly, sniffed me, and she even let me sniff her neck, and behind her ears . . .

"It was nighttime when we returned to our street. Back then, the people of Pondichéry would sit on their thinnai until very late in the evening, chatting to their neighbors. The thinnai is the most important part of the Tamil house: it's where everything in the district happens. It's a raised, open platform attached to the façade of the house. Sometimes, the thinnai is extended by a veranda with a tiled roof. This space separates the private area from the public area. Children play there, adults receive their friends there, and grandmothers sit there pounding areca nuts with a pestle and mortar. Sometimes, the thinnai also serves as a resting place for passersby. In short, a thinnai is always bustling with activity.

"Our passion had gradually increased as we progressed down the road, and I didn't want to let her go without having shown her my love. She didn't either, for that matter. But I could sense the gaze of all the people sitting on their thinnai; they knew what was going to happen. The thousand-year-old curse of Draupadi was becoming reality before their very eyes; there we were, our most intimate acts being observed by everyone on the street! However, I was blind and deaf to everything; this little corner of the pavement was to be our bed of love. But we were overcome by shame when we became aware of our situation.

"The people sitting on their thinnai were uneasy. The women went back into the house, and the men chased us away. A sort of malaise spread across the whole street. I tried, somehow or another, to drag my partner toward rue Cantine, which was darker and emptier. But she dragged me in the opposite direction, toward her house: she wanted to go back to her home.

We were ashamed; we wanted to hide, and I cursed Draupadi. I cursed all the characters of the *Mahābhārata* who were responsible for this situation. But what could be done? We just had to wait and see. The initial euphoria of the evening had now become suffocated by a mantle of shame. I sensed that even the stars and moon were seeking refuge beneath it. A light drizzle began to fall.

"What happened next was even worse, Lakshmi: I caught a whiff of the stench of alcohol mixed with beedi smoke, which was drifting toward us. A staggering silhouette appeared. Never, not even in my worst nightmares, had I imagined having to face this horrible situation. It was the rickshaw driver! His intolerable stench preceded him as he advanced toward us; his face was twisted into a malicious, mocking smile. At first, I saw only him, and then I noticed two other silhouettes following him: the lawyer and the servant. And so this dreadful rickshaw driver had gone to alert my partner's owner . . . The lawyer didn't stay for long. As soon as he saw us like this, he was overcome by shame and set off, murmuring something to his servant. As for my love, at the sight of her owner, she began to tug more and more in the direction of her house.

"As soon as the lawyer left, I saw the rickshaw driver set off for his pavement, and then return with something in his hand. I could sense danger. The road had become empty. The servant was holding a stick. In the light of the streetlamp, I saw the glint of a blade. The rickshaw driver was holding a knife, like the one I had seen at the butcher's. He was seeking revenge . . .

"At the same spot a few months ago, he must have experienced the same sensation. Fear of the blade. Now it was my turn. I had the feeling that my life story and that of the rickshaw driver had intersected somewhere along the line in the past. Perhaps our lives were linked by an invisible thread. Unfinished karma in a former life?

"The first blow was dealt. But strangely, it wasn't for me. The servant struck my partner with the stick.

"'Filthy dog!' he said. 'Look at what you have done. We raised you in the lap of luxury, and you went off to hang around with a mongrel! A stray dog!'

"My partner howled and bared her teeth to bite the servant. And I did the same with the rickshaw driver; I wouldn't let him come close. The second blow was dealt: this time, to my snout. We were still entwined, turning round and round in circles to escape the blows. Raindrops and blows showered us simultaneously. I dragged my love toward the small alleyway, but the rickshaw driver beat us to it, and he stood there, facing me. And just as I felt we were becoming separated from each other, the blade struck me.

"A trickle of blood blended with the rain that was flowing into the gutter. Half of my foreleg lay on the ground beside me. I could no longer stand. I was lying on the ground, howling with pain and shame. My partner had fled. All alone on this road, which had witnessed my birth, I cursed Yudhishthira's dog."

Chapter Eleven

TRIPOD DOG BABA continued his story:

"'Tripod. Henceforth, you will be called Tripod,' said my partner, smiling apologetically.

"I had been in this strange place for some days now. I was in a part of Pondichéry that I didn't recognize, beyond boulevard Nord. Ever since I'd met Jimmy, I had remained in the fashionable districts of the town, and this hidden facet of Pondichéry was unknown to me. What was I doing here, or rather, what were we doing here in this stinking location? For we were next to a public garbage dump. The biggest garbage dump in Pondichéry on the road leading to the Kottakuppam cemetery. A community of dogs lived here. A strange community, because no one knew where these dogs came from. They lived around the garbage heap—well, not even around it: they lived *in* it. It was an open-air garbage heap, and the dogs would climb it searching for food. The place stank. Very badly. It reeked so badly that I'm amazed that the gods and goddesses of the nearby Sengani Amman Temple hadn't absconded. I could imagine the statue of Madurai Veeran dropping his sickle from his right hand to hold his nose instead . . .

"Why was I here amid this stench? What was my partner doing here? Why was she here, rather than in her beautiful house? My head was reeling with all these questions, but I couldn't even think straight, for the stench was so strong. It was as if all this piled up garbage had numbed my mind. And also, who were this community of disgusting dogs that she had become associated with? They were all mongrels and mutts without any home or street. Their lives revolved around this garbage heap alone. This hill of bric-a-brac, where it was difficult to find food, was their kingdom. Of course they found food there, but it was rotten!

"My partner began to explain:

"'You see, after the incident, you became unconscious, and I fled. And when I tried to go back home, I was beaten, kicked, and punished for having been with you. They didn't want me anymore. I was thrown outside, and they closed the gates on me. I was thrown out onto the streets forever. But I'm not like you: I don't know anything about this town. So when I was thrown out, I came back to you. I found you in the same place, unconscious, next to your severed leg. I took pity on you and I didn't want to abandon you . . . Also, I didn't know anyone else! Where could I go? I roamed around aimlessly, disorientated. I was lost, and wandered from district to district, not knowing what to do. No one wanted to help me. Even worse: I was attacked and chased. When I accidentally stumbled on this community, one of the dogs understood my distress, and agreed to help me out. And that's how we brought you here.'

"My head was spinning. Not because of my injury, but because of the stench. I just couldn't get used to it. How could this dog who had been raised in luxury accept living in such conditions? And all because of me! I felt guilty. The contrast was truly startling: she was so beautiful, completely white and immaculate, next to this garbage heap, among these filthy, coarse dogs . . . I closed my eyes to reflect. I didn't even have any appetite. Plus, you'd have to be really starving to want to eat what you found here. We absolutely had to leave this spot: I couldn't spend the rest of my life in this community, as kind as its members were. It was true that they didn't fight among themselves. There were enough pieces of litter for everyone. They spent their time scavenging for food in the garbage heap, and each dog found their own happiness. In fact, they shared the heap among themselves. This was what made their community distinct from any other. Their world stopped there. They didn't venture beyond the dump. The only other place they visited apart from this one was the liquor store, which was situated a few meters away. This was the haunt of the rickshaw drivers, fishermen, rail workers, and the poor people of the town. Here, they were served an alcohol of poor quality known as arrack, and a palm wine, kallu, which the people of Pondichéry call cider. Some dogs would go and mix merrily with these drunkards, eating their dishes of tripe, and even daring to drink their revolting arrack. Jimmy must not have known this community, despite having led a life of vagabondage. I wondered what kind of distress had led these dogs here. You'd have to have absolutely no self-respect or be completely lost to live like this, among the pigs. Ah yes, I forgot to mention that the dump was also home to pigs. Dirty, fat pigs, which were completely black. And there were not only pigs, but also crows, vultures, and rats. Rats that were as large as cats.

"It was all too much for me. The more I looked at this garbage heap, the more it disgusted me.

"'Do you intend to stay here?' I asked my partner.

"'Do you have a better idea?' she retorted, defiantly. 'Returning to our street is out of the question. In any case, as you told me yourself, there's nothing to eat in that district.'

"'Yes, but I know other districts. I am famous throughout the town,' I added, with a sudden surge of pride.

"'Exactly, Tripod Dog Baba. Because you kept roaming around, you never claimed any district. You've never owned anything, and you never will. And look at what has happened, even to those who had their own district.'

"She pointed out to me some dogs at the bottom of the heap who were rummaging about in some plastic bags.

"'Don't you recognize them? Well, they know you. They even told me that you're a lazy good-for-nothing dog. It was because of a dog named Jimmy that they respected you. You've never achieved anything, and you've never deserved anything. They even told me that they have never seen you fight. It seems that you would roam from district to district, putting on airs and graces. To mock you, they called you an ascetic, a sanyasi. And now, how do you envisage the future? You're not going to be able to conquer the town again with three and a half legs . . . a town that you've never conquered, for that matter! Neither your bravery nor your charisma have earned you respect. It was more your lack of action. Yes, it was more the impression you gave of being above all that.'

"Sitting down, I listened to her, my head hung in shame. It was hard, Lakshmi, being judged by the person I loved. At this point, I didn't even know if I was still in love with her . . . But I was grateful to her for not having abandoned me on this road. Who knows? Maybe the rickshaw driver would have just finished me off! I was already beginning to feel that I was slipping toward a life of dependency. My life was going to change in a radical way. If I had understood correctly, I was going to become dependent on this dog. My recent handicap and the sudden transformation of this town were going to turn me into a nonentity.

"Hearing us talk about them, some dogs came up to us. I did, in fact, recognize some of them. They were mainly dogs from La Centrale, and the southern district. But it was understandable that I hadn't initially recognized them, for they were repulsively filthy.

"'How are you doing, brother?' one of them asked me. 'We haven't seen you for a long time. Since Jimmy's disappearance, we've only caught glimpses of you. We are sorry to see you in this state, because you're a good dog. You've never caused anyone any trouble.'

"'It's nothing, just bad luck. But what happened to you? Why didn't you go back to your respective districts after the state of emergency?'

"'If only you knew! When the state of emergency ended, all the dogs of the nearby villages began to invade the town.

Especially La Centrale and the quartier blanc. There were endless days of merciless fights. We weren't sure where these dogs had come from, but there they were. The youngest and the strongest dogs remained. Old dogs like us were forced to leave their districts again. Some of us already knew the garbage heap community. Each dog is so busy looking for their own food here that they don't have the time to think of others. We didn't have any other choice but to come here to spend the rest of our lives. At least we're left in peace here. It's true that it's filthy, but what would you have done in our situation?'

"I was lost for words; my mind was blank. I was utterly confused. I listened to them, but I couldn't make sense of anything. Were they expecting something from me? I had never had the makings of a leader or a boss. And this wasn't the time for me to take on such a task, with my three and a half legs. This situation was becoming difficult. What were we to do? Or to be precise, what was I to do? I wasn't sure about the others, but I certainly couldn't continue to live in such an environment.

"At nightfall, the road began to come alive. The men who visited the liquor store became increasingly rowdy. Fights broke out here and there. Competing with the stench of the garbage heap, the odor of fried food, tripe, and alcohol wafted through the air. The street was plunged into darkness; a lone lamppost projected the shadows of the drunkards, which grew and shrunk according to their gait. Some shadows collapsed along the temple wall, no longer able to stand. This whole scene was unbearable. Having previously lived in pleasant districts, there was no way that I was going to accept living like a maroon. Strangely, my partner, on the other hand, seemed to have got used to this environment. When she understood that I would never touch the garbage, she went to find me some pieces of tripe from the liquor store. My first reaction was not to touch this food that she brought back. Not because it was disgusting! No, it was more the feeling of guilt that kept me from eating. A dog who was so refined and well-bred was now condemned to live in this garbage heap because of me. I believe she could sense how I felt, because she gently pushed the banana leaf with tripe toward me.

"'Eat, Tripod,' she said. 'You've eaten nothing for two days, so you must be hungry. You need to get your strength back. Also, there's no point feeling guilty. There's no point crying over spilled milk. We need to look to the future. If you don't want to live here, you need to find us a solution. You know the town better than anyone, whereas I don't know anything about it. But rest assured: from now on, I'll take care of you. I'll never abandon you. Just find me a place where we can settle down, and I'll take care of the rest.'

"Her kind words did me a lot of good. This dog was truly devoted to me; she had even given me a name. Tripod! It was the first time in my life that I'd been given a name. I was no longer just 'the dog.' Of course, I'd have preferred Jimmy, Médor, or Zep. But the name Tripod was original. I wasn't going to make a fuss.

"Content with my new name, I shared the tripe with my partner, and I got ready to sleep. Lying along the temple wall, facing the mountain of garbage, I gazed at the stars and the moon, which had sought refuge behind a blanket of clouds to escape the stench."

■ ■ ■

"'The only place where we could settle is the Ashram district,' I said, after a few days.

"The days at the garbage dump were all alike. Apart from going round and round the mountain of trash, there was nothing else to do. No place to walk. There was the dump, the temple, the liquor store, some huts, and nothing more. Our days were interrupted by funerary processions. Every day. For the dump was on the same road as two cemeteries: one was Christian, and the other was Hindu. Not only were there burials every day (the burials were just about tolerable), but during the Hindu funerary ceremonies, bodies were burned, and that was altogether a different matter . . . When the breeze blew in our direction, the situation became unbearable. Imagine the cocktail of smells, Lakshmi. The stench of garbage, feces, alcohol, fried food, urine, and now on top of that, the odor of burning corpses. There were additionally dogs, pigs, rats, cats, cows, crows, and vultures who were making holes in the corpses of decomposed animals . . . Not to mention some humans searching for something or the other. Absolutely horrific . . . No creature on this planet deserves to live in such a place.

"'Why this particular district, Tripod?' My partner asked me, trying to get rid of a flea.

"Poor thing! Ever since she'd been here, she couldn't stop scratching behind her ears, and she kept shaking her head.

"'The Ashram district is rarely visited by dogs. That's because, firstly, there are no detached houses, and secondly, because there is no meat or fish.'

"'And what would we do over there?'

"This time, it was my turn to scratch my head.

"'Listen, to be honest, I don't have any plan or idea as to how we're going to get out of here. All I know is that it's the least populated district. We could go and settle there first, and then we'll see what we can do there.'

"'No. If we leave this place, we'd have to have a plan. I refuse to set off on an adventure. Especially with you and your three and a half legs. I wouldn't feel safe. Let me go and visit the district with *him*, and we can discuss it on my return.'"

■ ■ ■

"*Him*. I'd completely forgotten about him. He was the dog who had helped her bring me here. A dog without any great personality, just an ordinary mongrel who must have been born and spent his entire life at the garbage dump. He was of a tawny color, somewhat reddish-brown; thin, with ears folded back, he wore a mournful look. Not only was I going to have her with me, but *him* too. And however much my partner could be kind and attentive, she could also prove to be defiant and stubborn. In any case, *he* never interfered in our discussions; he was content to remain at a distance, growling as soon as someone came too close to us. He was to be our bodyguard. But for now, we had to get out of here.

"As she was about to set off, I asked:

"'By the way, what's your name?'

"'Mira,' she said to me proudly, looking at me gracefully.

"Despite the dump in which we were living, she still knew how to behave in a coquettish manner.

"'You were right,' she said on her return, 'the district you described seems to be ideal. There's no one there. We spent the day observing the area, and we noticed that this corner is very sparsely populated. The majority of the buildings are devoted to some aspect of the ashram. There's just one family who lives in the Foyer du Soldat, and two or three others who live near the temple. And there are two soldiers' houses on the same road as the ashram, just before the canal.'

"I was impressed by Mira's keen sense of observation; she'd even managed to spot the soldiers' houses, where there'd be a chance that we could feed ourselves adequately.

"'So, what do you think about it?' I asked, impatiently.

"She appeared to ponder over the matter. After a few minutes, she replied, looking at the other dogs.

"'We could go and settle in this district, but we mustn't go as a big group; we would risk attracting attention to ourselves. Whether we're with people or the other dogs of the neighborhood, we'll run into problems if they see us arrive as a group.'

"'But who says we're going as a group? There are only two of us. Well, three, if *the other* wants to come with us,' I said, pointing at *the other.*

"'Ah yes! *Him*, he's coming with us. I wouldn't be able to do anything without him. As for the others, that's not my business: I don't even know them. You're the one who knows them,' she answered, looking at her protégé.

"'Know them? I don't know them as well as all that! They're dogs whom I've just briefly met. I'm not very close to them.'

"This was partly true. Even if we had previously shared the same streets and the same trash cans on rue Montorsier or rue Laporte, we had never been friends. Of course, they had accepted me in their districts, but nothing more. I wasn't going to sacrifice my life and an opportunity like this in the name of a few pieces of beef shared between us. In any case, they knew the laws of the street better than I did: it was do or die. So, in this regard, I didn't feel bad."

■ ■ ■

"'From now on, this will be your spot. Come rain or shine, you will not move from here until I say you can.'

"As she spoke, Mira pointed out a place on rue Nehru, the arterial road of Pondichéry, located between the canal and rue Manakulla Vinayagar. Why there? There was absolutely nothing there. Not even houses. Opposite me, there was a bookshop named Vak, which sold spiritual books, and then there was the wall of the former house of the Gallois Montbrun family, the former mayor of Pondichéry, which had been purchased by the ashram. Behind me, there was a completely dilapidated house in which no one lived, and another building, where there were a few shops. What was I supposed to do here? And why wasn't I allowed to move? Was Mira out of her mind?

"Being right in the heart of town again filled me with joy. I rejoiced at hearing the symphony of buses, cars, motorcycles, and bicycles again. This sounded like music to my ears, which must have grown accustomed to the funerary music accompanying the processions. I regained my appetite for the scent of bread and the aroma of the cuisine prepared in the ashram's kitchen. The fragrance of cakes and other viennoisseries wafted from the pâtisserie on the corner of the road behind me. The stench of the nauseating mountain with its scavengers now appeared to be even more distant than before. I silently thanked Mira again for having pulled me out of this nightmare.

"But I still couldn't understand why I was here. Apart from me, there was no one in this part of the road. It was deserted.

"Actually, there was someone there. A few meters away from my designated location, there was a man. A bare-chested man, with long hair cascading down onto his shoulders, and he was sitting on a bedsheet. It wasn't even a bedsheet, but more a piece of cloth that men use as a towel and for other purposes. He was sitting on it, dressed only in his dhoti. He was sitting cross-legged, eyes closed, with his two hands resting on his legs. He didn't look like a beggar. I knew what they were like. They were our worst enemies. But not the ones who sit around temples . . . No, our worst enemies were the wandering beggars. Those who went from house to house, begging for food. They would throw stones at us, or strike us with their sticks, and we would chase them, barking at them or biting them. This man wasn't one of them. What was he doing here? I decided to observe him; at least this would give me something to do.

"Initially, it was difficult to stay still in the same place. The only time I moved was to go up to the canal to do my business. The rest of the time, I would spend my days observing the passersby. I saw all kinds of people. In the morning, there were students clinging onto their rickshaws for dear life, people on their bicycles going to work, pilgrims who were coming to the temple, policemen who went past me on their way to the Palais du Gouverneur, their red képis perched on their heads . . . And at around midday, I would see the same people again returning home for lunch; additionally, there were the ashram servants, who were coming to collect their masters' meals from the ashram kitchen. Between midday and four o'clock in the afternoon, the bookshop and some other shops closed. Only the man and I remained on the street, in the scorching sun. The man, like me, had not moved since my arrival. He didn't even leave to do his business! I hadn't seen him eat either. At around three in the afternoon, this matinée performance of students, office goers, and policemen to-ing and fro-ing would begin again, ending at around five in the evening, when everyone returned home. Finally, at sunset, those who were going to the temple, beach, or park would pass by. At nightfall, the man and I would find ourselves all alone in the twilight, between two lampposts.

"Was he aware of my presence? I wasn't sure. Initially, I was sitting a few meters away from him, but Mira, who came to bring me food between lunchtime and four o'clock, advised me to move closer to him. What was her plan? I had no idea, and so I drew closer to the man with great trepidation. He didn't stir. Though I had the impression that his eyes were always closed, I realized that he actually kept them open. But he had a vacant, unfocused gaze; he didn't look left or right. His gaze was suspended in a void. Indeed, he was staring into space. My presence must not have disturbed him, for he did nothing to chase me away. And so, I sat next to him, and I too began to gaze into space.

"'Well done, Tripod; you understood exactly what I was expecting of you!' breathed Mira.

"*The other* brought me a banana leaf with some biriyani and a juicy bone, and then he went to lie down at the other end of the road, in the shade of the power transformer.

"'What do you mean? I don't understand what you're getting at,' I said, attacking my bone.

"Ever since my leg had been mutilated, I had acquired a particular dexterity for holding a bone in one paw.

"'You must observe what's happening around you, Tripod, if you want to understand what I'm telling you. Do you see this man? Well, he has understood how to earn respect without doing anything. Look at him closely: he doesn't talk to anyone, he doesn't give big lectures, he's barely clothed, yet everyone admires and respects him. People passing by give him money. He doesn't move. No one sees him spending this money or eating, and no one sees him do his business. He's there every day, regardless of whether it's raining, the sun is scorching his skin, there's a cyclone, or the road is flooded; he's always there. So, you see, that's his secret: he does what other people don't do. That's what you should do: do what the other dogs don't do. Think about it: where's all the money that the passersby give him? Look, there are only a few coins in front of him. Where is yesterday's money, and the money from the day before yesterday? It's true that I had asked you not to do anything, but you could at least stay awake and observe what's happening around you,' she concluded, disappearing along with *the other*."

Chapter Twelve

"**EVER SINCE MIRA** had asked me to keep my eyes peeled, I'd begun to observe the man. It's true that upon arrival on rue Nehru, I had sunk into a state of idleness. This, incidentally, continues to be the case. What would you have done in my situation, Lakshmi? Spending entire days doing nothing inevitably makes you lazy. It wasn't easy for me, as I was used to wandering from district to district and roaming about the town. Now here I was, immobile, sitting from morning to evening, watching people pass by in front of me. I missed the walks, especially the nocturnal strolls. While Pondichéry was sleeping, I would enjoy strolling through the empty roads, listening to rickshaw drivers snoring. I liked to spot the shadows of the sewer rats who would emerge to look for food in the trash cans. Whenever I felt like it, I would delight in chasing them, pursuing them right up to the mouth of the gutter. Sometimes, I would take pleasure in accompanying the Gurkha on his rounds as he walked the streets with his whistle. I would trot next to this night watchman's bicycle; we would keep each other company. Now I missed all of this. Here, there was nothing to do, and I would sleep all day long . . .

"But Mira must have had something up her sleeve, otherwise she wouldn't have forced me to remain sitting next to this man. After a few days, I moved even closer to him, as if we were together. He said nothing and didn't even try to chase me away; it was as if my presence didn't disturb him in the slightest. I then adopted the same position as him. Initially, I remained lying down, but gradually, I learned to sit on my hind legs, and to stay still. I also learned to maintain a blank, unfocused gaze, like him.

"Previously, the people of Pondichéry would walk past the man indifferently, just throwing him a few coins now and again, but now they began to take an interest in him, well, in us; it was no ordinary sight to see a sadhu and his dog meditating. Before, the piece of cloth on which he was sitting would receive only a few coins. But ever since I had sat beside him, the cloth was never empty. Certain passersby even stopped in front of us, removed their shoes, and clasped their hands together in prayer, just as they would in front of any temple.

"Is it as easy as that? I asked myself. You just need to sit somewhere without doing or saying anything for people to start worshipping you? Any old fool can sit in a yoga position, but that's enough for people to believe that this man is a saint. They rush toward him, give him money and food. They show him respect and await a blessing from him. The man sitting next to me was proof of this. I didn't know his story. I didn't know where he was from, or what he was doing in Pondichéry. Was he going to stay, or was he going to leave? Maybe he really was a religious man? But I, Tripod Dog Baba, was only a mongrel, roaming about in the streets of the town looking for a bone in the garbage bins. Yet now I'd become the yogi's dog . . . and later on I'd become the yogi dog. That's what Mira had up her sleeve: to turn me into a guru dog. To make of me a well-respected dog. Respected by the other dogs and also by men. Respected without doing anything, without even lifting a paw! What a genius she was, Mira!

"I didn't need a lot of time, Lakshmi, to work out that the man and I were very similar. Ever since Mira had asked me to keep my eyes peeled, I had discovered his secret. In fact, he and I operated in the same way. Or you could say that I functioned like him. For the man who sat all day long in this yoga position underwent a metamorphosis at night."

■ ■ ■

"When rue Nehru fell silent, the signs illuminating Honesty Book House, Silk Palace, Ananda Emporium, and JBS Bus Transport grew dim, and the road was plunged into darkness, apart from the few streetlamps, the man would look left and right; and then, ensuring there was no one around, he would unfold his legs, while remaining seated. He would then stretch out his hands to touch his toes, remaining in this position for some time. I could sense his breathing. He would eventually get up and do all sorts of exercises to relax his muscles. I could hear his bones crack with each movement. Every finger, bone, and joint creaked. When he had finished, he would gather up his cloth, count up his money, take what he needed, and place the rest in a hole he had dug in the concrete where he was sitting.

"At the click of his fingers, I would follow him. He would fashion a turban for his head with his cloth to camouflage himself and would walk down rue Nehru toward the western part of the town. At the end of the road, when we'd got as far as the Raja Theater, where the only tricolored traffic lights of Pondichéry could be seen, we would turn right, where the Shakeela was located. It was a restaurant that, incidentally, still exists, and which remained open late into the night; we would go to have dinner there after the midnight film screening at the nearby cinema, called Kandan Talkies. The man had his own table there. He would always sit on the right, close to the entrance, opposite the cashier. And I would wait for him at the exit, standing along with the banana and betel leaf vendors. He would eat slowly, very slowly. He seemed to take forever, as I waited for him to come out with my package. Once his meal was over, he would stop at the stall opposite the cinema to buy beedis, and we would head toward the Ajantha Theater, where hot masala milk was sold. This sugary hot milk, prepared with cardamom, cloves, and other spices was the favorite drink of night owls; it was most delicious. At the tea stall on the corner of the boulevard opposite the Ajanta Theater, he would order two masala milks, and he would open up my package. While I ate my Ceylon paratha with mutton curry, he would enjoy his milk with a banana. And when I had finished my meal, he would pour me a bowl of masala milk, which was sufficiently cool to drink, and would begin to smoke his beedi. Next, we would go back down boulevard Nord until we got to the distillery, and then we would walk along cours Chabrol. He didn't walk fast. On the contrary: he took his own sweet time, as if he was savoring each step, every meter. Silence was our companion, interrupted only by the sound of stray dogs barking, echoing in the darkness. Once we had gone past the tennis court and the ashram boxing ring, we would sit down on the parapet, our backs to the statue of Dupleix, and gaze at the sea.

"Early in the morning, as dawn broke and the first glimmer of sunshine appeared, the sunrays threatening to scorch our skin for the rest of the day, we would return to our street."

■ ■ ■

This carried on for a while. Until the day when the man disappeared.

"As usual, he waited for nightfall to do his usual stretches, and he began to collect up the coins. I waited for him, happily wagging my tail, already savoring in my mind the curry that I was going to eat. This was my favorite moment of the day. Not only could I get sensation back in my legs, but I could also eat something that had been freshly cooked. I liked to eat this food coming directly from the kitchen, food that was still hot and had the aroma of fresh spices, because the food Mira would bring me usually had lost its flavor and had a dubious smell.

"On this particular evening, the man took longer than usual. I thought he was busy putting the coins into the hole, but actually, he was in the process of collecting up all the coins that were already there! He filled a large jute bag with them; I heard the coins fall to the bottom. Once the bag was full, he draped the cloth around his shoulder, and began to walk toward the canal. He was acting strangely. He wasn't wearing a turban, nor was he clicking his fingers. I was puzzled, but nevertheless decided to follow him. But he simply turned toward me as if he had just noticed me and uttered this phrase that I never thought I'd hear again: 'Hey, clear off, dog!' Initially, I thought I'd misheard him, and I continued to follow him. But he repeated: 'Hey, clear off, dog!'

"This was the first time I'd heard him say something. The first time I'd heard his voice, which seemed bizarre to me. He had a reedy voice that matched his frail physique exactly. Seeing that I was still sitting next to him, wagging my tail, the man put down his bag, and bent to pick up a stone. I knew this gesture well. It rekindled bad memories. But for some reason or another, my body refused to move, and I stood there, paralyzed, in front of him. Not finding what he was looking for, the man came up to me. I joyously yapped and went up to him. I wanted to rub my snout on his leg as a token of the friendship that had united us all this while, but I saw him move aside a little, and he kicked me on my side.

"I went crashing into the transformer next to which Mira and *the other* were sleeping, yelping in pain. This was the first time in a while that I had howled, and I myself was taken by surprise. Hearing this noise, Mira and *the other* woke up. They appeared to be as surprised as me when they learned what was happening. *The other* set off in pursuit of the man, barking all the while; Mira and I sat next to the transformer, not knowing what to do, watching the man vanish into the night."

■ ■ ■

"'Go back to the same place. Take up your position again as if nothing has happened, and I'll take care of the rest,' said Mira, sitting next to me.

"'But what am I going to do there, all by myself? There's no point. As long as the man was there, there was a reason to stay. But now that he's left, I'm going to feel ridiculous staying there all on my own,' I responded, trying to forget my pain.

"*The other* had returned. He was limping a little; he must have been kicked by the man too.

"'Are you afraid of looking ridiculous, now of all times?' Mira was shocked. 'Listen, you don't have much of a choice. Maybe you want to go back to the garbage dump?'

"Hearing her mention the dump, *the other* looked at me reproachfully.

"'Be sensible, Tripod. We're not going to take a step backward. People are used to seeing you there; you've already forged an identity for yourself as a yogi dog. Now is not the time to throw everything away. Half the dogs in Pondichéry already recognize you as such. I've heard them talk about you when I wander the streets to find you food. You can ask him if you don't believe me,' said Mira, pointing at *the other*.

"*He* nodded in agreement.

"'They talk of you with great respect, Tripod. They observe you from afar, but they're scared of coming close to you because of the man. Now that he has left, they would like to come up to you and find out who you are. Our aim has never been to earn the respect of humans; we're more interested in dogs. *He* and I have always had difficulty moving about in town; there are districts where we are not at all welcome. The "pleasant" districts, as you have the habit of saying, are still out of bounds for us. But that's where we find the best dishes, prepared in the way you like them. We only have access to the big bazaar and to some streets in the vicinity. It's not enough. We must succeed in conquering the whole town. And we won't get there by using force. We'll have to use stratagem. Our only trick is spirituality; we're on the right track. You'll see that once you have earned trust and respect, you'll be able to do whatever you want. I will make of you the most respected animal in the whole town.'

"I listened to her in amazement. Lakshmi, this dog really had the future planned out. She knew exactly what she wanted. I certainly couldn't complain about my fate: all I had to do was remain seated, or in a yoga position.

"'Do I really need to remain in this position permanently?' I asked Mira. 'It's rather tiring, you know. Also, you need to find me another spot that is less sunny; the sun is killing me.'

"I had spoken in a somewhat smug tone, for it had dawned on me during this whole discussion that through me, she and *the other* sought to take possession of the town without conflict or violence, which they weren't capable of themselves. Well, they couldn't do it without me. They needed me, as much as I needed them. A tacit understanding had been sealed between us."

■ ■ ■

"What is life, Lakshmi?"

Noticing that I was taken aback, Tripod Dog Baba waited for a few seconds, and then continued.

"Life is merely a series of seconds, minutes, days, months, and years. Along with life, time was born. This complex, cruel, and merciless time dictates our existence. From the very moment man became aware of the reality of time, he has ceased to live. Since then, all he has been doing is fleeing from the past to run toward the future without stopping in the present. For it is impossible to live in the present. It's so subtle that it's practically imperceptible. The world can change in a split second. Life resembles an enormous hourglass that can't be reversed. And the present is this fleeting moment situated between two grains of sand that are falling; it lies between the grain that has fallen and the one that is yet to fall. Can we live between these two moments? No. It's impossible. All that we see and feel is the consequence of our experiences and hopes, which shape us. Yet we're constantly told that what exists today will no longer exist tomorrow, and that what existed yesterday no longer exists today. Only the present is true, real and tangible. Yesterday is like a newborn wave that breaks on the rocks and perishes there, making place for the next day. Between the two, the present exists. The wave that crashed into the rocks no longer exists, and tomorrow's wave does not yet exist. However, it's the same sea, unchanging and eternal, that makes us aware of the passing of time."

As Tripod Dog Baba spoke, he was attempting to gaze far into the distance. But his wandering gaze came to a standstill in front of the shop opposite him. Had he lost his focus? Had his gaze become suspended in a void? Was he putting on his philosopher's act? His words seemed to make sense, but when you listened to them closely, you realized that they were completely incoherent. That's how he must have earned respect among the dogs: through philosophical words that I, Lakshmi, am sure even he does not understand. For these are nothing but nonsensical words that sound clever as long as you don't pay attention to their meaning.

"Why are you talking about time, Tripod Dog Baba?" I asked.

"What's that? Ah yes, time . . . because time is a curious matter. Did you know that I'm the vehicle of Kaala Bhairava?"

Once again, he thought the whole world revolved around him. Whatever was he going to come up with next?

"No," I simply said, even though I knew that Kaala Bhairava's dog was called Shvana. But I wanted to know where he was going with this.

"Well, I'll tell you now. Kaala Bhairava is the ferocious aspect of Lord Shiva; his dog is Shvana. And Shvana is considered to be the gatekeeper of the underworld. Moreover, Kaala Bhairava is the most important god in our life; he's the one who governs and possesses the secret of time. Life is nothing without time! And what's more: I am also Yama. Without me, life would not exist. I am the master of life and death. I also represent the four dogs who accompanied Lord Dattatreya; these dogs symbolize the four Vedas. And finally, I am Sarama, mother of all the dogs; she was the one who found Indra's herd of cattle that was stolen by the barbaric Panis. And why am I telling you all of this? Because in the history and religion of this country, there was a time when I was cherished, and my role as the vehicle of Kaala had a very philosophical dimension."

"Why are you telling me all this, Tripod Dog Baba?"

"Because despite occupying such an important role in mythology, I was ignored and abandoned in the middle of this road, without anyone paying any attention to me. And do you know why? Ironically, by a strange twist of fate, time itself, which I carry on my back, threw me into oblivion. Over time, people have forgotten how important I was in cosmogony."

I understood that all this had a connection with his story.

"So, what happened next?" I asked. "With all your allusions to mythology, I've lost the thread of your story."

I was curious to see how all this was linked to his tale.

■ ■ ■

"After the man's departure, I returned to my position. At first, the passersby glanced in my direction. Not to look at me, but more because they were wondering where the man had gone. After a few days, they started to walk straight past, without even glancing at me. It was as if I didn't exist. Whereas they had previously stopped to throw coins at the man, they now completely ignored me. However, I was still in the same position, with a vacant stare. Days went by without anything happening, whatever that was supposed to be. I knew Mira's aim, but what was her plan? Was something supposed to happen? How long was I going to remain like that? I was sure Mira didn't know either: when I asked her, she told me to wait patiently, and she said that she and *the other* would go through the town to spread the news of the yogi dog. Some curious dogs did, in fact, begin to show up. Initially, they would just observe me from afar, but after a few days, they eventually came up to me. They came and walked around me; some of them sat next to me, while others sat a little farther away. My silence and asceticism intrigued them. The number of dogs who came to visit began to increase day by day.

"The moment we had so hoped for finally came one day, thanks to the Gurkha with whom I used to roam the town during my nocturnal wanderings. You should know, Lakshmi, that the flower garland, the tilak, and the color of saffron are the three most powerful things in our society. Anyone or anything who adorns themselves with these three things will be worshipped and respected. And that's how an ordinary tree that has been decorated with a garland and a tilak can become a sacred tree. A stone or a milestone decorated with flowers and a tilak can become a temple after some time. And any old idiot who sits cross-legged with a garland around their neck, a tilak on their forehead, and dressed in a saffron-colored garment or in a langoti can become a guru, as this color embodies purity, the quest for truth, and asceticism. Any old crook wearing a tilak and a garland can become a politician, and even end up as a minister. So why not me? I, Shvana, am the faithful dog of Yudhishthira who transforms himself into Yama at the entrance to heaven. I, the vehicle of Bhairava and Kandhoba, also have the right to my sacred status."

He paused for a moment and nibbled his tail to get rid of a few fleas, and then he continued:

"I'm going to tell you a story, Lakshmi. Do you see the temple in the park?"

"Which park, which temple?" I asked him.

"Come now, Parc de Pondichéry. You know the park, don't you?" he looked at me reproachfully.

"By the sound of things, you know nothing about my life, Tripod Dog Baba," I said to him in a mournful voice. "You know very well that beyond these two roads, I know nothing of this town. My life is restricted to this route, and to these two temples. No one beyond these two roads has heard the tinkling of my bells. I have never set foot in La Centrale, the ville blanche, or the Muslim district that you talk of. Ever since I arrived in this town, I've only been living through my imagination. Standing between these two columns, which are my prison, I imagine the vastness of the ocean with its beautiful waves gently lapping against the shoreline. When I feel this soft breeze caress my skin, I imagine the beauty of the trees in the park you mention. When I sense the quivering of the coconut palms of the Eswaran Kovil, I imagine the beautiful moon coming to settle on the pond's surface, waiting for Veeran's kiss. I only see the world through my imagination. Reality is quite different."

Tripod Dog Baba glanced at me, then carried on as if nothing had happened. He hadn't even been listening to what I'd been saying. I had the sense that my words had fallen on deaf ears. Sighing, I began to listen to him.

"Well, you see, if you carry on straight in that direction," he said, pointing right, "when you get to the end of the road and reach the former pâtisserie, take a left. And after a few meters, there's a park. A very pretty park, incidentally. It's the favorite spot of the locals and tourists, who come and sit in the shade of these magnificent trees to escape the searing heat. And right at the bottom of this park, there's a tiny temple. Originally, there was nothing here, just a small play area for children, surrounded by some stone columns that the colonizers brought back from Fort de Gingy. You must be wondering why I'm telling you this whole story. Your impatient mind must be going mad, dying to know what the connection is between the tilak, the garland, and the color of saffron. Let me tell you.

"A poor Brahmin priest with a large family lived in rue Muthu Mariamman Kovil. For some unknown reason, he didn't belong to any temple of the town. Perhaps it was because he wasn't originally from Pondichéry, or because people considered him a simpleton. After all, the Hindu district wasn't exactly lacking in temples. But this priest spent most of his time outside his district; he would come and sit in this park, spending his day talking to the trees and the crows. And one day, when immersed in his spiritual musings, he noticed the image of a deity sculpted on one of the Gingy columns. Instead of only seeing a decorative motif there, carried away by his religious zeal and the frustration of not having a temple, the poor priest began to worship the sculpture. A tilak and a garland placed on the sculpture did the trick. From that day onward, he would come and sit down next to the column, light an incense stick, and devote himself to his column puja.

"Initially, no one paid any attention to it. People were more interested in snoozing and snoring under trees than listening to the incantations of a deranged priest. But as time went by, he finally managed to attract the attention of some policemen whose headquarters were nearby, along with people who were on their way to the town hall. From one day to the next, the priest had become an object of curiosity. The passersby stopped in front of the park and came to attend the column puja. Of course, that's all it took to capture the attention of all these people, who had been brainwashed by centuries of superstition. The priest heightened the effect by telling them the story of Prahalada.

"Prahalada, the son of the demon Hiranyakashipu, was awestruck by the presence of the Lord Vishnu. His devotion toward Lord Vishnu was unrivaled, to the great dismay of his father. Hiranyakashipu tried to kill his son several times, but never managed. In desperation, he promised to spare his son's life if Prahalada recognized that his father was the supreme being and the master of the universe. Prahalada refused. Upset and enraged, Hiranyakashipu said to his son: 'Oh, unfortunate Prahalada! You insist that there is a being who is stronger than me, a supreme being who is superior to everyone, who is the master of the universe. But where is he? If he is omnipresent, why isn't he here, facing me? Why isn't he in this pillar that is before me?' On hearing these words, Prahalada responded calmly: 'He was, he is, he will be. He is in this pillar, just as he is in every speck of dust.'

"No longer being able to control his rage, Hiranyakashipu smashed the pillar next to him with his club. With a deafening din, Lord Vishnu immediately appeared in the form of the half-lion, half-man Narasimha, and killed the demon Hiranyakashipu.

"By alluding to this mythological tale to support his act, the old priest managed to convince everyone that god was present within this column.

"From that day onward, this column became a temple. Anyone who was tired of going back and forth from the town hall in pursuit of some trivial document would come to pray in this temple. People would give offerings to the column in the hope that they would be able to obtain some kind of official document that a fat lazy civil servant refused to hand over. His main job, after all, was to unblock his ears with a pen. It would have been simpler to bribe him with a baksheesh than to give offerings to a nondescript column. Those who were on their way to the general hospital came to the temple to pray for the cure of some family member whom an incompetent doctor didn't know how to treat.

"And that's how the poor, deranged priest had managed to change the course of his destiny. He should have died impoverished and senile, but instead he became prosperous, and was recognized by the entire town. A tilak, a garland, a piece of cloth of saffron color, and some incense sticks. A forgotten column hidden away somewhere in the Fort de Gingy, which had been brought back by the colonists who had nothing else to do, ended up being transformed into a temple. Raja Desingh, the former king of Gingy, must have been laughing in his tomb.

"You see, Lakshmi, these three things are the most dangerous elements of our society."

This story amused me a lot. Encouraged by the grin spreading across my face, Tripod Dog Baba continued:

"One day, late in the afternoon, I saw the Gurkha arrive. I hadn't seen him for a long time. He went past me on his bicycle, with his trusty stick under his arm. He had gone a few meters past me, when he stopped suddenly, and then retraced his steps, pushing his bicycle. I watched all this out of the corner of my eye . . . he stood in front of me smiling, and began to speak to me as if he were addressing a human being.

"'Are you OK, dog? It's been a long time since I saw you,' he said, crouching down in front of me and stroking the top of my head. "What happened to your paw? What are you doing here in this position? Have you become a yogi dog? Did you know that I've missed you? I used to value your presence a lot during my rounds . . .'

"He stroked and massaged my mutilated paw, as he continued to talk to me kindly.

"'Wait, dog, I'll be back in a minute.'

"Leaving his bicycle near me, he set off toward the temple, which was just beginning to open. The sweltering afternoon heat was beginning to melt into the balminess of the evening. People were heading toward the park or the seaside. The pilgrims were scurrying toward the temple to beat the large crowd. The road was thronging with people.

"The Gurkha returned a few minutes later with a small temple basket in which there was a garland of marigolds, a small box containing vermilion, and some sweets. He shifted the bicycle, which was just in front of me, set the basket down next to me, and began to perform a puja. I couldn't believe my eyes. What had the world come to? Who was more out of their mind?

I, who was toying with the idea of becoming a yogi dog, or he, who had seen goodness knows what in me?

"While the man was busy placing the garland around my neck, a small group of people had gathered around us to spectate. It was an unusual sight to see a man doing a puja to a dog. The Gurkha didn't seem to be bothered by the gathering. He even seemed to enjoy the attention. He then took out a small bell from the basket and circled it around my head while uttering a prayer. He lit a few incense sticks and applied a tilak to my forehead. Those around him didn't know how to react. But the sound of the bell and the smell of incense made people automatically clasp their hands together in prayer. With their heads bowed, hands joined together, and eyes closed, they began to worship me. This sudden turn of events took me by surprise. I had expected everything, but not this, and I didn't know what was going to happen next. But I was reassured by the sight of Mira and *the other*, who were weaving in and out between the spectators' legs, beaming victoriously.

"At the end of the puja, when the incredulous and hesitant crowd were reluctant to disperse, a man spoke up, addressing the Gurkha.

"'Hey, Gurkha, have you lost your head? It's just a dog! Also, he must be very stupid to stay on there, when his master, the yogi, has left. It's a mystery as to why he continues to remain in that position. But why do a puja to him?'

"The Gurkha was now sitting cross legged next to me, and he gave me the sweets that were in the basket. With one hand, he stroked me, and with the other, he fed me.

"'Eat, dog,' he said. 'You really need to; it's been a long time since you ate. Today, it's your festival day; it's the ideal day to put an end to your penance.'

"He then turned toward the gathering.

"'You know, a very long time ago in our religion, the dog occupied a position that was as holy as the cow or the elephant. The dog was worshipped just like the other animals who are vahanas, transporting our gods. In this part of the country, over time, you have all forgotten to celebrate the festival of the dog, and you have only focused on other animals, whom you believe to be noble.

"'However, the dog is the vahana of Bhairava. You have forgotten him, but we haven't, we Gurkhas. In my native land of Nepal, we still worship him and celebrate the festival of Kukur Tihar in honor of Shvana. That's why I did a puja to him.'

"'And why particularly him? Why this dog, and not any other?' Another man in the crowd queried.

"The Gurkha appeared to ponder for a few seconds, and then, pointing at me in front of the crowd, he said:

"'Look at this dog closely. Don't you see that he has something unique about him? Look, he has three legs, exactly like the statue of Ganesh inside the temple.' With surprise, I discreetly looked at my third leg, which was dangling down. 'Haven't you noticed that this dog is a yogi? How do you explain the disappearance of his master? Surely you must know what has happened to him, at least?'

"The crowd fell silent. Everyone was waiting for the Gurkha's explanation. More and more people flocked to the scene, and the rows of onlookers multiplied. Some people stood on their tiptoes to see what was happening, while others asked the people next to them about the man who was normally there. Conscious that he was now dealing with a small crowd, the Gurkha got up, dusted his khaki uniform, and continued:

"'The man who was there was a baba, and he went into a deep state of meditation, leaving the fruit of his penance, his soul, to this dog.'

"A murmur ran through the crowd. People looked at each other, knowing neither what to believe nor what to say.

"'And how do you know?' asked someone in the crowd.

"The Gurkha knew that this was his moment of glory. Previously, he had been invisible, audible at night only because of his whistle and the screech of his poorly oiled bicycle. He was the nighttime watchman of the town, earning just a few rupees at the start of every month like a common beggar. No one knew his name, and no one knew about his life; living in obscurity, he wandered through the town at night, armed only with his stick to chase away thieves. But now, he was going to become visible. The Gurkha then turned toward me proudly, and pointed out the dark hole that I was sitting next to.

"'How do you account for this hole at the location where this holy man was previously sitting? Do you think that this dog has hollowed it out with his three paws? And where was this hole previously? It appeared the very day the baba disappeared. Can anyone explain this? I'm telling you: the spirit of the baba lives on in the body of this dog. Otherwise, why would he still be there? Do you often see yogi dogs?' he concluded, triumphantly.

"But he didn't wait for an answer; he quickly mounted his bicycle, broke up the crowd, and sped off around the corner."

■ ■ ■

"On this auspicious day, I became the yogi dog. On the very evening of this famous puja, Mira and *the other* thanked me with a sumptuous chicken vindaloo, which they must have found in the Creole district. Mira was very excited; I was too, for that matter, but I ate in silence, awaiting the next series of events.

"'You see, Tripod, you have harvested the fruit of this lengthy wait, as if by a miracle. Thanks to the Gurkha, you have just attained a holy status. Nothing can ever make you come down from this status as long as we don't commit any faux pas. Those people who were there just now are convinced that you're the soul of the baba. Only we know that this imposter wasn't a saint. As long as the secret remains concealed, everything will be fine. We will be able to live in peace, without worrying about what the next day might bring. Already, the dogs of the town were beginning to recognize you as a saint; today, they have had confirmation of this. You'll see: from tomorrow onward, they'll all come to pay homage to you, and they will obey your orders.'

"Hearing these words, *the other* wagged his tail in approval. I'm sure he could already picture himself parading through the streets of the town, proud to be the first disciple of the yogi dog.

"Personally, I, Tripod Dog Baba, was skeptical. Of course, people's attitudes after the puja had been very positive. Some had gone to buy more garlands, which they had then put around my neck; others had lit incense sticks, which they had then placed next to the hole. Some people had bought me even more sweets. I had never eaten so many in all my life. But at the end of the evening, the crowd had dispersed with mixed feelings. I was curious to see what was going to happen over the next few days.

"To my great surprise, the very next day itself, early in the morning, a man stopped by in front of me. Surely, he must be going to the temple, I thought. But after taking his shoes off, he came up to me and removed the withered garland round my neck. He then began to clean around me, took away the burned incense sticks, and set off toward the temple. I recognized him: he was the man who had asked the Gurkha the first question the previous day. I was suddenly panic-stricken. What was going to happen next? Had I been stripped of my status as the yogi dog already? I glanced at Mira and *the other*, who were sitting next to the transformer; they were also watching and waiting to see what was going to happen . . . And when I saw the man return, holding a basket with a fresh, new garland and incense sticks, I was relieved. 'Nothing can stop my progression toward my holy status now,' I said to myself proudly, sporting my yogi position. In fact, the man performed the same gestures as the Gurkha. Once the puja was complete, he served me a sweet, closed his eyes, with his hands clasped together in prayer, put his shoes back on, and headed toward the temple. Some people who were passing by paused to see this new spectacle. No one talked to this man; they just attended the puja, and then set off again, glancing back at me.

"Over the next few days, more and more people came to light incense sticks in front of me. More people stopped and took their shoes off. Some beggars who had caught whiff of a good business opportunity came to settle next to me. Meanwhile, all the dogs of the town had heard of the yogi dog. A number of them also came to visit me. Some spent entire days on the streets wandering about, but they never came close to me. Not one dog ever showed even the slightest sign of aggressive behavior. I felt they respected me; as long as I remained silent, they didn't know how to react.

■ ■ ■

"This new cult of the yogi dog even caught the attention of the priest, who came to visit me one morning. I began to tremble. He was a middle-aged man of average height, with a protruding belly covered by a yellow silk cloth that he wore above his dhoti. He was otherwise bare chested. His body and forehead bore three horizontal streaks, commonly worn by temple priests. When he arrived, a man was already in the process of lighting incense sticks, which he would circle around my head. The priest paused and stood a few steps away, and began to observe the man. He waited for him to finish his puja, and then came up close to us. I don't know why, but the man stepped aside for the priest, as if to apologize, and he handed over the incense sticks he was still holding. The priest was surprised by this gesture; he had just come to see what was happening but ended up doing the puja himself! He had no other choice but to take the incense sticks that the man handed over to him, and to carry on from where the man had stopped.

"Fate was on my side that day. It was the time of day when the road starts to awaken from its slumber; it was the time of day when all the students and office goers went by. They had grown used to seeing the pujas performed in my honor, but they were nevertheless surprised to see the priest himself officiating the puja. From then onward, everyone was convinced that I was indeed a yogi dog. By performing this puja no one had ever dreamed of, the priest had just affixed his seal, confirming my holiness. He himself was surprised by the turn of events; he applied a tilak to my head and set off, patting his stomach on his way to the temple, without understanding what had just happened."

Tripod Dog Baba fell silent and stretched out his limbs at length. He glanced at me mischievously, as if to say how easy it had been for him to become a yogi dog. He then got up, shook himself, and made it clear that he was getting ready to go somewhere or other. Sometimes he would just set off like that. He would come and go as he pleased, sit next to me if he wanted to, or go for a walk whenever he felt like it.

"But where are you going, Tripod Dog Baba? You still haven't finished your story!" I said, trying to hold him back.

"Oh, this whole story has tired me out, Lakshmi . . . Incidentally, while telling it, I just realized that it's been a long time since I took a stroll in town. I'm going to go and have a little wander."

I felt most jealous seeing him set off. This dog was free to do what he wanted. He could go anywhere and do whatever he liked. Unlike me, who was chained up from morning to evening, forced to beg. What difference is there between the beggars at the other end of the temple and me? None at all. Apart from the fact that I bestow blessings on people, whereas they don't. My only consolation is telling myself that I have a job, although it isn't even a job.

I was relieved when I heard the noise of the key turning in the temple door. I needed some rest.

■ ■ ■

When I returned to the temple at the end of the afternoon, Tripod Dog Baba had still not returned from his walk. I had grown so accustomed to listening to his story these last few days that I dreaded spending the rest of the day all alone. As time passed by, I was overcome by boredom. There was nothing to entertain me; it was always the same pilgrims, the same beggars, and the same pedestrians. To kill time, I began to think about Tripod Dog Baba and about life in general.

"Life is indeed curious," I said to myself. "Here's the story of a dog who had never once dreamed of becoming famous, and who never had any ambition, apart from wanting a name and a collar around his neck. All he wanted was some bins full of bones, and a life of vagrancy. Even when he had the opportunity to have a master, a roof over his head, and a sign saying 'Watch out, vicious dog!,' life had led him to opt for vagabondage. Why had he deviated from this path that he had so yearned for? What was it that made Tripod Dog Baba decide not to take this path? A hunch that the future could be better? No, I don't think so. I believe, quite simply, that Tripod Dog Baba had just thrown himself into life, without pondering too much, without worrying about what the next day would bring. He had let life decide for him. And this is what life had chosen. A set of circumstances had led him to meet Jimmy and had led Jimmy to show him another facet of the town, revealing another way of life to him . . . Otherwise, he would have remained in the yellow house, spending the rest of his life there. Then, the state of emergency had led him to return to his district of origin, where he had met Mira. Owing to unfinished karma involving the rickshaw driver, he had lost a paw, which made him dependent on Mira. And finally, Mira's ingenuity and craftiness had enabled him to become a yogi dog, idolized and respected by all. Had he thought of all this in advance? Had he skillfully planned and plotted his life? No. Life had dictated his trajectory. That was his fate. Fate, a curious concept indeed."

When we manage to successfully achieve something we have wanted and have worked hard for, we attribute this success to our hard work, perseverance, and self-confidence. But when we fail, we blame this very outcome on fate and destiny; it is synonymous with defeat. Ultimately, fate serves to free us of guilt in the case of failure. For a long time, I, Lakshmi, refused to believe in fate, because it had a negative connotation. Ever since I was little, I've wanted to escape my fate of becoming a temple elephant, and God only knows how hard I tried to achieve this! My decisions have always been made consciously, in the knowledge of what has led to them. And what happened? Nothing. I came back to square one. But when I think about it, I haven't made many choices; in fact, I only made one: to escape from the gurukulam. The rest has been nothing but a set of circumstances. Fate caught up with me just when I thought I'd escaped from its grips; that was when I was a film star. Despite some unexpected twists and turns, my life has simply followed the path already sketched out by fate. However, everything led me to defy my fate: my aspiration for a different life, my escape from the gurukulam, my encounter with Veeran and the Gajarastas, being captured, and my cinema career. But despite all this, I have become a temple elephant again. Whereas Tripod Dog Baba, who made a decision unconsciously, and had never hoped to become a guru, ended up becoming the most respected dog in town. Fate definitely exists. It's simply the encounter between the unconscious and a set of circumstances that produces this extraordinary thing located between what has been anticipated and what actually happens. Fate is neutral; it's neither positive, nor is it negative. We each interpret it in our own way.

I was so consumed by all these musings that I lost track of time. The black mantle of the night had begun to cloak the town, plunging it into gloom. A yellow, full moon rose from the ocean, and one by one, the stars began to illuminate the sky, as the neon lights of the town grew dim. As I set off on the path returning to the Eswaran Kovil, I saw the ashram devotees paying their final homages of the day to the tomb of Aurobindo. Tripod Dog Baba still hadn't returned. What could he be doing at night? While all the stray dogs were attempting to conquer the town and were fighting for bones around garbage cans, Tripod Dog Baba was surely snoring somewhere after enjoying a hearty meal.

Chapter Thirteen

"YOU NEVER TALKED TO THEM?" I asked, pulling on my chain.

For some time now, I had begun to develop this tic—like Rambo the circus elephant, whom I'd met when I was with Veeran. I hadn't noticed it at first, until the day when Tripod Dog Baba had pointed it out, saying, in irritation: "Stop pulling on your chain, Lakshmi! This sound is preventing me from sleeping."

"No, never," said Tripod Dog Baba, in response to my question. "Not one yap or bark. I never spoke to them. What did I have to say to them, in any case? Nothing. I was happy to remain silent."

"But how did you manage to earn respect without any communication?"

Tripod Dog Baba had just dismissed one of his disciples who had come to greet him. He had woken up and was in a good mood. Normally, he looked sullen, wouldn't stop yawning, and would fall asleep as soon as he could. But when he was in a good mood, his eyes would twinkle, he would wag his tail incessantly, and he would do a little parade in front of the shops. He was in this kind of mood today, and he came and sat next to me with a banana in his mouth. On days like these, Tripod Dog Baba could prove to be really kind.

"Here, Lakshmi, eat this. I don't feel like it, and I know you're always hungry," he said to me, placing the banana in front of me.

I took it and looked at him gratefully, while he let himself be petted by Tokuram.

"Yes, as I told you, I had never spoken to them. Mira was responsible for communicating with them. I'm sure she passed on the stupid things I told her. Like the discussion we had about time, and other things I tell her when I get bored. To be honest, I never gave a thought as to what she might say to them. After the priest's famous puja, all the dogs of the town came to pay homage to me. I received so many sweets throughout the day that I would have ended up diabetic if I'd eaten all of them! As soon as one incense stick went out, someone would come to light a new one. The news of the sanctity of the yogi dog had spread like a streak of vibhuti. From this day onward, the doors of the town had opened up to Mira and *the other*. They could walk wherever they wanted without being attacked. They could go wherever they liked. Previously, they would look from afar at the dogs who would gather around the best restaurants to feast on a good biriyani or a mutton curry. Now, the best locations were reserved for them. The best dishes and leftovers were offered to them by the other dogs. Aristo, Salem Biriyani, Satsanga, La Promenade: these restaurants were no longer unattainable dreams; for Mira and *the other*, they had now become a daily reality."

"So why all this drama about your vegetarianism?"

"That's because of the temple," he said, lost in thought. "It's no good being a dog. I'm not sure the disciples would have tolerated my consumption of meat in the temple surroundings. Also, the staging of this drama only serves to emphasize my unique qualities."

"I see. And what about Rameswaram in all of this?"

I was happy we'd reached the end of the story. Not because I didn't find it interesting; on the contrary, Tripod Dog Baba's life fascinated me. There was, of course, nothing exceptional or extraordinary about him, but I liked the way his life had turned out, without him being the master of his destiny. His whole life had been dictated by fate. Nothing had been thought up in advance, planned, or even wished for. Yet here he was, adored and respected by everyone, without even having lifted the tip of his tail. It was his lack of action that had led him to this situation.

Tripod Dog Baba gazed at me for a long time, tried to say something, but then changed his mind. Then, sitting back on his hind legs to scratch his ear, he said to me, grinning:

"Rameswaram? I've never set a paw in Rameswaram. I don't even know where it is, for that matter."

"Oh really? But people say you became a saint after you returned from Rameswaram."

"No, Lakshmi. Those are all stories invented by Mira."

"And why would she have invented all of that?"

"You know, all saints need myths and extraordinary stories to get worshipped. Every single bit of this story about pilgrimage in that sacred location was made up by Mira to prove my sanctity. And all the dogs believed it."

"No one even doubted it?"

"Not in the slightest! That's what people need; they need mysteries to believe in something. Simple things have no value in their eyes. Holiness is only of value when it is complicated, incomprehensible, and inaccessible. My silence, too, is part of the mystery, for silence is the language of the gods. You can interrupt someone who is talking or making noise, but interrupting someone's silence is sacrilege. That's why I adopted this tactic. What's more, people leave me alone. What do I have to say to them, in any case? I don't know anything. I can talk all day long about food. But as for philosophy, spirituality, and meditation, I don't know anything about those matters. No one asks me any questions, no one expects an answer from me . . . apart from you, who hasn't understood anything. But I like you a lot, Lakshmi, for you are neither a dog, nor a human, and you don't mean to cause me any harm. By the way, did you know that you and I both came to the temple at practically the same time?"

"No, I didn't know that," I said, trying to remember. "But it's true you weren't here when I first arrived."

"Ah yes! I was still on the other side of the road. But I think that the priest must have been afraid of a new temple coming up next to his, as more and more people were beginning to flock toward me! One devotee had even built a small makeshift shelter for me, with some bricks and a corrugated iron roof. When the priest saw the shelter, he sensed danger.

"One day, he came over and beckoned to me to follow him. Initially, I didn't know how to react, so I stayed put, wagging my tail. But I sensed that he didn't mean any harm. He went away, and then returned with a piece of barfi in his hand. He placed half of it in front of me and kept the rest. As soon as I had gobbled up my piece, the priest set off toward the temple, holding the other half of the sweet. I glanced over at Mira to see if I should follow him or not; she nodded by way of approval. And so I followed him.

"The priest took me on a walk around the temple by the canal, and he motioned to me to sit down next to Ram, the coconut seller, who was on the street corner. He protested violently.

"'Hey, priest, what are you doing? I don't want this dog next to me!'

"'But he's not like the others, Ram,' the priest said to him. 'He's a yogi dog. He is sacred, you know.'

"'Sacred or not, I don't like dogs. As long as I pay for my spot in the temple, I have the right to decide whom I want to have next to me,' muttered the merchant.

"Unwilling to pursue the discussion further, the priest then led me toward the main entrance. It was early in the morning, and the shops were gradually opening, one by one. The shopkeeper who was running the souvenir shop just opposite the entrance spoke up.

"'Hey, priest, why are you breaking your head? Put him next to Lakshmi, the new temple elephant.'

"'Really? Do you think it's a good idea?' asked the priest, scratching his head.

"'I'm not sure if it's a good idea. But at least both of them will be together,' said the shopkeeper, rubbing his hands together in glee; what he had in mind was the fact that the proximity of his shop to the two animals would attract more people toward him.

"'Yes, maybe you're right,' answered the priest, indicating that I should sit down next to the two pillars, where you are right now, Lakshmi.

"He then gave me the rest of the sweet he was holding and went back inside, wiping his fingers on the yellow cloth he wore around his waist, looking very pleased with himself.

"Mira and *the other*, who were following all this drama, were in heaven. In fact, they couldn't have hoped for better: now, I had officially become the temple dog. Mira was very proud of me; she looked at me appreciatively. I could sense her feeling of relief at having accomplished her task. As for *the other*, he was already running through the streets of the town to announce the news that the yogi dog had officially been recognized as a saint. As a result, a pack of dogs came to visit me to receive their first darshan. The priest, who had come out of the temple just then to ensure that I was still there, was panic-stricken at the sight of so many dogs. But *the other* had already anticipated this. He barked to break up the pack of dogs, then made them come to me one by one, ensuring that the smooth running of the temple was not disrupted. Seeing all this, the priest was delighted that the dogs had managed to organize themselves in this way, and he valued the presence of Mira and *the other.*

"At first, I was worried about your presence, Lakshmi. I was afraid that you'd be my rival. I didn't want you to become the center of attention: this would have made me lose my fame. In fact, sometimes I forgot that my objective was to earn the respect of dogs and not humans. I had just taken advantage of humans so as to target dogs! Now that I had succeeded, humans weren't of much use to me . . . Mira reassured me and told me that I had nothing to fear. To be honest, I no longer need to spend my life here at the temple. I could settle down anywhere in this town, and I'd still enjoy the same privileges. I'm free to do what I want. It's just that I'm old, lazy, and can't see very well anymore. All I want now is to be left in peace for the little time that remains for me to live."

■ ■ ■

I remained pensive as Tripod Dog Baba finished his story. The temple was soon about to close its doors. I heard the clinking of the coins in the bowls that the beggars were shaking frantically to attract the attention of the last few pilgrims. Opposite us, the owner of the souvenir shop was scratching his nose at leisure, waiting for the temple to close. On the street corner, I noticed Mira and *the other*, who were also awaiting the end of the day. The curtain was falling, the scene was drawing to a close. Now, Tripod Dog Baba could return to his normal life. He would accompany his friend the Gurkha for a bit, go and eat his mutton curry at the Shakeela, and maybe he would go and sit down on the parapet of cours Chabrol to gaze at the sea. Or perhaps he would simply eat what Mira brought him, and doze off under the watchful eye of Ganesh.

Chapter Fourteen

I COULDN'T SLEEP A WINK all night long. The pitter-patter of the rain on the rooftop kept me awake. The monsoon had begun. Along with it came gale-force winds that set the trees dancing, a rain-soaked gray sky, and roads flooded by nocturnal downpours. I'm not sure why, but I prefer the monsoon to the intense heat of summer. Perhaps it's because the monsoon has this sense of sadness and melancholy about it that matches my mental state? Whenever there's a deluge, I enjoy listening to the thunder, catching a glimpse of lightning, and observing the children play with their little boats through a curtain of rain. The roads are deserted, and the few remaining pedestrians out in the rain scurry home, huddled under their umbrellas.

On the way to the temple, an army of dragonflies flew around me to herald the onset of the monsoon. I could feel the first drops of rain. Tokuram stopped by at the shop on the corner of rue Gandhi to buy something. As we waited for the shopkeeper, who was busy covering his newspapers with tarpaulin, I observed the people sitting on the pavement in front of the Nallam hospital, sheltering from the rain. The road was practically deserted. I didn't feel like going to work.

I trudged down the road, attempting to dodge the puddles that had formed overnight. Instead of sleeping on the streets as they usually did, the dogs were now lying on the pavement in front of the houses, idly watching me pass by. The Chettiar who lived in the house next to the poet Bharati's house was waiting for me as usual with some bananas. That was our routine. Ever since my first day in Pondichéry, this man would perform a ritual of offering me some bananas on my way to the temple, so as to receive my blessing. He was always the first to receive it.

In the temple, I noticed there were fewer people than usual. The beggars had left to seek shelter from the rain. The coconut seller was absent, as the Kramanis don't climb coconut palms on rainy days, hence the lack of coconuts in the markets and the temple surroundings. Some shops remained closed. Tripod Dog Baba was nowhere to be seen either. The day threatened to be dull. To amuse myself, I diverted my gaze to a nest. A few days ago, a pair of birds had started to set up their home in the eaves between the left-hand pillar and the roof of the shop on the other side of the road. They relentlessly flew back and forth with twigs and straw in their beaks, constantly chirping. In a matter of a few minutes, this sound transported me back to my former gurukulam.

In my mind, I tried to piece together an image of rainfall in the Bandipur Forest. The quivering of the trees, caressed by the wind, the concert of the frogs in harmony with the drumming of the waterdrops falling upon the leaves, the chorus of the birds with their rain-soaked feathers sheltering in the foliage . . . This whole scene gradually came back to me as I listened to these birds. How far away my forest now seemed to be! I hadn't thought about this phase of my life for a very long time. Not that I had missed it. On the contrary: these memories had sought refuge in the deepest corners of my mind. Tucked away in a forgotten drawer. And now, the sound of the birds chirping had pulled open the drawer. I wanted to close it immediately, expelling these images from my mind—otherwise I'd be sad—but it was difficult. Like a horse dashing off on a race, these images galloped through my mind. Manmath, Veeran, the Gajavasis, the Gajarastas, the chameleon, and all the other animals of the forest invaded my mind. It was as if they had gathered in a room that was too small for all of them, and they were jostling for space. I closed my eyes.

When I opened my eyes again, I saw that Tripod Dog Baba had returned. He was soaked through. If it hadn't been for his three and a half legs, I wouldn't even have recognized him. He didn't have his garland around his neck, nor did he have his tilak on his forehead. Soaked to the bone, he looked just like any other stray dog. He sat down next to me and shook himself dry. He looked tired.

"Terrible weather," he concluded, breaking into a sneeze.

"Yes, Tripod Dog Baba. I can sense the cyclone. Where have you been?" I added: "You're completely drenched."

"I too felt the cyclone approaching. That's why I went to take a stroll in the fishing village to observe the sea. It's the best spot to admire the large waves. Well, I can tell you that things are looking grim. I saw waves as tall as houses. Vaitikuppam and Kurussukupam look like ghost towns. The boats have been put away, and the roads are desolate. The men had gathered in the temple, while the women were returning home from the market with empty baskets. It was the final market day. They'll have to wait a few days before going back. The atmosphere was as morose and as bleak as the sky."

"You're lucky," I said, sighing. "I've been in this town for some time now, and I'm just three roads away from the sea, yet I still haven't seen it . . . I spent my whole childhood breathing in the sea air. Lulled to sleep by the sound of the waves. My first dreams took shape on the cliffs overlooking the Arabian Sea . . ."

A large tear like a raindrop began to trickle down my trunk. I turned away so that Tripod Dog Baba wouldn't notice. But it was too late; he had raised his head to look at me, hearing my voice full of sadness.

"Why, you're in tears, Lakshmi! What's wrong? Are you unhappy?" he asked, taken aback.

I remained silent. My voice tried to emerge from my trunk, but remained stifled. My tears gushed forth like a torrent of rain, washing away all the sadness that I'd kept locked up within me over the past years.

"Tell me what's wrong, Lakshmi," Tripod Dog Baba begged, appearing to be genuinely moved. "I've never seen you unhappy. The very thought that you could be sad has never even crossed my mind. And now that I see you weeping, I don't know how to console you. Please answer me . . ."

"I feel miserable, Tripod Dog Baba. If only you knew how painful it is for me to be here. I feel as if no one notices my sadness. These thousands of disciples who come to this temple to receive my blessing, rejoicing at the sight of me standing up and begging, have no feelings. The hypocrisy of these pilgrims who come to pray and worship Ganesh—who looks just like me—fills me with disgust. They have absolutely no compassion for me. I'm on my feet, tethered from morning to evening, just to give them their stupid blessing. As part of their worship, they tap their cheeks, knock their temples with their fists, and tug at their earlobes, standing in front of me, but they have no clue that I'm suffering. It doesn't even occur to them that I don't belong here, that I could have a family, raise my elephant calves, and look after my lot, and above all, be free. Just like them. But no, instead, I'm their toy, their entertainment. In fact, to them, I'm nothing but a poor beast without feelings, and I should consider myself lucky to be here instead of in the wild."

Tripod Dog Baba was watching me, shocked to witness this outburst of anger and sadness.

The wind picked up and began to blow even stronger, sweeping into its whirlwind the leaves of the bougainvillea trees that decorated the houses of the district. In the distance, I could sense the roaring of the sea. I could hear the wind howling through the branches. Realizing that it was about to rain, some passersby came to seek shelter in the temple entrance, and they took my blessing while waiting for the rain to abate.

"What terrible weather," said the priest, standing at the temple entrance.

He said this patting his stomach, addressing nobody in particular. Then, turning toward Tokuram, he added:

"It looks like this cyclone is going to be formidable. I'm thinking of closing the temple this afternoon. Look, everything is flying away! But don't worry, your Lakshmi won't fly away. Hahaha! But it would make sense for you to take the afternoon off. What do you think?"

"What do I think? I've nothing to say. If the temple closes, then I don't need to be here," answered Tokuram, scratching his chin.

There was a tone of irritation in his voice. Firstly, he didn't find the priest's joke funny, and secondly, if the temple were to close, he'd lose his income. He raised his head toward the sky to curse the rain.

Ignoring Tokuram, the priest continued:

"I sincerely hope the cyclone doesn't wreak too much havoc and the rain stops soon. Otherwise, we'd have to cancel our annual festival. What on earth shall we do? May God protect us from the dark fate of Kali Yuga! Come on, let's wait a little longer and then we'll close the temple. Besides, I must go and find the committee members to make a decision regarding the festival," he concluded, and he set off.

"Yes, yes, do hurry back home, you fat priest. You're so fat you could soon replace the statue of Ganesh!" muttered Tokuram under his breath. "Off you go, your wife will be waiting for you with some delicious ghee sambar; you can eat and drift off to sleep in front of your favorite TV series. What does it matter to you if it rains or if it's windy? You've got a salary at the end of the month, whereas we depend on the temple."

The shopkeepers began to close their shops; they did so reluctantly, for they too were affected by the priest's decision, while the beggars gathered their few worldly possessions to settle down in the space between the shops, protecting themselves from the rain. All of this happened in a leaden silence; no one was in a mood to talk.

"And what about you, Tripod Dog Baba, what are you going to do?" I asked the dog, breaking the silence.

"What about me? I don't know. I'll wait for Mira. She'll be able to find a place where we can take refuge. As for food, it's going to be difficult if all the restaurants start closing. But we've always got the Creole district, so I'm not worried. I'm more concerned about you, Lakshmi."

"That's really kind of you, Tripod Dog Baba," I said, genuinely touched by his kindness. "But you don't need to worry. Tokuram has stocked up enough food for a week. I'm not going to starve to death."

"That's not what I'm worried about. I'm more concerned about your state of mind. It pains me to see you sad. As I just said, it had never occurred to me that you could be unhappy! To be honest, you're the first creature I've ever had sympathy for. Like these people, I too was blind, thinking that the lifestyle of the temple elephant could be nothing but a bed of roses. Appearances are deceptive, Lakshmi."

"It's true, Tripod Dog Baba: appearances are deceptive. I'd always seen you as someone who was cynical and lazy, who just takes advantage of any situation. I didn't know that so much gentleness and goodness could be concealed beneath your fake guru carapace."

"It's not your fault, Lakshmi. We're all like that. We aren't capable of seeing the true qualities of those around us. We cannot perceive this inherent goodness that is within us before life corrupts us. For we are corrupted by life! Life is so hard that it can throw us off course. And others judge us in relation to our journey; they care only about our deeds, and not our inherent qualities. Of course, not everyone can look beyond appearances and actions. Now, I believe that we should try to return to our original path, despite going astray. I say 'try,' because it isn't easy to get back on the right track after all these detours. Some will carry on down the wrong path, knowing perfectly well that this will only lead to their downfall, while others will return to the correct path, even if they never reach their destination."

Tripod Dog Baba's speech took me by surprise. This was the first time I'd heard him speak in such a profound manner. A thought crossed my mind that made me smile. He noticed this, and asked:

"Why are you smiling, Lakshmi?"

"I fear that by playing the role of a fake guru and philosopher, you've actually turned into one!" I said, winking at him.

Tripod Dog Baba remained lost in thought as he heard this. For the first time, I saw his expression becoming vacant. That's how he must have been when he aspired to become a guru. Sitting on his two hind legs, one foreleg folded, and the other half leg dangling down, he looked completely different. For the first time, without his garland and tilak, however, Tripod Dog Baba earned my respect.

In the distance, the thunder picked up, and a flash of lightning struck an electric pole on the corner of the road, in the coconut seller's spot. An electric cable fell to the ground; it zigzagged like a snake on fire toward the canal, where it fizzled out.

"I think you're absolutely right, Lakshmi. I think I'm ready to go back on the right path for the rest of my life," said the dog, after a long silence. "By talking to you, and by sympathizing with your pain, my true nature has just become apparent to me. I feel as if a weight has been lifted off my shoulders, Lakshmi. All these years, I had kept this version of myself locked up within me, buried under layers of ignorance and greed. And this other lazy, mean, and cynical version of myself, who was fearful of uncertainty, has just escaped like an evil spirit, imprisoned for too long. All that remains for me now is to choose between becoming a real guru or returning to my life as a stray dog. But whatever I decide, I'll now take up the path of truth. But what about you, Lakshmi, how will your future shape up? I'm not sure if you have a choice in the matter. I'm worried about you. You can't spend your whole life shouldering this burden of sadness and misery."

"One always has a choice, Tripod Dog Baba. I don't believe in life without choices. Since the hardest part is selecting the right one, I'm going to take advantage of these few days of rest to think it over. I really must find a solution. I can no longer accept this predicament of spending the rest of my life in these conditions."

I was determined to find a solution.

The sound of the key turning in the temple door cut short our discussion. Huddled under his umbrella, the priest headed toward his scooter. The beggars were scurrying back and forth between the shops to find the best place to shelter from the rain and wind. Tokuram and I set off on the path toward the Eswaran Kovil, leaving behind us a content Tripod Dog Baba.

EPILOGUE

THE RAIN PERSISTED for three days, accompanied by gale-force winds that swept away the corrugated iron roofs. I heard tiles crashing to the ground with a deafening din. The doors of the motorcycle workshop and other shops behind our temple banged to the pulse of the wind. From my room, I could see the water level in the temple pond rising. Spending three days enclosed within these four walls had driven me crazy. At the same time, as I listened to the rain, my mind was searching for a way out. I couldn't sleep until I had found a solution.

On the last day, when the wind had died down, and the rain had subsided to a trickle, until only the occasional raindrop fell, it was apparent that the cyclone had ended. Even the sun was timidly peeking through the charcoal clouds.

I had made up my mind. I knew what I was going to do. I had devised my plan!

On that final night, as the last flash of lightning pierced the sky, I heard a sharp sound, as if something had just crashed onto the roof. I heard it despite the sound of the last few water droplets drumming on the roof. At first, there was a bolt of thunder, followed by a flash of lightning. The unknown object then fell to the ground at the room's entrance. In the twilight, I couldn't see anything: for three days, I had been immersed in the darkness, without electricity. But something had just fallen to the ground. It didn't bother me, as I was in the process of putting the finishing touches to my plan. And for the first time in three days, I was able to sleep. A regenerative and peaceful sleep.

I woke up to the sound of the priest ringing his bell, and to the first scents of camphor and incense. The temple had just reopened. Tokuram came to fetch me; he untied me and led me to the pond for my bath. He would normally wash me in the room. As he washed me, he murmured into my ears:

"Oh, how happy I am to return to work, my dear Lakshmi! These past three days have been horrible. And what's more, today is the festival day at the temple. You're going to be spoiled, admired, and pampered by all the pilgrims. We're going to recover all the money we lost over these last three days."

I already knew that it was the festival day at the temple. Incidentally, my whole plan depended on this. During these past three days, like Tripod Dog Baba, I had given myself two options: the first was suicide, and the second was to escape.

Suicide was the simplest to execute. All I needed to do was to feign madness. It wouldn't be the first or last time that a temple elephant went mad. Especially during this festival period!

All I needed to do was toss some pilgrims—or other objects within my trunk's reach—into the air for people to think I was mad. I was ready to face death; it would be better to die than to live this life as a slave and a beggar. And if for one reason or another my plan should fail, then I would escape during my next vacation. For we have holidays too! Once a year, all the temple elephants are driven to different reserves to experience a semblance of life in the wild. This time, I would take advantage of the vacation to escape at all costs.

Having made this decision, I let Tokuram apply my makeup and bathe me. Suddenly I remembered the sharp sound I had heard the previous evening. I was eager to know what could have slipped along the roof.

Tokuram had finished applying his finest makeup on me and he led me outside to stand in front of the room so he could go and get changed, and then I saw something glistening on the ground. A silvery object that had lost its original luster.

Oh my God! It was Alphonse! My poor Alphonse! The dear flying fish must have been struck by lightning. Struck by the last bolt of lightning before the end of the monsoon rain. I was sure he had come to visit me to give me advice. I wanted to cry, but at the same time, I restrained myself, so as not to spoil my makeup. I just couldn't wait to get to the temple and be done with this life.

We were among the first to arrive at the temple. The shops were already open, and the shopkeepers were grinning broadly. The beggars had begun their noisy ritual, rattling their bowls for coins. The fat priest came to welcome me with great pomp, and he smeared the three horizontal streaks on my forehead.

People were busying themselves with various activities around the temple. Some were busy decorating the golden chariot on which Ganesh was to be transported in the procession. Others were finishing repair work on the electricity generator, while some were putting the finishing touches on the decorations around the temple, putting up banana stalks, and hanging neon and fairy lights between the pillars. Pieces of coconut and palm leaves lay scattered on the floor, and children gathered armfuls of these, running about helter-skelter.

Amid all this chaos, I hadn't noticed that Tripod Dog Baba was missing. He was no longer there! His spot was empty. I didn't have too much time to think about it, for the musicians and firework crew had just arrived. My worst enemies! However, I was going to be able to escape from this hellish situation exactly because of them . . . They positioned themselves to the left of the temple entrance and began their deafening music. The day was going to be really trying . . . Already, thousands of pilgrims were flocking toward the temple. The line was never-ending: it stretched right from the temple entrance, where I gave my blessings, up to the souvenir stall. People were jostling with one another. The odors of camphor, incense, sweat, hair coated with coconut oil, talcum powder, and flower garlands wafted throughout the temple. I glanced from left to right: Tripod Dog Baba was still nowhere to be seen.

What had happened? Had something happened to him during the cyclone? Or had he simply made up his mind? If this were the case, when I had last seen him, he had been leaning more toward wanting to become the guru that he had never been. In any case, that was the impression he had given me. The thought that something terrible had happened to him tormented me. Or perhaps he had chosen to return to the street? I kept turning these questions over and over in my mind when I saw the flower seller arrive with a garland in her hand. She made her way through the crowd of pilgrims and managed to come over to Tokuram and me.

"Tokuram, periyanna," she said, addressing him as her big brother, "have you seen Tripod Dog Baba, by any chance? I've been looking for him all morning and I can't find him. On this fine festival day, I crafted my most beautiful garland for him. I'm heartbroken that I can't find him!"

"It's true, Maha! With this huge crowd, I hadn't even noticed that he was missing. But between you and me, Tripod Dog Baba is very fond of sleeping. I am sure he'll wake up and will come and join us soon. Leave the garland with me; I'll put it round his neck when he's here, and I'll call you so you can come and apply his tilak," said Tokuram, slipping a one-rupee note into his bag.

Normally, he would put the money into his shirt pocket. But during festival days such as this one, he would have a cloth bag with a picture of Lakshmi on it (not of me, but of the goddess Lakshmi) dangling from his wrist.

The day flew by at an alarming pace. When I returned to the temple at around four in the afternoon, it was even busier than it had been in the morning. The first thing I did was to check if Tripod Dog Baba had returned. No sign of him. He would usually sit behind the generator, but this had now been shifted and attached to the chariot in front of the entrance, so his spot seemed emptier than ever. I was saddened; I had just lost Alphonse the previous day, and now I was going to leave this world without saying farewell to Tripod Dog Baba. The only two creatures I knew in this world.

Dusk came upon us. The twinkle lights attached to the pillars and banana stalks lit up the entire road. The frenzied pilgrims were pushing and shoving one another, right from the ashram up to the post office, which was on the corner of rue Rangapillai. The first fireworks hurtled into the sky. The fat priest, accompanied by others who had come to assist him during the festival, carried out the statue of Ganesh. The frenzied crowd was overcome by religious zeal; the disciples tapped their temples with their fists and pulled at their earlobes, while simultaneously crossing their arms in prayer. The musicians played even louder.

The priests placed the statue on the throne of the chariot, and the fat priest sat next to it to perform the puja. Hundreds of disciples then positioned themselves in front of the chariot, holding the rope, ready to pull the chariot along. The procession was about to begin. The fireworks team went first, the musicians next, and finally me, followed by the chariot and its generator. On either side of the procession, men carried neon lights mounted on long bamboo sticks.

The procession set off. All day long, I had strived to conceal even the slightest trace of anxiety, not letting anything show. However, deep down in my heart, a storm was raging. It wasn't death that worried me; no, it was failure. I was prepared to confront death peacefully. Besides, I had never considered death as a finality; our entire society is based on the cyclical concept of reincarnation. But what worried me was failure. I couldn't suffer yet another one. I had spent so many stages of my life trying to become something other than what I was destined for . . . Since life wouldn't grant it to me, I would obtain it through death. Too bad for life.

After turning right upon leaving the temple, the procession then went up rue Nehru. The evening was still young. After three days of rain and shop closures, the usual activities had resumed on the street. There were people everywhere. The neon lights of the first shops beyond the canal glimmered in the distance. We had only got as far as the Ramana restaurant. Some customers came out of the restaurant to pay homage to the procession.

I still hadn't decided when and where I was going to set my plan into action. I needed a signal. What kind of signal, I couldn't say . . . Every ten meters, the procession stopped to let the crowd give their offerings. This festival was tiring; it was stop, start, stop, start, each time. The procession crawled at a snail's pace. I absolutely hated it. Fortunately, it was the last one, or at least, I hoped so.

As we arrived at quai d'Ambour, the procession stopped to let some buses pass by. Passengers stuck their heads out of the window, and some clasped their hands together in prayer for Ganesh, even while seated inside the bus. The policeman who was controlling the traffic gesticulated wildly and let out long, piercing whistles to urge the bus drivers to hurry up. But he didn't have much success, for the driver had to pray too. The procession took longer than usual to set off again.

Just then, a small group who had gathered at the corner of the canal caught my eye. Half a dozen people were standing in a circle, looking at something, not paying any attention to the procession. I was curious to know what was happening, and was fed up of seeing the musicians' backs. This huddle of people seemed to be mournful and kept shaking their heads. Some of them were gesticulating angrily at the buses. Tokuram was also curious about this gathering, and as he too could not see what was happening, he advanced a few meters. I followed him.

Between the legs of the bystanders, I noticed the body of a dog. Well, what remained of the body, for there wasn't much left: the head was completely flattened, and the remains were swimming in a pool of blood. Poor thing, he must have been run over by a bus . . . The first thought that crossed my mind was death. Was this the signal I had been waiting for? Was fate beckoning to me by placing this dead dog in my path? I took my eyes off the corpse and scanned the road. At the sight of this spectacle, I became aware that this was perhaps the last time I would see this world. It was the last time that I would cross this canal, that I would see all these roads, all these people. The last time that I would see the moon and the starry sky.

These thoughts were interrupted by the continuation of the procession, which then stopped again, almost immediately, after just a few meters. More buses, cars, and auto-rickshaws . . . The policeman was going crazy. As we had come as far as the police station, some of his colleagues came out to help him.

I looked again at the gathering. The sight of this dog reminded me of Tripod Dog Baba. I was grief-stricken not to have seen him one last time, saddened not to have bid farewell to him. What would he have thought of my decision? Would he have approved of it? Would he have understood it, at least?

My mind was wandering . . . The last bus had just passed by. The policeman stood in the middle of the road to stop other vehicles from crossing. The procession was about to resume. With my eyes, I followed the beams of the headlights from the last bus; I noticed two shadowy figures sitting on the section of the pavement in front of the police station near the bus stop, and my heart skipped a beat.

These two shadows were, in fact, two dogs. One of them was lying down, and the other was sitting upon his hind legs. Even before fully identifying them, I'd already jumped to a conclusion. I looked back again at the corpse, and this time, I examined it in panic. The crushed head hung to one side, attached to a blood-soiled body, which was still in one piece. To my horror, I noticed that the dog only had three and a half legs . . .

My body went into a spasm, as if I had just been struck by lightning, or had experienced an electric shock. Oh my God! What had happened? In the space of a few hours, I had lost the only two creatures I'd known in this world. My mind was in turmoil, and tears flowed from my eyes. I didn't care about my makeup. I hadn't been able to mourn Alphonse; I would now weep for Tripod Dog Baba. Through my tears, I spotted Mira and *the other*, who were weeping too. I still didn't understand what could have happened. Why had Tripod Dog Baba ventured out into this part of the road, which he knew to be dangerous? He never risked coming here after nightfall, because of the traffic and his bad eyesight. So why was he here? My mind was frantically searching for an answer when I noticed the trash can. Tripod Dog Baba was lying next to a trash can. And then I understood everything.

■ ■ ■

So that's what had happened: Tripod Dog Baba had decided to resume his life as a stray dog. His life had come to an end when he decided to live an honest life. He had been safe while he lived a life of falsehood. And now he had just paid the price of truth. Among the bystanders, I recognized Maha, the flower seller, who had just left her most beautiful garland of white and yellow flowers on the body, and as she couldn't find the head, she applied her final tilak to the half leg of the dog.

How utterly absurd this world was! With the death of Alphonse, the reincarnation of the soul of the famous Paradesi Swamigal had met its end like a common fish, scorched by a bolt of lightning . . . Had Alphonse come to visit me to transfer his soul to me, knowing about his imminent death? Or had his soul simply reached the end of its cycle? I had no idea, and I would never know. One of life's many mysteries.

Tripod Dog Baba had lived half of his life as a fake guru, and by choosing to take the path of truth, he had just met with death. He had been hit by a bus, exactly like his mother. The mysterious and retributive hand of fate. But retribution for what? For whom? Punished for having defied fate? For having wanted to experience something other than the path carved by some unknown hand? Would Tripod Dog Baba have experienced a less tragic death if he had only ever been a stray dog?

As for me in all of this, I was ready to confront my fate a final time, uncertain of everything. I still didn't know whether this would mean death. Until the end, doubt would be my only companion. And doubt accompanied me as I took my last steps.

The procession resumed. The fireworks team fastened their string of firecrackers next to La Boutique d'Auroville. The musicians played louder and louder, as they gazed at a shopwindow display of ice-cold milky kulfi. To my right, bicycles and motorcycles were lined up. Drivers in parked cars waited for the procession to pass through. Everyone in this entire section of the road, between rue de la Cantine and the kulfi shop, were enthusiastically watching the procession pass by.

When the first firecracker exploded, I pushed against the vehicle to my right with all my might. The metal crumpled and crackled like tinfoil. I then placed my leg on the first car and felt the steel of the bonnet melt, giving way under my weight. Then, turning around, I raised my trunk as high as I could, and I trumpeted my final farewell salute to Ganesh.

TRANSLATOR'S AFTERWORD

WHILE *LAKSHMI'S* *Secret Diary* is a work of fiction, the story of Lakshmi's real-life counterpart is well-known in Pondicherry. Lakshmi the temple elephant was donated to the Sri Manakulla Vinayagar Temple as a calf in 1995, and she worked there long hours throughout her life. She tragically collapsed and perished in 2022 at the age of thirty-two, after suffering from ill health.[1] Gautier imagines a more colorful, eventful life for Lakshmi, with an alternative manner of dying, but he nevertheless illuminates the pain and sadness of Lakshmi's real life as a temple elephant in captivity and encourages the reader to contemplate the plight of countless other elephants across India who continue to suffer a similar fate. Tripod Dog Baba's narrative in turn highlights the violence faced by stray dogs. But *Lakshmi's Secret Diary* also underscores the complexities that surround animal and human relationships in India, where animals such as elephants and dogs are abused, but are also paradoxically worshipped, owing to their status in Hindu mythology and religion.

The French East India Company arrived in India in the seventeenth century. Lakshmi's chronicler, Ari Gautier, was born in Madagascar in 1965 and raised in postindependence Pondicherry, a South Indian town and the former capital of French India; the town was also occupied by the British on several occasions, and was transferred to the Indian Union in 1954.[2] Like numerous denizens of Pondicherry, during the French colonial rule of the town, Gautier's grandfather opted to be governed by French civil code, and adopted a French family name.[3] Gautier, who was educated at the Lycée Français in Pondicherry,[4] subsequently emigrated to France, and is now based in Norway; he has adopted French as his primary literary language, and he describes it as his mother tongue.

Gautier is part of a small constellation of Indian Francophone authors[5] that includes contemporary writer K. Madavane from Pondicherry, who composes theatrical and prose works in French.[6] Indian Francophone writing, however, has been composed not only by writers from former French territories of India but also by a minority of Indian writers from other regions; these writers with an affinity and a passion for the French language, its literature, and culture include Manohar Rai Sardessai from Goa, and Toru Dutt and—more recently—Shumona Sinha, both originally from Calcutta, Bengal.[7]

Gautier's writing represents a distinct voice in contemporary Indian fiction, not only because of his adoption of French as a primary literary language, which is unusual, but also because of his captivating depictions of various facets of Pondicherry and

India's oft-neglected French colonial history. He is the author of multiple works of different genres, which have recently begun to garner acclaim from literary critics, reviewers, and translators worldwide.[8] Gautier's novel *Le Thinnai* (2018) sheds light on the cultural and linguistic legacy of Pondicherry's French colonial history, and it has recently appeared in an English translation by American translator Blake Smith.[9] Gautier is also the author of *Nocturne Pondichéry* (2021),[10] a collection of short stories set in Pondicherry, and his poetry collection entitled *Négrodalitalité* (2021) has recently been translated into English and Italian by translators based in the United Kingdom.[11] Gautier's first novel, *Carnet secret de Lakshmi* (2015), appears in an English translation for the first time in this volume.[12]

In *Lakshmi's Secret Diary*, Gautier offers the reader colorful vignettes of Pondicherry. Through the unique perspective of animals, we are offered insights into numerous fascinating moments of Pondicherry's history, along with glimpses of the districts and life on either side of the canal that divides the town into the "ville blanche" (white town) and the "ville noire" (black town). Gautier's writing shines a spotlight on the radical contrasts between the architecture, sights, soundscapes, atmospheres, and culinary and cultural traditions of the town's diverse districts and locations, including the Sri Aurobindo Ashram, the Sri Manakulla Vinayagar Temple, the Hindu, Creole, Catholic, and Muslim districts, and the fishing village of Kurusukuppam. Pondicherry, as Gautier demonstrates, is a world full of unexpected quirks and dissonances; a Hindu shrine can be found in the Catholic district, and a Ganesh temple in the white district. Alongside these urban portraits that showcase the diversity of Pondicherry, Gautier paints vivid descriptions of areas of natural beauty in South India. We are immersed in a sensory world, experiencing a profusion of powerful sounds, scents, and colors in the Bandipur Forest, and we are offered a bird's-eye view of Villianur and the natural beauty around it.

In addition to telling the story of Lakshmi the temple elephant, Gautier pays homage in this novel to the life and works of the Tamil poet C. Subramania Bharati (1882–1921).[13] Bharati originally resided and worked in British-ruled Madras, but owing to his political activities, which opposed the British Empire, he was soon under threat by British authorities, and therefore fled to Pondicherry, where he developed his knowledge of the French language, literature, politics, and culture. His Tamil writing was shaped by French thought and literature in various ways.[14] His death, caused by a temple elephant, is not only documented in Gautier's narrative but is also somewhat reflected in the novel's depiction of Lakshmi's plight, for Lakshmi also displays violent and unpredictable behavior at the end of her life as a consequence of her dissatisfaction with her enforced captivity and life as a temple elephant. Furthermore, the intersections between French and Tamil cultures that shaped Bharati's writing are mirrored in *Lakshmi's Secret Diary*, for Gautier similarly builds a bridge between France and India in his multicultural and multilingual writing.

■ ■ ■

French is a major, global language, with a dominant status in numerous former French territories across the world. Yet in contemporary India, French is an endangered language with a fragile status. In 1965, Tamil and English were imposed as languages to be employed for official purposes in Pondicherry.[15] These languages remain dominant in Pondicherry today.[16] Not only does French have a precarious status in Pondicherry, but architectural traces of the town's French colonial history are also gradually undergoing erosion. The town, like Gautier's characters, is constantly in flux, experiencing transformations. French colonial buildings such as the town hall have recently fallen to ruin,[17] and French road names have been replaced with Indian ones; rue Dupleix, for example, has been renamed Jawaharlal Nehru Street.[18] To counter such processes of erosion, acts of French heritage preservation are currently underway in Pondicherry; the town hall and the iconic statue of Dupleix have recently undergone restoration, and there are also plans to restore the French colonial building of the Collège Calvé, which features in Gautier's work.[19]

Echoing these urban acts of French heritage preservation, Gautier's writing memorializes the vanishing traces of the French Empire through a literary medium. By writing in French, Gautier counters the loss of a colonial language of India, and revives the linguistic legacy left by the French Empire in Pondicherry. Moreover, Lakshmi's narrative unearths and restores certain French features of Pondicherry's landscape that no longer exist; the history of the street name rue Manakulla Vinayagar is unveiled, and its former French name rue d'Orléans is memorialized in *Lakshmi's Secret Diary.*[20] Gautier's work—in both content and medium—may therefore be interpreted as a literary act of French heritage preservation.

Gautier's writing reminds us that Pondicherry is a translational space, sculpted by processes of translation, visible in the act of renaming roads.[21] But the novel itself is also shaped by processes of translation, exemplifying the notion that "Indian literary traditions are essentially traditions of translation."[22] Multiple elements of the ancient Sanskrit epic *Mahābhārata* are translated into Gautier's novel, such that Gautier's work may be described as both original and derivative. The poetics of anthropomorphism, employed in the *Mahābhārata*, are present in Gautier's book, in which animals embody human experiences, characteristics, and thought.[23] Similarly, the structure of the *Mahābhārata*, in which one tale is frequently contained within another, is translated into the structure of Gautier's novel.

Mythological tales from the *Mahābhārata* are retold in Gautier's text, serving various purposes. The tale of Draupadi is retold by Tripod Dog Baba, and as it intersects with his life, the original tale becomes embellished and extended. A priest retells the tale of Prahalada and Hiranyakashipu in order to convince onlookers that a nondescript architectural structure is of spiritual value. Retold in Gautier's novel, this latter tale from the *Mahābhārata* highlights the extent to which Indians are frequently brainwashed into believing that mundane objects, events, animals, or people are associated with the divine, owing to the powerful and influential role of mythology and religion, which are deeply engrained in the nation's consciousness and society.

Gautier's act of retelling aspects of the *Mahābhārata* may be described as a poetics of "transcreation," a term that is frequently employed in the Indian context to describe the long-standing tradition of retelling and adapting Sanskrit mythology.[24] Transcreation may also be described "as a rebirth or incarnation (avatar) of the original work,"[25] as G. Gopinathan suggests.

Gautier provides an allegorical depiction of this very process in his novel. In the sixth chapter of *Lakshmi's Secret Diary*, the concept of reincarnation from the *Bhagavad Gita*, part of the *Mahābhārata*, is described as follows: "Just as a man casts off his worn-out garments and adopts new ones, the soul rejects its spent body and enters others that are new."[26] This process is dramatized in Gautier's writing; a kingfisher who is the reincarnated form of a saint transfers his soul to a fish. The kingfisher perishes thereafter, but his soul lives on in the reincarnated form of a flying fish. The kingfisher is therefore reborn with new features (the body of a fish), yet he also retains aspects of his previous features, including his ability to fly, and his yogic powers.

This depiction of rebirth may be interpreted as a trope for the process of transcreation in Gautier's writing. This process is visible in Gautier's reincarnation scene itself, in which the concept of transmigration from the Sanskrit epic is reborn with new characters and a new plotline. *Lakshmi's Secret Diary* is therefore shaped by processes of transcreation and it simultaneously illustrates these very processes.

The Hindu philosophy of reincarnation, then, is central to Gautier's writing, which reflects its significance in Indian society; as Lakshmi remarks, "I had never considered death as a finality; our entire society is based on the cyclical concept of reincarnation." In this English translation, Gautier's work undergoes a further reincarnation as it travels into another language, and Lakshmi, the real temple elephant, who tragically passed away during the translation of this novel, is reborn in this translation.

NOTES

1. "32-Year-Old Puducherry Temple Elephant Dies," *Times of India*, December 1, 2022, https://timesofindia.indiatimes.com/city/puducherry/32-year-old-puducherry-temple-elephant-dies/articleshow/95897312.cms.
2. For an overview of the writer's life and works, see Ari Gautier, "About Ari Gautier," https://arigautier.com/about/. For details of the British occupation and the French history of Pondicherry, see Jessica Namakkal, "Chronology," in *Unsettling Utopia: The Making and Unmaking of French India* (New York: Columbia University Press, 2021), xv–xvii.
3. Gautier's ancestral history of conversion, set in its historical context, is detailed in Aditi Sriram, *Beyond the Boulevards: A Short Biography of Pondicherry* (Delhi: Aleph, 2019), locs. 1019–63, Kindle. Such conversions are also described in Gautier's semi-autobiographical novel *Le Thinnai*; see Ari Gautier, *Le Thinnai* (Paris: Lys Bleu, 2018), 119–23.
4. Gautier's education background is recounted in Sriram, *Beyond the Boulevards*, 1019.
5. For an overview of Indian Francophone writing, see Vijaya Rao, "Ecrire l'Inde en français en Inde," in *Ecriture indienne d'expression française* (New Delhi: Le Germ, 2008), 11–20; Blake Smith, "Translingualism in Francophone Writing from South Asia," *L'Esprit Créateur* 59, no. 4 (2019): 68–80.
6. For an analysis of the work of K. Madavane and other Indian Francophone writers with a connection to Pondicherry, see Vijaya Rao, "Globalizing the Spiritual and the Mythological: Indian Writing in French from Pondicherry," in *Francophone Literature as World Literature*, ed. Christian Moraru, Nicole Simek, and Bertrand Westphal (New York: Bloomsbury, 2020), 95–105. Madavane's collection of French short

stories has recently been translated into English by Blake Smith. See K. Madavane, *To Die in Benares*, trans. Blake Smith (New Delhi: Pan Macmillan, 2018). For an overview of the writer's life and works, see also K. Madavane, "Penser dans la langue de la mère; écrire dans la langue du père; vivre le mythe comme un agent interculturel," in *Ecrire en langue étrangère: Interférences de langues et de cultures dans le monde francophone*, ed. Robert Dion, Hans-Jürgen Lüsebrink, and Janos Riesz (Québec and Frankfurt: Éditions Nota Bene and Iko Verlag, 2002), 505–23.

7. This phenomenon has been observed by Rao and is highlighted in her anthology, which presents works by Toru Dutt and Manohar Rai Sardessai. See Rao, *Ecriture indienne d'expression française*.
8. For example, see Ananya Jahanara Kabir, "Creole Indias, Creolizing Pondicherry: Ari Gautier's *Le Thinnai* as the Archipelago of Fragments," *Comparative Literature* 74, no. 2 (2022): 202–18. Gautier's writing has been reviewed in the Indian press; see Geeta Doctor, "Diamond and Rust: Geeta Doctor Reviews Ari Gautier's 'The Thinnai,'" *The Hindu*, October 9, 2021, https://www.thehindu.com/books/diamond-and-rust-geeta-doctor-reviews-ari-gautiers-the-thinnai/article36891799.ece; Anamika A., "A Window to a Melting Pot of Confused Cultures," *Hindu Business Line*, November 10, 2021, https://www.thehindubusinessline.com/books/reviews/fiction/a-window-to-a-melting-pot-of-confused-cultures/article37415607.ece; Annie Philip, "Lakshmi, the Protagonist of French Fiction," *The Hindu*, January 7, 2016, https://www.thehindu.com/news/cities/puducherry/Lakshmi-the-protagonist-of-French-fiction/article13985403.ece.
9. Ari Gautier, *The Thinnai*, trans. Blake Smith (Delhi: Hachette, 2021).
10. Ari Gautier, *Nocturne Pondichéry* (Paris: L'Harmattan, 2021).
11. Ari Gautier and Ananya Jahanara Kabir, "Négrodalitalité," trans. Ananya Jahanara Kabir, Luca Raimondi, and Rosa Beunel, *Il Tolomeo* 23, no. 1 (2021): 35–61.
12. First published in 2015 by Edilivre, the novel was republished in 2018 by Lys Bleu; Ari Gautier, *Carnet secret de Lakshmi* (Paris: Lys Bleu, 2018).
13. For a discussion of Bharati's life and Tamil writing, see Bernard Bate, "Subramania Bharati and the Tamil Modern," in *Protestant Textuality and the Tamil Modern: Political Oratory and the Social Imaginary in South Asia*, ed. E. Annmalai, F. Cody, M. Jayanth, and C. V. Nakassis (Stanford, CA: Stanford University Press, 2021), 85–109.

14. For details on the work and life of Bharati, including French influences on his Tamil writing, see Pugazhendhi Kumarasamy, "Bharati's Adaptation and Appropriation of French Thoughts," *Translation Today* 10, no. 2 (2016): 74–83.
15. "The Puducherry Official Languages Act, 1965," April 5, 1965, https://www.indiacode.nic.in/bitstream/123456789/6117/1/the_puducherry_official_languages_act%2C_1965.pdf.
16. For more on the status of French, English, and Tamil in postindependence Pondicherry, see Helle Jørgensen, "Between Marginality and Universality: Present Tensions and Paradoxes in French Colonial Cultural Heritage, Civilizing Mission, and Citizenship in Puducherry, India," *Heritage and Society* 10, no. 1 (2017): 51.
17. "Mairie Building to Be Ready by Jan.," *The Hindu*, August 25, 2018, https://www.thehindu.com/news/cities/puducherry/mairie-building-to-be-ready-by-jan/article24774645.ece.
18. Jørgensen, "Between Marginality and Universality," 51. For an analysis of similar processes in other cities, see Sherry Simon, *Translating Montreal: Episodes in the Life of a Divided City* (Montreal: McGill-Queen's University Press, 2006), 204; Sherry Simon, *Cities in Translation: Intersections of Language and Memory* (Oxford: Routledge, 2012), 118.
19. "Mairie Building to Be Ready by Jan."; S. Prasad, "Facelift for Dupleix Statue," *The Hindu*, December 29, 2014, https://www.thehindu.com/news/cities/puducherry/facelift-for-dupleix-statue/article6734988.ece.
20. For an overview of former and current road names of Pondicherry, see Jean Deloche, "Appendice: Noms des rues anciens et modernes," in *Le vieux Pondichéry 1673–1824: Revisité d'après les plans anciens* (Pondicherry: Institut français de Pondichéry; École française d'Extrême-Orient, 2005), 128–30.
21. Here, I draw on the work of Sherry Simon, who investigates processes of translation, including the rewriting of urban signs in various cities of the world such as Montreal. See Simon, *Translating Montreal*; Simon, *Cities in Translation*; Sherry Simon, *Translation Sites: A Field Guide* (Oxford: Routledge, 2019).
22. Ganesh Devy, "Translation and Literary History: An Indian View," in *Postcolonial Translation: Theory and Practice*, ed. Harish Trivedi and Susan Bassnett (London: Routledge, 1999), 187.
23. For a discussion of the role of animals in the *Mahābhārata*, see Wendy Doniger, "Zoomorphism in Ancient India: Humans More Bestial Than

the Beasts," in *Thinking with Animals: New Perspectives on Anthropomorphism*, ed. Lorraine Daston and Gregg Mitman (New York: Columbia University Press, 2005), 28–47. See also Anirban Bhattarcharjee, "Reason, Death and the Animal: The Mahābhārata and the Eruption/Interruption of the Ethical," *Journal of Dharma Studies* 5, no. 1 (2022): 63–81.

24. G. Gopinathan describes transcreations as "creative translations of the ancient Sanskrit spiritual texts into modern Indian languages." See G. Gopinathan, "Translation, Transcreation and Culture: Theories of Translation in Indian Languages," in *Translating Others*, vol. 1, ed. Theo Hermans (Manchester: St. Jerome, 2006), 236. For a further discussion of transcreation in the Indian context, see Sujit Mukherjee, "Transcreating Translation: An Indian Mode," *Kunapipi* 19, no. 3 (1997): 85–93. See also Susan Bassnett and Harish Trivedi, "Introduction," in Bassnett and Trivedi, *Postcolonial Translation*, 9–10.
25. Gopinathan, "Translation, Transcreation and Culture," 236.
26. There are multiple versions of the *Mahābhārata*, but for one well-known version of the concept of transmigration, see P. Lal, *The Bhagavad Gita* (Delhi: Roli, 1994), 33.

ACKNOWLEDGMENTS

I AM GRATEFUL to all those who have contributed to this volume. For the opportunity to translate his work, and for his valuable insights and our discussions, I would like to express my gratitude to the author, Ari Gautier. I am especially grateful to Blake Smith at Chicago University, who encouraged me to translate this novel. I am deeply grateful to Judith Woodsworth and Sherry Simon at Concordia University, Montreal, for inspiring me to translate and to pursue research in the field of translation studies, and for our fascinating discussions on various aspects of translation. I would like to express my thanks to all the generous translators who have contributed to my thinking about translation, including Ros Schwartz, Sophie Lewis, Émile Martel, Adriana Hunter, and Marilyn Booth. I am very thankful to the three anonymous reviewers of my work, whose thoughtful feedback and thorough reading of the manuscript contributed to its enhancement. I thank Andrea Meyer

Ludowisy for all her help in procuring materials for my research at the Senate House Library, London. I owe a debt of gratitude to Christine Dunbar at Columbia University Press for her exceptional support, excellent ideas, and input. I am very grateful to Leslie Kriesel and Adriana Cloud for their rigorous editorial work. Finally, I thank my family for all their support and patience, and for their help with proofreading the translation; in particular, I am grateful to my parents, and to Amruta and Vivek Mahadevan. I am indebted to my grandparents, Ammamma and Thatha, for sharing their vast knowledge of South Indian culture and Sanskrit mythology with me.

GPSR Authorized Representative: Easy Access System Europe, Mustamäe tee 50, 10621 Tallinn, Estonia, gpsr.requests@easproject.com

www.ingramcontent.com/pod-product-compliance
Lightning Source LLC
Chambersburg PA
CBHW031649100726
47898CB00006B/2039

* 9 7 8 0 2 3 1 2 1 2 0 5 2 *